Alien on a Rampage

Alien on a Rampage

by Clete Barrett Smith

illustrated by Christian Slade

Disney • Hyperion Books
New York

First Edition

Printed in the United States of America

1 3 5 7 9 10 8 6 4 2

G475-5664-5-12074

Reinforced binding

Library of Congress Cataloging-in-Publication Data
Smith, Clete Barrett.
Alien on a rampage/by Clete Barrett Smith;
[illustrations by Christian Slade].—1st ed.
p. cm.—(The Intergalactic Bed & Breakfast)
Summary: Spending another adventure-filled summer in the
Pacific Northwest at his grandmother's hotel for visiting space aliens,
eighth-grader David uncovers a plot to destroy the Earth.
ISBN 978-1-4231-3448-0 (hardcover)
[1. Extraterrestrial beings—Fiction.   2. Grandmothers—Fiction.
3. Bed and breakfast accommodations—Fiction.   4. Science fiction.]
I. Slade, Christian, ill.   II. Title.
PZ7.S644633Al 2012
[E]—dc22   2011014716

Visit www.disneyhyperionbooks.com

For Mom & Dad

When the taxi pulled up to Grandma's place, I opened my door before the driver had even come to a complete stop. "Whoa, buddy, take it easy," he said. "You'll get there on time—it's not going anywhere."

Then he stopped at the curb and got a good look at the Intergalactic Bed & Breakfast. His mouth dropped open, forming a circle that matched his wide eyes. I guess some people just aren't used to seeing a huge Victorian-style house covered in a mural of swirling galaxies, with silver spaceship sculptures jutting up all over the front yard. Especially at the edge of a forested wilderness on the outskirts of a tiny Pacific Northwest town.

"Ummm...okay...on second thought, that place looks like it could blast off any minute. I guess you better hurry up."

I hopped out of the taxi, pulling my suitcase off the back-seat. "Thanks for the ride," I said, handing the driver a wad of cash through his open window. The driver nodded and collected the money but kept his eyes fixed on the house.

Jogging along the white picket fence, I thought about how different this was from my arrival last year. Back then the only thing I had to worry about was starting seventh grade in the fall. But that was before Grandma gave me my summer job and put me in charge of defending the biggest secret on the planet.

I stopped at the front gate and took in the view. I had been a little worried that things might've changed since I was last here. But everything looked to be in the right place, just the way I remembered it.

Well, okay, maybe not the *right* place. Grandma's house could only be in the right place if it was hosting a Klingon birthday party on one of Jupiter's outer moons. But it looked the same as last summer, and that was good. Seeing it again felt like coming home.

But as I looked up at the porch...I don't know, I guess I felt a little disappointed. It's not like I expected a big WELCOME BACK! banner and a marching band playing under a blizzard of confetti. But maybe I had expected *something*. Maybe someone sitting on the front porch, waiting for me. Maybe Amy. I mean, I'm pretty sure she knew I was flying in today.

No big deal. This would give me a chance to surprise them. If I had planned it better, I could have brought an alien disguise and mingled with the dinner crowd in the dining room, to see how long it took Grandma to figure out I was in there with the rest of her customers. But I'd have to settle for sneaking in through the back door and catching someone off guard.

I left my suitcase just inside the gate and darted between the spaceship sculptures for cover. When I reached the side of the house, I ducked below the first-floor windows and made my way to the back. As I tiptoed up the back porch stairs, I heard someone rustling around in one of the sheds behind me.

Perfect. I could sneak up and startle them and then we'd laugh about it . . . unless it was Sheriff Tate. I mean, "Head of Security" Tate, or whatever his official title was, now that he was working here. Last summer I had devised a secret plan to humiliate him in front of the entire town. But only because he had led everyone in Forest Grove to the front lawn of the bed-and-breakfast, threatening to storm the place and drag Grandma's customers off to jail, or worse.

So it was probably not a real good idea for me to give that guy another big surprise. Ever.

The door to the shed stood partially open, and some-one was kneeling on the ground, hunched over a scattering of spare parts. The carcasses of an old computer, a lawn mower, and a carpenter's nail gun rested against the far wall. It looked like pieces had been stripped from all three and mashed together to form the device in the center of the shed.

I crept forward for a better look. The figure inside the

doorway was wearing a pair of black coveralls. A pale hand punched a string of numbers into the computer's keyboard. Instantly the blade from the lawn mower whirred to life and rose in the air, a mini helicopter propeller. Attached below was a sheath of tubing that held a cartridge of nails. The gadget hovered in the air in the middle of the shed.

The figure in coveralls grabbed the computer's mouse and whipped it back and forth, clicking furiously at the button. The floating thing rotated in the air and spat out a machine-gun stream of nails.

Yikes! I jumped back in case one of those nails flew right out the doorway.

Then I heard a noise over the whirring of the blades. It might have been laughter, but it was so harsh it almost sounded like someone choking. I had a pretty good idea this wasn't Grandma or Amy. Or anyone who called Earth home. Not even Tate.

I looked up and saw paper targets spread across the walls of the shed at varying heights. Although the device had only been in action for a few seconds, each target had at least a dozen nails slammed through its bull's-eye. The nails were sunk into the wood all the way to their heads.

Bzzzzt! Sparks shot from the computer's mainframe where the casing had been cracked open to expose the circuit boards. It sizzled, and the smell of burning plastic was awful. The figure in the coveralls shouted, "Curse these cave dwellers and their primitive toys!" just before the flying device spun out of control and smashed into a wall. The wreckage crashed to the ground in a smoky heap.

"Whoa." I barely breathed the word, but the being on the

ground jumped up as if he'd been electrocuted. He stepped out of the shed and slammed the door.

Then he turned and loomed over me. His skin was bone white and smooth all over, making his head look like a skull. The dark purple lips and black eyes didn't help much. I stumbled backward and almost fell onto the grass.

But I recovered quickly. Sure, it had been almost a year since I had seen an alien, but you only had to remember they were pretty much just like us inside. Even the really creepy-looking ones. "Hey, sorry if I startled you," I said.

His upper lip contorted into a sneer, revealing sharp teeth. "You are equipped with neither the cognitive capacity nor the physical dimensions necessary to alarm one such as myself." He made a shooing motion with the back of his hand. "Now, return to your little village of like-minded dirt-crawlers."

Excuse me? First, no welcoming committee—and now this? I stared at him for a moment before I could even muster a response. "Oh, no. I'm not from Forest Grove. I just got here from—"

"Your point of origin is irrelevant. Despite a few insignificant biological variations, humans are the same everywhere." The smile he gave me would have looked fake and condescending on any planet. "My meaning—and here I shall speak very slowly to aid your limited comprehension—was that you should vacate the premises immediately. Your ultimate destination means little to me."

I took a deep, calming breath. Usually Grandma's customers were really nice, but occasionally you came across a rude one. And then you had to remember the best thing about meeting them at a bed-and-breakfast: they would be gone in a day or two. "You know, you're not in a very good mood for someone on vacation." I tried to keep my tone light; it would kind of spoil my arrival if I got into a big argument with a Tourist before I had even seen Grandma.

He made a face like he had just noticed that my clothes were made of flaming manure. "Vacation?" he said. "You presuppose that I would choose to spend even one moment here of my own free will?"

What was this guy's problem? "Well . . . you're here, right? And this is a popular vacation spot for those who are, you know"—I leaned in and whispered so he would know that I was in on Grandma's secret—"*like you.*"

The alien cleared his throat. "There exists no one in this pathetic little galaxy who is"—he leaned in and did an impression of my voice that was very unflattering and highly accurate—"*like me.*" He straightened back up. "And certainly you did not say *popular?*" The alien scoffed so forcefully it sounded like he was hawking up a big wad of phlegm. "Your species' affinity for self-delusion is appalling."

Okay, so I might not have known what some of those words meant, but I could tell he was trying to insult me. And probably everyone I've ever met. But I remembered my training from last year. No use getting mad. Time to just start over. "Look, I think we got off on the wrong foot, with my sneaking up on you. Sorry about that." I stuck out my hand. "I'm David. I'll be working here this summer."

"Oh, I have managed to deduce that all by myself at this point in the conversation." He glanced at my hand distastefully. "There actually exist a few of us in the universe who put our brains to more use than obsessing over matters of fancy and trivia. You must be the visiting earthling child, two generations removed from the proprietor here."

I dropped my hand. Despite how rude the alien was acting, I was kind of glad that Grandma was apparently excited enough about my visit to mention it to one of her customers. "Right. So, I'm David. And you are..."

"Your barely evolved vocal mechanism could not begin to pronounce my true name."

I noticed the lettering stitched above the pocket on his coveralls. "So...I should just call you 'Bob,' then?"

His black eyes narrowed into slits. Little gray spiderweb lines appeared on his throat, creeping out of his collar and up his neck. They looked like cracks in his skin. "If a cockroach could insult a king, then I might be offended by that comment."

I couldn't help but snort a little. Maybe this is what passes for humor on the Planet of the Sarcastic Skull-Faces. I figured that since I wasn't officially on the clock yet, there was really no point in trying to get along with this guy anymore. Soon he would step into one of the transporters and get beamed back home. Maybe somebody there would be willing to listen to his antihuman tirades.

"See ya," I said.

I started to turn away, but he stepped closer. "The average life span of a human is laughably brief." He glanced up at the house, checking the windows, and then leaned in even closer. Two small red dots glowed in the center of his black eyes. The spiderweb lines turned darker and reached up past his jawline. He whispered, "If you ever sneak around and try to catch me unawares again, yours will be much shorter than average."

The look in those eyes totally freaked me out. But I forced myself to stare right back at him. "Don't worry about it," I said. "We'll probably never see each other again."

"How I wish that were true." The crack lines on his skin faded and his face was smooth and white again. He pulled on a cap that matched his workman's coveralls. "It is the great shame of my existence to admit that we are fellow employees at the moment."

My mouth fell open. "Fellow employees?"

The alien sighed heavily. He looked straight up and addressed the sky. "Why must these humans repeat everything as if the veracity of a statement will be altered somehow through its repetition?"

"Fellow employees?" I said again. I couldn't believe this. Any of this.

He looked back down at me. "Yes, that's right. Say it a few more times and you might just get it." He leaned even closer. "But here is something I shall only say once. Tell no human of the circumstances of our meeting here. And stay as far away from me as possible."

He straightened back up and marched away, along the side of the house and up the steps to the porch out front.

I just stared after him. I don't think I blinked for over a minute.

So much for my big *Welcome Back!* party.

2

When I finally got over my shock, I climbed the back porch steps. I was still excited to see Amy and Grandma again, and maybe I could figure out what was going on with that creepy alien. He had to have been messing with me about the "fellow employees" part. No way would Grandma hire someone like him.

The sounds of a heated argument drifted out through an open window. I hurried over and peeked inside.

Robert Tate may have been an ex-sheriff, but he was still a man in uniform. His khaki getup looked like a modification of his scoutmaster uniform, decorated with lots of badges that he had probably made himself. The brick-red patch on his upper arm matched the color of his face as he yelled, "Are you kidding me? There's no way he leaves this house."

Grandma stood right in front of Tate, hands on her hips and chin stuck out as she glared up at him. "This is my place of business, and I say he comes and goes as he pleases."

"Now, this here might be your place"—Tate plucked the toothpick out of his mouth and pointed it at Grandma—"but I don't work for you." He tapped a badge on his chest. "By the power vested in me by the Intergalactic Police Force, I forbid him to step even one of those feet outside of here."

Grandma scoffed. "The power vested in you isn't enough to run a night-light."

Tate puffed out his chest and wrestled his tortured belt higher up on his vast belly. The leather couldn't have been that strained when it was still on the cow. "You never seem to give the proper respect to my employer." His voice dropped dangerously low. "Keep this up, and I'll see to it that you answer to the most powerful law enforcement agency in the universe."

Grandma threw her hands in the air. "Ha!" Her bamboo bracelets rattled all around her skinny arms and her tie-dyed hippie tunic billowed around her. "And what do you suppose will happen then, Tate? Six months later some space bureaucrat will stop by and hand me a sternly worded warning in triplicate?"

"What will happen is that you'll be shut down. Or don't you remember what Commander Rezzlurr said last summer? After your grandson let pictures of alien customers get splashed across the front page? I swear, if you allow that kid's carelessness to rile up another mob—"

"No, Tate, it was *you* who did that."

I was glad Grandma stuck up for me, but I still felt bad. I *had* made some mistakes last summer. But it would be different this time.

Tate took a deep breath. "All I'm saying is that if you keep up this lackadaisical attitude about security, it'll be someone else investigating next time. And then we'll both be out of a job." He pulled a handkerchief out of his pocket and mopped at his brow. "You've always had a head full of strange notions, but I swear, you gotta be able to see sense right now. I mean, just *look* at him, will you?"

Tate gestured to the corner of the room. Squeezed into an oversized leather recliner was a huge brown beast completely covered in hairy fur. Or furry hair. He yawned and stretched out one tree trunk of a leg to rest his foot on a coffee table.

I stared. The foot dwarfed the coffee table. From the base of the heel to the tip of the shaggy big toe, it measured at least a yard. Probably longer.

And that foot looked very familiar.

"Yes, I see him, Tate," Grandma said. "He's been coming here for years and years. In fact, he's—"

"I know he's been coming here for years and years." Tate's voice was rising now. "And can you guess how I know he's been coming here? Because *everyone* knows he's been coming here. He's had his picture taken! He's been filmed strolling around in the woods! People have taken plastic molds of his footprints—why, you can buy one at the Forest Grove flea market this Saturday if you like!"

"Oh, come on, now, Tate. Pretty much everyone thinks all of those things are hoaxes."

"Is that so? Go on and type 'Bigfoot' into that Internet and you'll find people who believe, right enough. Millions of 'em."

The beast cleared his throat. "Actually, I prefer 'Sasquatch,' if you don't mind. It sounds a little more dignified." He shrugged his massive furry shoulders. "You have a name that your mother gave you, correct, sir? So how would you like it if everyone on this planet called you Roundnose? Or Giantbelly? To be reduced to a mere body part is a little depressing."

Grandma smirked. Tate shuffled his feet and avoided the beast's gaze. "I don't intend any disrespect, it's just that—"

"You know, the funny thing is that back on my planet, my feet aren't even that big. They're considered average, at best. You want big feet? Then you should see my brother-in-law. He laughs so hard when I tell him about my nickname here."

Tate turned back to Grandma. "See, that's exactly what I'm talking about. He's got a *nickname* here. And there's books and movies and T-shirts and-and-and"—Tate's face was getting purple now, and little flecks of spittle flew from his lips—"and coffee mugs! With his face on them! We're trying to keep a mighty big secret up here, and one of your guests is *famous*."

Sasquatch stood up, his head brushing against the ceiling. Tate took a step backward, and his face went several shades lighter. Sasquatch turned his shaggy head to Grandma. "I've always loved my vacations here." He spread out his hands, enormous palms upward. "But if it's going to cause problems for everyone now..."

"Oh, nonsense." Grandma reached up to pat the alien's arm, and her hand got lost in his fur. "You are always more than welcome here, you know that. Don't pay him any mind."

Sasquatch placed his hand gently on Grandma's shoulder, and most of her back disappeared under a blanket of shaggy hair. "Thank you. I do enjoy my visits. My home planet is getting so crowded, and there's just so much open space here." He glared at Tate. I noticed that the ex-sheriff dropped his own hand to his belt, but there was no longer a gun there.

Sasquatch's voice came out a little growly this time. "It would be a shame to stop these visits now. Especially when I've never been captured. Not even close."

Tate shrank back a little against the wall. "Well, now, maybe we can work something out."

"That's more like it," Grandma said. She smiled sweetly at Tate, but it was a little too big to be genuine. "I knew you were capable of seeing some sense."

"But you can't disguise him like you do the others, you know."

"Oh, of course not. I don't even try that. He'll just slip quietly into the forest, like always."

"I'm not gonna let him just wander out of the house by himself." Tate stepped away from the wall and tried to reclaim some of his swagger. "We're too close to town, could be some hikers real close by. Or people fishing at the river, kids building forts in the woods, whatever."

Sasquatch crossed his arms over his barrel chest and loomed over Tate. Grandma stepped in between the two of them. "So what do you propose?" she asked.

"He can squeeze in the backseat of the Jeep, and I'll throw a few blankets over him. Then I'll drive him through the forest and up to the end of that old logging road. Nobody's used it in years. He can hop out up there and have his vacation, as long as he promises to stay well away from any humans. But if—"

I couldn't stay quiet any longer. "Can I come?" I said.

They all turned. "David!" Grandma said, throwing her arms wide. I scrambled through the window and she rushed over and gave me a big hug. "It's so good to see you."

I hugged her back. "You too, Grandma." I stepped away and gave a little wave to the man in uniform. "Hi, Mr. Tate." I wasn't too excited to see him, obviously, but he was Amy's dad, after all. It was probably a good idea to be polite.

He touched his finger to the brim of his hat. "Hey, kid."

Grandma took me by the arm. "David, I'd like you to meet one of my most loyal customers. Sasquatch, this is my grandson. David will be here for the summer."

Bigfoot stuck out a woolly paw and I shook it. "Hi there," he said. "Any relation of your grandma's is a friend of mine."

"Thanks. I mean, hi," I said. I had never met someone famous before, and I was a little nervous. "I'm ... well, I'm a big fan."

Tate rolled his eyes. "See what I mean?" he muttered to the ceiling.

"So, what do you do when you visit Earth?" I asked.

"I usually head up to Nooksack Falls first. The salmon up there are spectacular." He licked his lips. "And there's a great maze of deep caves near the top of Mount Baker. I'm a bit of a spelunker." He glanced sideways at Tate. "Don't worry, the humans can't visit these caves. They'd have to come in by helicopter, and there's no place to land."

"That sounds fun," I said.

"How long will you be staying with us?" Grandma said.

"It's just a quick getaway this time—maybe a day or so. I'll need to be back at work soon."

Whoa. Bigfoot had a job? "What do you do?"

Sasquatch looked at the ground and cleared his throat. "You'll laugh."

I shook my head. "No way. I'm really curious."

The huge beast shuffled his feet back and forth. "Well, on my home planet . . . I manage a shoe store."

Tate chuckled. Sasquatch's head jerked up and he pointed at the security officer. "But that doesn't give you a license to perpetuate stereotypes by using my earthling nickname."

"Wouldn't dream of it," Tate said, smirking. He crossed to a trunk sitting against the wall and pulled out some blankets. "Time to head out. Getting dusky out there, and I don't want to be on that logging road in the pitch black."

"I'm coming with you," Grandma said.

"Oh, no you don't," Tate said. "We're not leaving him in charge of this place." He tilted his head in my direction.

"I trust David's judgment a lot more than that of some other people around here," she said. Tate's face went red again. He opened his mouth for a rebuttal, but Grandma cut him off. "Besides, the Director of Tourist Entertainment is on duty tonight. Practically running the whole show, as usual. And we do have additional adult help around here now, remember? This place will be in great hands, and we'll only be gone a half hour or so."

Director of Tourist Entertainment? How many aliens did she have working here now? Because there was no way she was talking about Skull Face. Or was she? Man, I couldn't think of anyone less suited to a job like that. Except maybe Tate.

The security man harrumphed. "There you go proving my point again. This is just the kind of slapdash approach to security that I'm talking abou—"

"Oh, go use some of that hot air to warm up the Jeep."

Sasquatch barked out a laugh but tried to disguise it as a cough. I bit the inside of my cheek to keep from busting up.

Tate gave us both a sour look. "Here, carry these." He thrust the armful of blankets at Sasquatch, fished the Jeep keys out of his pocket, and kicked open the back door.

Sasquatch looked at us with raised eyebrows after Tate stalked off. "I suppose I should follow. I'd hate to see what happens if he ever gets in a bad mood."

"Have a good vacation," I said.

"Thanks. Nice to meet you, David." The big alien smiled and gave me a wave before ducking his head to get through the doorway.

Grandma put her hands on my shoulders and looked at me. "I'm sorry not to be able to welcome you properly. I just don't trust that man to be polite to my guests if he's out on his own."

"It's okay. I understand."

She winked at me. "Thanks, David. We'll have time for a nice chat later. It is so wonderful to see you again." She gave me another hug.

"Oh, before you go, just one question," I said. "I met an alien outside. Tall guy, white face? He said he works here?"

"Oh, yes. That's Scratchull. He's our new repairman."

"Scratchull?"

"That's a shortened version. His proper name is too long and complicated for us Earth types. I'm glad you got a chance to meet him, though."

"But . . . he actually works here?"

"Yes. We were having so many problems with the transporters that I had to bring in some off-world help."

"Really? What, did you put a classified ad in an alien newspaper or something?"

Grandma smiled. "Scratchull comes highly recommended from some administrative folks with the Collective. In fact, a group of them escorted him here for the interview, and then—"

"Let's get moving," Tate barked as he stuck his head back in the door. "Your friend's all scrunched up in the backseat. You don't want him to get a cramp, do you?"

"All right, all right," Grandma said. "I'm sorry, David, we'll catch up later." She took a few steps toward the door, then turned back to me. "Amy is working tonight." Grandma winked. "She's around here somewhere. I'm sure she'll be happy to talk to you again."

Tate took his wet toothpick out of his mouth and pointed it at me. "You see that talking is all you do, boy. I'll be back soon." His eyes narrowed into slits. "Real soon."

I wandered around, looking for Amy. A series of muffled *bangs!*, like a string of firecrackers going off under a pillow, came from the kitchen.

I nudged open the swinging door. There was Amy, overseeing pans of popping corn on three stove burners. She divided her attention expertly between all three, stirring this one, adding salt to that one, lowering the temperature on another one.

She looked great. It had been less than a year since I had seen her last, but it was like she had time-warped ahead to a much older version of herself. A more developed version.

The same thing was happening to all of the girls in my grade back home in Florida.

It made me kind of nervous, actually. Because I had barely grown an inch since last summer. I know, because I measured myself every week of the basketball season. Sometimes twice a week.

But still, it was great to see her. I pushed the door the rest of the way open and watched her from the doorway. She had cut her hair shorter, and I think that's part of why she looked so much older. She was wearing cutoff denim shorts and a tank top, and she looked taller even though her flip-flops had really thin soles. I hoped she wasn't taller than me now. She also had—

"David!" Amy bounced over and hugged me around the neck. But before I had time to put my arms around her, she pulled away and hurried back to the stove. "Sorry, I have to make sure none of this burns."

"That's okay. It's nice to see—"

"Can you grab a couple of bowls for me? Quick?" The lids on top of the pans were being pushed upward by the bubbling mass of popcorn underneath. I moved to the cupboards. "No, they're over there now. I've moved things around a little bit." I stopped and tried to see where she was pointing. I crossed to another wall of cupboards. "No, they're right there." I stopped again, confused. "Never mind, I'll do it."

Amy dashed away from the stove, grabbed a few oversized plastic bowls from a bottom row of cupboards, and thrust them at me. "Here, hold these."

Freshly popped corn spilled over the sides of the pans and scattered across the stovetop. Amy wrapped her hand in a towel, then grabbed the pans and dumped hot popcorn into the bowls. I tried to keep them steady in my outstretched arms.

When the pans were empty she set them back on the stove and turned off the burners. "That's great. Follow me." She took one of the bowls and marched through the swinging door and down a side hall. But why bring all of this popcorn down here? If I remembered right, the only thing at the end of this hall was a dingy spare room full of cardboard boxes and dust.

Amy eased the door open, and I almost dropped the bowls. The room was so clean it was shiny, and the walls were painted in bright colors. They were also covered with crayon drawings on notebook paper. It looked like a kindergarten classroom . . . only here the simple, childlike pictures depicted alien beings of every shape and size standing in front of exotic planetary landscapes. The room was also filled with toys and stuffed animals and helium-filled balloons.

"I did a little decorating while you were gone," Amy whispered.

"I guess so," I breathed. The transformation of the room was amazing, but what really caught my eye was the group of aliens huddled around the TV. They were all very small, so I guessed that they were either from pygmy planets, or, more likely, they were kids. There was a big cozy pile of them on the floor, maybe a dozen altogether, lounging against beanbag chairs, pillows, and one another.

And it was pretty obvious that they were all from different planets. A little alien with fluorescent-orange skin rested his head and antennae against someone else's scaly red shoulder as they watched TV together. Another young Tourist sat cross-legged (only she had three legs and a tail, so it looked like she was sitting on a big pretzel) and braided the long yellow tentacles sprouting out of the neck of the alien sitting in front of her.

"What the...?"

"It's Movie Night," Amy whispered, clearly not wanting to disturb the little crowd of Tourists. "I host it every weekend. The parents drop their kids off for the evening and then have a little time to themselves—dinner in Forest Grove, or a hike in the woods, or whatever."

"Really?"

"Yeah. It helps with repeat business for your grandma. I think some Tourists come here for the weekend just so they can get away from their kids for a little while."

"So when did you—"

"Wait, watch this part. It always gets a big reaction," Amy said. The TV screen was black and white and sort of grainy. "Alien kids love these old sci-fi movies from the fifties. They always get the biggest kick out of seeing what humans think aliens might look like. Or act like."

On-screen a young couple stared wide-eyed at the mouth of a cave. The background music swelled to a crescendo, and the woman put her hand over her mouth in a close-up, stifling a scream. The alien kids all leaned forward as one, completely silent.

Suddenly the movie "alien" lumbered out of the cave. It was an actor in a ridiculous gorilla suit, only he was wearing what looked like a fishbowl on his head with two metal antennae sticking out of the top. Talk about cheesy. I wondered if kids in the fifties knew what they were missing with the complete lack of realistic CGI.

The alien kids erupted into an explosion of sound. Some were making squealing noises, and others sounded like they were barking, but it was clear by their faces that they were all laughing as hard as they could. They pointed at the screen and slapped each other on the back, and the whole colorful pile wriggled with their happy hysterics.

The woman on-screen finally let loose with her scream while the man picked up a stick and tried to subdue the shuffling, badly costumed space beast, and it all made the alien kids laugh even harder.

One of the little Tourists—he looked sort of like a cross between a big lizard and a small kangaroo—jumped up in front of the TV. He grabbed a container of Legos, dumped them out on the ground, then jammed the clear plastic tub over his head. He stuck his arms straight out in front of him and lurched toward the crowd in a perfect imitation of the actor in the stiff gorilla suit.

The kids let loose with fresh shrieks of laughter. Another alien, the one with the yellow tentacles, jumped up and grabbed a plastic Wiffle Ball bat to "protect" the others, swinging as wildly and inaccurately as the B-movie actor.

"All right, all right," Amy shouted over the laughter and screams, stepping all the way into the room. "You could hurt someone there, you little space slugger."

"Amy!" The whole mob converged, hugging her legs. They completely encircled Amy and jumped up and down in excitement. I just stood outside the circle and watched.

"And she brought Earth treats!" The little aliens reached for the popcorn.

"You know the rules: no snatching at the food." She lightly swatted at red and scaly hands as they reached over the rim of a bowl. "And Xantork, no extending those grabby arms of yours." The little red alien, who was the shortest of them all, let go of the bowl. He gave Amy a sheepish grin and sucked his wiry arms almost all the way back into his torso with a slurping sound. "Now, everyone sit down nicely, and you can have your snack." The alien kids flopped back on the floor around the TV. Amy passed out the bowls. One roundish, greenish kid stuck his long snout right into the bowl and sucked up popcorn like a vacuum cleaner.

"Gross!" the orange alien said. "Amy, he's hogging all of the corn explosions and getting his slimy spit all over them!"

Amy shook her head in mock sadness. "Oh, well . . . maybe I'll just have to turn off the movie . . ."

"No!" they all cried.

"All right, then get along. And only take your fair share, you." Amy pointed at the green alien, who began gingerly picking out one kernel at a time with the tip of his snout.

The kids turned back to the TV. The plodding movie alien was chasing the humans and somehow gaining on them, even though they could have crawled away much faster than he could lumber around in that big rubber suit. The kids howled and pointed and crammed popcorn into various facial openings.

Amy motioned toward the door. We stepped out into the hall together.

"Wow. You do this every weekend?"

Amy nodded. "It's kind of fun. They have a lot of energy and it can get a little crazy sometimes, but they're great."

"But none of them are in their earthling disguises."

"Yeah. We decided that in the evenings, as long as they weren't going outside for the rest of the night, they could take those off. Just inside the B-and-B. Let them be themselves, you know? It can get stuffy wearing a disguise and unfamiliar clothes all the time, especially for kids."

Man, she seemed different. More grown up, or something. Definitely more confident. Had *I* changed that much? It didn't seem like it.

We had e-mailed back and forth during the school year, of course, so why did it feel kind of awkward to see her again? It's probably because I'm not the best e-mail correspondent— I'm mostly good for forwarding along funny videos or sharing music downloads, but that's about it. I guess I'm just better face-to-face. And speaking of being face-to-face...

"So, do you have a little time to catch up while they finish the movie? We could sit out in the backyard." She didn't immediately say yes. I was sort of expecting her to immediately say yes. "The stars should be coming out pretty soon," I added. I realized it was pretty shameless to use her obsession with astronomy to try to get some alone time with her, but it had been so long since I had seen her.

Amy made the *Eeesh-I'm-really-sorry* face. "I'd love to, David, but I have a few more jobs tonight. You can tag along if you want, though. Follow me."

Tag along? That made me sound like someone's little brother. But I found myself following her down the hall anyway. "More jobs? On a Friday night? Let me guess: you're the official Director of Tourist Entertainment."

"That's right." Amy smiled at me over her shoulder. "It's a big job. Too bad I can't put it on my college application."

"Grandma's really cracking the whip on you."

Amy pushed through the swinging door and opened the refrigerator. "Oh, most of this stuff I set up on my own." She took a pitcher of iced tea from the top shelf and handed it to me. "In fact, your grandma is always telling me to take some time off and hang out with friends, or do more school things. *Normal* things." Amy grabbed a stack of plastic cups from the counter and rolled her eyes. "But who needs boring, normal stuff when you can hang out here, right? Come on."

I followed her down the main hallway and up the stairs. She knocked lightly and pushed open the door to 4B.

There were aliens in this room, too, but they were bigger, and their varying colors were muted. Tinged with gray. Many of them sat in rocking chairs.

Amy set the cups on a table in the center of the room. Four aliens sat around it playing a card game. She motioned to me, and I placed the pitcher of iced tea beside the cups.

"Oh, thank you, dear," said one of them, and she reached out and patted Amy on the back with a many-fingered hand.

"You're welcome," Amy said. "Everybody, this is my friend David. His grandma owns the bed-and-breakfast, and he'll be staying here this summer."

Most of the aliens in the room glanced up and gave a quick wave (or nodded, or shook their jowls, or buzzed, depending on the mode of greeting on their home planet) but returned quickly to their games. A few pairs of aliens sat at little tables spread around the room playing checkers or chess, and there was a group sitting in the corner, knitting.

"Aha! I trump your human queen-person!" A grayish alien with a head so squished it was almost football-shaped slapped a card on the table.

"Mr. Nikto..." Amy put her hands on her hips and raised her eyebrows.

"What? What did I do?" the gray alien said.

"When your eyes flash green like that, it means you're using your X-ray vision, doesn't it?"

The other aliens groaned and threw down their cards.

Amy stepped back to where I was standing by the doorway. "Aren't they cute?" she whispered.

"Sure," I said. "So, is this another, you know, thing you've set up?"

She nodded. "Seniors Night. Twice a week. They aren't very mobile, so I figured I'd start teaching them some quiet Earth games. Bridge, pinochle, there's even a shuffleboard court out back. That sort of thing."

Amy poured iced tea, handed out refreshments, and made small talk with the elderly aliens.

I just stared at her. I couldn't believe she had done all of this. How did she have the time? Or the energy? When I was working here last summer it was all I could do to keep up with the GRADE jobs (that stands for Greeting and Review of Alien's Disguise for Earth). I felt so exhausted at the end of each day that there's no way I would have been able to do stuff like this.

And let's be honest, even if I had had the time... I never would have thought of setting up activities. I should have known she would be much better at this job than I could ever be.

Amy finished making her way around the room and said good-bye to the aliens. I followed her into the hall. "I think it's really cool that you're doing all of this for them. And for Grandma's business."

"Thanks," Amy said. We walked down the stairs. "But I'm no saint or anything. I mean, I'm not just doing it for them. It gives me so many chances to talk to a wide variety of aliens. It's fascinating. We have so much to learn from them."

She pushed through the swinging door into the kitchen and washed out the pitcher in the sink. I moved in closer to help, but it was really a one-person job, so I just sort of watched her.

"You're probably tired from your long day of travel. And it's really three hours later for you, right? You must be exhausted." Amy glanced at me over her shoulder. "Grandma said you'll be in the same room as last year. I understand if you want to crash. I can see you in the morning."

"Actually, I'm more hungry than tired. Does Forest Grove still have that diner that's open late? Maybe we could walk into town and get something to eat. You know, after you finish up your jobs?"

"That sounds like fun. Really." Amy placed the pitcher on the rack and wiped her hands on a towel. "But after the movie I promised the kids I'd read them some bedtime stories. Then I'll have to clean up the playroom and help the seniors wrap up and get to bed. The diner will probably be closed after all of that."

She must have seen the disappointed expression on my

face, because she stepped closer and kind of patted me on the shoulder. It was a little awkward. "I'm sorry you got here on such a busy night, David. But we'll have all summer to hang out. Okay?"

"Sure." We just looked at each other for a minute. "Well, I guess I'll head up to my room."

"All right. I'm going to get a few things ready in here for the breakfast rush tomorrow."

I turned to walk out of the kitchen but stopped at the swinging door and looked back at her. "Hey, about this new guy. The one that fixes the transporters or something?"

"Oh, you mean Scratchull."

"Yeah, what's up with him?"

"He got here a few weeks ago. And just in time, too. Three of the transporters didn't work at all, and one of them kept short-circuiting and bringing in Tourists that were trying to go somewhere else. It was a mess."

I shrugged. "That's good, I guess. But—"

"And he doesn't use a translator chip. Isn't that amazing? Already speaks perfect English. Apparently he knows thousands of languages. He's crazy smart."

"Okay...but isn't he a little...?"

"What?"

"I don't know. I got a weird vibe from him."

Amy waved away my concerns. "Oh, he might not be as bubbly as some of the customers, but he's fine. And I know your grandma is glad that he's here."

"All right. Well...good night."

"'Night. See you in the morning."

I left the kitchen and plodded my way up the staircase.

My room was chilly. I had forgotten how quickly the air cooled down in the Pacific Northwest after the sun went down. Back home in Florida it stays warm all night, especially in the summer.

I went to close the window but paused for a minute, looking out at the first stars showing in the darkening sky over Forest Grove.

It's good to be back, I told myself. Really. Now I just had to figure out how I'd fit in around here this summer.

A thumping sound woke me up way too early in the morning. Someone at the door? My feet untangled themselves from the quilt, and I shuffled across the room. I eased the door open. The hallway was empty.

Thump! Thump! Thumpthumpthump! Ka-chunk!

What the ...? It sounded so close. I crossed the hall and peeked into the alien bathroom. Also empty.

Rubbing the sleep out of my eyes, I went back into my room.

A blue light, the size of a dinner plate and set in the center of the transporter door, glowed brightly. That usually meant a new arrival.

Had Scratchull missed this transporter repair on his rounds? I like hanging out with most of the aliens, but I definitely did not need them randomly showing up in my room at the crack of dawn.

I walked over and put my ear to the door.

Thump! Thumpthumpthump!

Whoa. Definitely coming from in there. But what kind of alien could be making all that noise? And why didn't they just open the door—were they trying to bust their way out?

"Hello?" I called. The sounds cut out completely for a couple of seconds, then started up again double time. The heavy door shuddered in its frame.

I took a couple of steps backward. Staring at the door, I remembered how nervous I was last summer to meet my first alien Tourists. That had turned out all right, but this seemed . . . different. Whatever was in there sounded pretty agitated.

I considered going to get Tate, but only for about half a second. Admitting to him that I was scared and needed his help was not a good way to start off the summer. And it's not like I would ask Grandma or Amy to do something I wouldn't do.

So I gripped the metal handle, counted to ten, and tugged the door open.

All I could see was a blur of purple. After a moment my eyes adjusted to the rush of motion, and I could make out a round-ish mass, about the size of a beach ball, ricocheting crazily from wall to ceiling to wall to floor. *Thump! Thumpthumpthump!*

I was about to slam the door shut when the ball launched out of the room and smacked me in the sternum. The force of the blow knocked me flat on my back, my head banging off the wooden floorboards. Something slimy slurped across my face.

The purple beach ball stood on my chest, balancing on six little legs. Its tail was going a million miles an hour, but it wasn't exactly wagging. More like twirling. Its eyes were wide and green and only a few inches from my face. And its whole body bounced up and down as it panted, a long tongue slipping in and out of its mouth.

Slorch! That tongue dragged across my face again. I reached up to wipe the slimy trail from my cheeks when the beach ball shot off my chest and scampered around the room.

When it hit the corner it scaled straight up the wall, then dashed to the middle of the ceiling. It hung there, upside down and panting, scanning the room with those wide eyes.

Suddenly it dropped from the ceiling, hit the floor on its back and bounced in the air, then flipped over and landed on all six feet. I caught a glimpse of a double row of sharp teeth as it panted some more. Then it was swarming around the room again like a cyclone, rebounding off the walls, the bed, the chest of drawers.

I inched along the wall to get closer to the door and make my escape. Now I didn't feel too embarrassed about finding Tate. He could earn his paycheck this morning.

But as I eased the door open I paused and studied the thing. If it kept zooming around the room like that, sooner or later it was going to smash right into the window. Right *through* the window, probably. It could get hurt, I suppose, but that was the least of my worries. I could imagine that thing rocketing down the street into downtown Forest Grove. Not good. Keeping Grandma's secret about her customers was the only way to keep her in business . . . and the rest of us out of jail. Or out of a super-secret-military science lab a mile underground somewhere.

"Hey," I called. "Settle down."

The little purple alien stopped short. He was standing on the wall above the headboard of my bed. There was a smattering of light blue dots on his back, near his tail. Their coloring was so bright, the dots almost seemed to sparkle.

The thing looked down at me, his round body pulsating with his heavy panting.

"Do you speak English?" I said. He cocked his head and regarded me curiously. "Do you speak anything?" His tongue slipped in and out of his mouth in time with his heavy breathing. I could almost swear he was smiling.

I dropped to one knee and snapped my fingers near the floor. "Come here, boy. Right over here." I felt a little embarrassed, talking in that high-pitched voice that people use with puppies. But it seemed right. And what else could I do?

The alien tilted his head from one side to the other, studying me. "That's right, boy," I said. "I'm not gonna hurt you." Hopefully the feeling was mutual. Who was to say the thing didn't have a set of retractable tusks and a taste for raw earthling flesh?

Although, somehow I wasn't too worried about that. As weird as the little guy seemed, there was something about him that was . . . well, I might call it *cute*, if that was a word I ever used. But I don't.

The purple beach ball shuffled its feet down the wall, gazing at me the whole time, and then hopped onto the top of the headboard. "Good job," I half whispered. "That's a good boy. Now, come right on down here." He studied me for another minute, then fell sideways off the headboard, bounced off the mattress, and landed on all sixes on the floor a few feet away.

"That's it." I eased forward. Slowly. Just as slowly, the alien shambled backward.

I stopped. He stopped.

I patted the floor in front of me. He did the same with one of his front feet.

"Come on, now. Don't play games with me." Every time I inched forward, he backed up the same amount. We made a full circle of the room that way.

Time to try something different. I stood and walked to my suitcase. He took that as his cue to zoom all over the room again.

I looked at the candy-bar selection in my bag. Which would be most enticing for a nonverbal, hyperactive mini-alien? I unwrapped a chocolate bar, a nut roll, and a pack of licorice. He could decide.

I knelt down again and held up the treats. The alien froze in place on top of the chest of drawers. A small cave opened up underneath his green eyes, and a few wispy tendrils snaked out and danced in the air, making a sniffing noise. Then they sucked back into his face, and he hopped down on the floor.

He crept toward me, very slowly, head tilted toward the ground but eyes looking up. I held out the treats. I tensed up my muscles, ready to grab him when he was close enough.

But before I had time to blink, he darted forward, inhaled all three candy offerings, jumped up, used my forehead as a springboard, and did a backflip onto the bed.

He sat still for a moment and we stared at each other. *Gulp!* He swallowed the food. Then he shook all over, took a run at the headboard, bounced off of it, and did a double backflip. Then he was racing all over the walls and ceiling again.

Enough with the bribes and sweet talk. Time for a more direct approach.

I crawled over, tugged the quilt off the bed, gathered it up in my hands, and knelt on the floor in a sprinter's crouch. Watching the little alien zoom around the room, I tried to make out a pattern in his chaotic path.

He seemed to be passing by my side of the bed every three or four laps, although that wasn't exact. I was going to need a little luck.

I coiled the muscles in my legs. The purple blur hit the ceiling, then the wall over the headboard, then bounced on my side of the bed—

I pounced, throwing the quilt over him like a net. Got him! A round lump shot up in the middle of the quilt, and I tackled it, scooping up the alien in a wriggling ball underneath the cloth. I hoped this wasn't the part where some horrible alien defense mechanism kicked in and things got ugly.

Finally the alien stopped struggling and settled down. Slowly, keeping a tight grip on him, I pulled back some of the quilt until his little face poked out. He started making a whistling noise and short bursts of high-pitched sound.

However—and this might seem weird—they sounded like *happy* whistles. His tongue shot out of his mouth and gave me a big slurp on the cheek again. It was a little gross, but it was better than hydrochloric acid shooting out of his eyes or something.

I relaxed my grip. I didn't want to hurt the little guy. Keeping him wrapped up in the quilt and holding him to my chest, I nudged the door open with my foot and stepped out into the hall. Time to show him to the others. Hopefully somebody would know what to do.

Grandma was in the kitchen when I made my way downstairs with the wriggling lump of quilt-covered alien. She was pulling something out of the oven, and it actually smelled really good. If you know anything about Grandma's organic-tofu-centric cooking skills, then you know how surprising that was.

"Ah, you're awake. A pleasant new day to you, David," Grandma said. "And what do you have there?" She crossed the kitchen, holding a steaming pie in two oven-mitted hands.

I kept a firm grip on the alien, pinning him to my side

with one arm while I used my free hand to pull back a corner of the quilt. The little guy peered out from underneath with those wide green eyes. "He was banging away on the transporter walls in my room this morning," I said. "I opened the door and he spazzed out. He doesn't talk and I think he might be, like, somebody's pet or something. But he was all alone."

Grandma moved closer, bent down, and peered in at him. "Well, my stars and comets. He's a cute little creature, isn't he?"

"I don't know. I guess so."

A few of those wispy tendrils snuck out of the blanket and sniffed the air. I barely had time to notice how close that pie was before a long tongue shot out, wrapped itself around the dessert, pie tin and all, and sucked it back inside the quilt. Furious chomping sounds came from underneath while the whole quilt shivered, and then the pie tin flew back out and clattered on the kitchen tile.

"Sorry, Grandma. I should have been more careful—he did the same thing with some of my candy bars." I peered inside the quilt and tried to look stern. "Bad...thing! You hear me? Bad!" It was hard to scold him with a straight face, though. He was slurping pie filling off his purple lips and not even pretending to try to look ashamed of himself.

"Actually, that's a good sign. I'm flattered he liked it so much," Grandma said. "It means I must be one step closer to winning the big contest!"

"Contest?"

"Oh, I forgot, you haven't been here. The whole town has been getting ready for weeks." Grandma picked up the pie tin and brought it to the sink. "The annual Pioneer Day Festival is a bigger deal than usual this summer. Forest Grove is celebrating its centennial."

Wow. A hundred years of Forest Grove. Maybe in another century or so they'd get a second stoplight in this town. Or if they dreamed big, some cell-phone service.

Grandma ran soap and water over the pie tin while she scrubbed it. "They hold a baking contest every year. It was Tate's idea that I sign up to compete this time—fairly forced me to do it. Claims I need to be a more active part of the community. The *human* community, that is. After . . . well, after what happened last summer . . . with everyone showing up and almost storming the front—"

"I remember." My face got hot. Yes, the whole thing had been my fault, but did it have to keep coming up? It had turned out all right in the end, hadn't it?

Grandma cleared her throat and finished quickly. "Anyway, he thinks maintaining friendly relations with the townsfolk is the first line of defense in keeping our little secret."

She dropped the pie tin into the dish drainer and crossed the kitchen floor to me. She lowered her voice to a whisper. "Now, don't tell Tate this, but I'm actually glad he's gotten me into this contest. I think it will be a real hoot." She grinned and looked around, checking the kitchen for eavesdroppers. "But I don't want to give Tate the satisfaction of knowing that I think he actually came up with a good idea for once."

"Your secret's safe with me," I said. "*All* your secrets. Promise."

I shifted the alien so I could use both arms to hold him. He had settled down since eating two big snacks—he might have even been asleep—and the deadweight was making my arms tired.

"Well then, maybe I can let you in on another little secret." Grandma grinned mischievously. She walked over to where another pie was cooling on the counter. "Try a taste of this." She lifted out a slice and plopped it on a plate.

"Okay...um, you did use sugar, right?" You could never be too careful when sampling Grandma's cooking.

"Didn't need to. That's part of the secret," Grandma said.

Uh-oh. Knowing her, she might have used anything to sweeten that dessert—raw molasses, condensed goat's milk —anything.

I covered up the little alien's head with the quilt so he wouldn't wake up and snatch any more food. Grandma got a forkful of pie and held it out to me. I closed my eyes, mentally prepared myself for the worst, and took a bite.

"Hey...that's actually pretty good," I said. "I mean, that's really good."

Grandma laughed. "Don't act *too* surprised, now." She scooped up some more with the fork and offered it to me. I finished the whole piece in three more bites.

Grandma wiped off my chin with a paper towel. "It's nice to know that someone other than an uninvited purple alien pet appreciates my baking skills."

I licked the last bit of pie filling from the corner of my mouth. I'm not real good at describing how things taste, but it had a deep sweetness with a little bit of tartness around the edges. "You know, I can honestly say I've never tasted anything like that," I said.

"I shouldn't think so." Grandma winked at me. "Unless maybe you've been doing some traveling to the planet Kernta in the Mahkker galaxy."

I suddenly became very aware of the pie's lingering aftertaste. "Wait a minute . . . do you mean that you actually used . . . ?"

"I certainly did!" Grandma opened the fridge and took out a plastic bowl. "Sweet and juicy Kerntaberries. After a hundred years of tasting the same old apple pies and strawberry tarts, the taste buds on those Pioneer Day judges are liable to hop up and start dancing right on their tongues. I might be declared the undisputed winner all the way until the bicentennial gets here." Grandma grinned at her own joke.

"But isn't that sort of like cheating?"

"Now, David." Grandma used an overly serious tone. "I've read over the baking contest rules three times now, and not once did I see mention of a ban on berries harvested on other planets. If something like that had been included, I promise I would have followed it." She waggled her eyebrows and held the bowl up for me. "Try one. They're good in the pie, but I like them even better plain."

I peeked into the bowl. The berries were fat, round, and so fluorescent pinkish-purple, they almost glowed. "I don't know, Grandma . . . couldn't that be, like, dangerous or something?" I leaned forward and sniffed at the alien berries. "And should you really be baking those up and serving them to the entire town of Forest Grove?"

"Oh, come now, you're starting to sound just like Tate.

I've been eating these for ages—one of my returning guests always brings them as a gift." Grandma grabbed a berry and popped it into her mouth. Then she stretched her arms out and twirled around on the kitchen floor tiles, the colors on her rainbow tunic swirling like a kaleidoscope. "And don't I look healthy? Why, I can't remember the last time I had anything worse than the sniffles. In fact, I can't remember the last time I even had the sniffles. If anything, this will be good for the people of Forest Grove."

The door swung open, and that creepy ghost-faced alien in dark coveralls walked in. He stopped in the middle of the kitchen, closed his eyes, inhaled deeply, and then let out his breath with an *aaahhhhhhh*. "I have visited thousands of planets throughout hundreds of galaxies," he said in that deep voice of his, "but never encountered such an enchanting aroma. Whatever can that be?"

Grandma giggled. Actually giggled. "It's my soon-to-be-award-winning pie recipe." She nudged me with her elbow and nodded at the alien. "Scratchull here is my number one fan when it comes to my cooking."

Scratchull opened his eyes, swept up Grandma's wrist in his bone-white fingers, and kissed her on the back of the hand. "Never were words more true."

Oh, please. Where was the Ego Monster from Planet Disdain that I had met in the shed yesterday?

Grandma giggled. Again. I didn't know which was worse: how he was acting, or the fact that Grandma was falling for it. I instinctively took a few steps backward. The air seemed colder around that guy.

"Would you like to take a break and sample a piece, Scratchull?" Grandma said.

"Indeed I would, madam. But I have much important work to do for you today. And, if truth be known, that smell is so intoxicating, I fear I would be unable to stop myself from devouring the entire dessert, serving dish and all."

Grandma grinned and shook her head. "Such a teaser, Scratchull." She playfully swatted at his hand, which still held hers. "But that reminds me. Believe it or not, we had someone do that very same thing, just a moment ago. Maybe you can help us identify the little creature." She motioned to the bundle in my arms.

Up until this point, Scratchull had not acknowledged my presence in any way—had, in fact, not even glanced at me. But now he turned and sneered in my direction. "How may I be of service?"

Grandma nodded toward me. "David's holding a little extraterrestrial friend under there. Found him in the transporter this morning. We think he might be a pet of some kind—he's friendly and hungry but he doesn't speak."

Scratchull stroked his chin for a few moments. "Is it housebroken?"

"Well, I guess we're not sure yet," Grandma said. "He's only been here half an hour."

"I was referring to the earthling child."

Grandma giggled yet again. "Oh, didn't I say he was a teaser, David?" I scowled at Scratchull, and he gave me a withering smile. "Earthling children get that figured out by the time they're two or three years old," she told him.

"You must be so proud."

Grandma pulled back a corner of the quilt. "Maybe you could take a look at him? You might have seen one of these before. I know you to be a well-traveled gentleman."

"Indeed." Scratchull lowered his head to have a look, but remained a safe distance away from the alien's tongue range.

"Do you recognize it?" Grandma asked.

"I do. What you have there is a common snarffle," he said to Grandma. "Domesticated household companion on several planets throughout the Axomedian galaxy."

"I'm assuming they're safe, then. Tame?" Grandma said.

"Yes, it's harmless. The snarffle is a gentle creature by nature," Scratchull said. "Tendency to be hyperactive, low IQ, short attention span." He looked right at me. "You two should get along just fine."

I glared at him, but he was pretending not to notice me again.

"Maybe you could take a look at the transporter in David's room," Grandma said. "I figure that either the little fella jumped into a transporter on his home planet and knocked into the buttons, or else there was a malfunction and his owners were sent one way and he went the other. Either way, his family is sure to be worried about him."

I didn't like the thought of that pale-skinned alien in my room for any reason. I'd have to remove anything of value before he went up there.

"I would be delighted to help. At the moment I am on my way to assist your head of security with a task, but I shall move directly to the transporter as soon as I am finished."

"Thank you, Scratchull."

"Good day." He gave a little bow and then left through the swinging kitchen door.

"I tell you, David, I feel so fortunate to have found reliable off-world help," Grandma said. "That Scratchull is—David, whatever is the matter?"

I was glaring at the kitchen door, imagining all sorts of nasty things I'd like to say to him. "I just don't like that guy."

"What? Why?"

"I don't know. . . . He creeps me out. I don't trust him."

Grandma gave me a funny look. "I must say, David, I'm surprised at this attitude. I thought you learned last summer to be more tolerant of those who are different."

"I did. I just . . . That doesn't mean I have to like everybody."

Grandma frowned slightly. "I suppose not. But you just arrived, David. I do wish you would give everyone here more of a chance."

I considered pressing it, telling her all of the reasons that guy didn't feel right, but I knew it wouldn't do any good. It's not like I was going to change Grandma's peace-and-love-make-the-cosmos-spin philosophy. And besides, there were times last summer when I was glad that she found the good in me even when I couldn't find any there myself. "Okay. Whatever."

I shifted the quilt-covered bundle for a better grip. Grandma inclined her head toward the kitchen table. "Let's sit down, shall we? Looks like he's getting pretty heavy."

We sat at the table and munched on berries. I felt like Grandma thought I was being a jerk about Scratchull, so I tried to change the subject.

"So, what kind of jobs do you want me to do around here this summer? Should I start out by helping you with the GRADE duties like last year, help get the Tourists disguised and ready to leave the B-and-B and mingle with the earthlings?"

"Actually, Amy has that chore pretty much covered," Grandma said. She scooped up a few more berries. "She's updated the *Your Vacation on Earth* brochure to give potential visitors much more information, and then—"

"She did? Really?"

"Oh, yes. She had to wade through months of requests and red tape with the Interstellar Tourism Bureau, but she finally got it done. She's tenacious, that one. And then she made a little self-service tutorial booklet for each Tourist when they get here. We still drop in and check out their disguises, of course, but it's mostly to give them a quick personal greeting, see if they have any questions. It takes up much less time than it used to."

"And now you have more time to experiment with alien recipes and enter baking contests?"

Grandma smiled. "Exactly. Isn't it wonderful? I'm so lucky that you brought her into my life last summer. She's perfect, David, just perfect. And she also helps me keep Tate in check"—Grandma lowered her voice—"although he has been surprisingly useful at times. But don't ever tell him I said that." I nodded and tried to smile back, but Grandma must have seen something on my face. "David . . . is anything else wrong, dear?"

I shrugged. Remembering my semi-awkward interaction with Amy, I wanted to ask if maybe she had met someone else during the last school year. Someone else who happened to be a guy. Maybe someone taller and older and who knew almost as much about science and stuff as she did. But there was no way I was going to ask Grandma all of that.

"I don't know ... I just want to be able to help you out. I know I made a few mistakes last summer, but I think I can be a good worker."

"Oh, David, of course you're a good worker." Grandma scooted her chair closer and offered me another berry. "It will just take a while for everyone to find their places with a new routine. And until then, you can have a chance to enjoy yourself. I worked you so hard last summer that I was worried you weren't having any fun at all. You can actually have something like a real vacation this year."

I tried to smile. "Okay."

Grandma put her soft hands on either side of my face and tilted my head up a little bit until I was looking at her eyes. "And have patience with Amy, as well. I know she's really been looking forward to having you come back. Sometimes it just takes a little while to get readjusted."

Hmm. I didn't know if I trusted Grandma's definition of "a little while" when it came to relationships. After all, she had been waiting over forty years for the alien dude who helped her set up the B&B to step out of one of those transporters and back into her life.

But it was nice of her to say encouraging things about Amy, so I just nodded. "Thanks, Grandma."

"And how is everything going back home?"

"Actually, pretty good," I said. And I meant it. "Dad and I have had a lot of interesting conversations over the past year."

"I bet you have." Grandma winked at me.

"That reminds me. He gave me some instructions for this

summer." I fished a piece of notebook paper out of my pocket and unfolded it. "What does 'Never go swimming with a Flibbinhooxle' mean, anyway?"

Grandma just looked puzzled for a second, then she threw her head back and laughed. "Oh, I had forgotten all about that!" She wiped laugh tears from the corner of her eyes. "Don't worry, David. The Flibbinhooxles didn't mean any harm. That was just a big misunderstanding."

I rolled my eyes. "Dad told me you'd say that."

A few weeks before I flew out, he had let me skip school so that we could hang out all day and have this big man-to-man talk about me coming back to the B&B. We went out to lunch and then he even took me fishing, which was cool, because we didn't usually do that kind of thing, just the two of us.

Anyway, I could tell he had spent a long time putting his instructions together. (It was certainly more coherent than the awkward birds-and-bees lecture he had come up with last year. And probably more useful.)

I ran my finger down the list. "Okay, how about 'Never turn your back on a Koogruu'? He underlined that one and put two stars by it. Sounds important."

"Why, no Koogruuians have visited here since . . . my stars, your father must have been in kindergarten. How does he even remember that?" Grandma shook her head. "Oh, well. They sent the nicest apology note afterward. No need to worry about them, either, David. Another misunderstanding is all."

Uh-huh. I think I was starting to understand what Dad meant when he said that Grandma's tolerance of loony alien behavior was maybe the biggest danger I'd face out here. "She means well, David—always has—but she tends to just chalk everything up to Interstellar Culture Shock," he'd said. "So it's up to you to be the voice of reason out there. Keep your eyes open, okay?" I intended to do just that.

Grandma took the list from me and scanned it, smirking and muttering to herself. "Well, it certainly sounds like sharing our little family secret has brought you two closer together."

"Yeah, we've definitely talked a lot more lately. It's been good."

"I'm so glad." Grandma handed back the instructions. "And your mother...? How has she been handling all of this?"

"Um...she still doesn't know. I think Dad figures she'd sort of freak out, you know? She's pretty conservative about everything."

"Everything in good time." Grandma patted me on the hand. "Maybe it would be best if they come with you to visit one summer. Seeing it up close seems to be the easiest way."

I nodded, but it was pretty hard to imagine my mom mingling with a bunch of aliens.

The bundle in my lap squirmed. Just a little at first, but then it wiggled out of my grip, bounced up on top of the table, and started blindly nudging up against the bowl of berries.

"Looks like someone is hungry again," Grandma said. "I think he wants some of those Kerntaberries. Can you blame him?"

"Should we give him some?"

Grandma scooped out a handful of berries. I got a tight grip on the alien and then pulled back a corner of the quilt. First those wispy tendrils came out and sniffed at the air, and then his tongue shot out and slurped up the food in Grandma's hand.

She laughed and looked at her palm. "He's got quite the slimy tongue, doesn't he? And what an appetite for such a little thing." She pushed the bowl closer to us. "He can have the rest. There's more in the fridge for my next attempt at the award-winning recipe."

I picked up the little alien and held him over the table. His tongue dangled out of the quilt and lapped in and out of the bowl. In a few seconds he finished up the rest of the berries.

"Well, David, since you're looking for a job, I think we have your first one right here." She gestured toward the purple alien.

Great. Babysitting someone's pet was not exactly the type of big, important job I was expecting this summer. But how could I tell Grandma that right after I'd asked how I could help out? "Yeah, okay."

"Why don't you go around to the rooms and ask the guests if they are missing a pet?" Grandma said. "Now that I think of it, I suppose there's a chance he was already at the inn and he ran into your bedroom and got stuck in the transporter by mistake."

"Sure." That didn't sound too bad.

"If we come up empty there, then Scratchull can go ahead and take a look at the transporter," Grandma said.

I hoped it wouldn't come to that. I wanted as little to do with that creepy skull-face alien as possible. But I had to admit, it might be worth it to get the hyper alien-pet home. I had a limited survival stash of candy, and when it was gone I would have to live entirely off Grandma's cooking, and there's only so much alienberry pie a guy can take.

6

After an hour of knocking on guest-room doors and showing the little purple alien to the Tourists, I still hadn't made
any progress. He was starting to get frisky and all of the
wriggling around made him harder to hold.

I had to think of a way to let him run around a little
without giving him a chance to escape. The front yard was
no good; anyone who happened to walk by would be able
to see him, and he could easily jump over the white picket
fence and scurry into town. The backyard was private but
entirely surrounded by forest. If he got loose in there it
would be impossible to find him. Frustrated, I was tempted

to throw him into the nearest transporter, say good-bye, and push some random buttons on the input console, when Tate walked in the front door.

Tate nodded once at me. "'Mornin', boy." He was holding a handmade sign and a hammer.

"'Morning. What's that?"

He turned the sign around. HAPPY 50TH ANNIVERSARY, MR. AND MRS. OLSON. THANKS FOR CHOOSING THE INTERGALACTIC BED & BREAKFAST FOR YOUR PARTY!

"Grandma hosted a party for someone named Olson? A *human* party?"

Tate scoffed. "No, no. It's all part of the evasive tactics." He raised one eyebrow and pointed at me with a thick finger. "Something you never figured out last summer, by the way."

One more thing I did wrong? Big surprise. "What are you talking about?"

"Evasive tactics, boy. Keeping up appearances, making it look like actual humans stay here. You follow me?" Tate lifted up the sign. "I got dozens of these—*Welcome, Seattle Hiking Club* and *Enjoy Your Stay, Northwest Fly Fishermen*, that sort of thing. I put 'em out front for a day or two, and the stray passerby citizen-type from Forest Grove figures we're host-ing some get-together or another. A *normal* get-together. Puts his mind at ease, you know? Even if it's only subconsciously."

"Oh. Got it." That was actually a pretty good idea.

"Yep, I spend lots of time on evasive tactics these days. Got a friend who runs a used-car lot down in Bellingham. For a few bucks he lets me borrow a different two, three cars a week to park out front. Make it look like people are actually showing up. Humans don't usually travel too much by transporter, in case you hadn't noticed." Tate opened a storage room door and placed the sign and hammer inside. "I got all sorts of little tricks like that. We don't want a repeat of last summer's unpleasant incident."

Did everyone have to keep mentioning that? I sighed and nodded, but didn't say anything.

Tate closed the storage room door and glanced at the quilt bundle in my arms. "You're a little old to still be carrying a blankie around, aren't you?"

"It's not a blankie. I'm just making sure this guy doesn't escape." I drew back a corner of the quilt so Tate could get a look at him.

Tate studied the alien with a sour look on his face. "Now, I know how you're feeling, boy. Some of these things look pretty shifty. Dangerous, even. But I'm afraid you can't just go wrapping 'em up and taking 'em hostage, much as I'd like to sometimes."

"Oh, no. This guy's different. He—"

Tate grunted. "They're *all* of 'em different, trust me."

"No, this one is different even for an alien. He doesn't talk, and he scampers around like a little pet or something."

Tate took the toothpick out of his mouth and rolled it carefully between his fingers, clearly thinking things over. He bent down to get a better look at the purple alien. As soon as he got close, that long tongue shot out and slurped Tate's face from his second chin all the way up to his eyebrows.

"Yeechhh!"

I've never seen a big man move so fast. He shot upright and lunged for a hand sanitizer dispenser on a nearby end table. I had noticed two or three of those in every room;

now I saw why. Tate furiously pumped a lump of gel onto his meaty palm and then scrubbed it all over his face. He repeated the process two more times, spluttering away and swearing under his breath.

"What are you grinning about?" he said when he was finished. "You think your immune system can handle germs and microbes and who-knows-whatnot from a million miles away? You won't be smiling when you come down with some crazy strain of space flu, I'll tell you that. They won't have any medicine for it at the Forest Grove Pharmacy."

"Sorry." I hid my smile behind a fake cough. Why does trying not to laugh at something make it ten times funnier?

"I know your grandma thinks it's all peace and love and commingling in perfect harmony around here, but we still need to keep our guard up, you follow me?"

I nodded. I actually *was* following him for once. And I suddenly realized that maybe Tate would be the perfect person to talk to about my concerns regarding Scratchull. Grandma could be tolerant to a fault with her customers, and Amy was easily impressed by all things alien, but Tate could be counted on to be a skeptic. He would listen to me, for sure.

"Mr. Tate, would you mind if we had a talk for a minute? A private talk?"

He studied my face for a moment, then slowly nodded. "All right. But see that you keep that thing covered up while we do."

"Okay." I stuck my head under the quilt for a minute and tried to talk soothingly to the purple alien, told him to just wait for a minute and then I would find him a place to run around. I was rewarded with a big lick across my forehead and a couple of happy whistles. I bundled him up, and Tate and I moved to some chairs in the corner of the sitting room.

Tate crossed his arms over his chest, resting his elbows on his belly, and looked at me without expression. It felt very strange to be confiding in him, but it seemed like the only way to get some help.

I glanced toward the kitchen door, then up at the empty staircase. I finally looked back at Tate and lowered my voice. "I'm a little worried about one of the aliens."

Tate looked much more interested at that. He leaned forward and whispered back, "Me too. Is it that squishy bluish-green fella up in Three-C? I've had my eye on him the last couple days. Don't like the way he looks at your grandma."

Okay...that was a little weird. "No. It's the one who just started working here, actually."

Tate straightened back up and gave me a funny look. "Scratchull? Why would you be worried about him? He's the only one of these aliens that's ever been useful. The others just sit around and lollygag all day long."

"Well...they *are* on vacation...."

Tate harrumphed. "Oh, they lollygag at home, too. I can tell. But that Scratchull's okay. He's been right helpful."

"Really?"

"Yep." Tate scratched at his jowls and studied my face. "But why are you so worried about him? You seemed right chummy with all of these creatures last summer, if memory serves."

"When I first got here, I was sneaking in the back way and I saw him messing around in one of the sheds. So I went over to check things out." I lowered my voice even more. "And he was building something pretty strange. It looked like a weapon of some kind. And when he saw me standing there and watching him, he totally freaked out."

Tate frowned and scratched some more. "Totally freaked out? That doesn't sound like Scratchull. I've found him to be a pretty cool customer."

"Well, he did. And then he—"

"What did this so-called weapon look like?"

I remembered the alien's grating laughter as that thing flew around and spat out nails. I shuddered. "It was like a cross between a mini-helicopter and a machine gun. It could float in the air and—"

Tate held up a hand for me to stop, then shook his head slowly and pushed himself out of the chair with a grunt. "Come with me, boy."

I followed Tate down the hall and through the back door. He led me around to the far side of the house.

Whoa. There was a huge wooden structure being built back there. It was a tower attached to the side of the house, constructed of a series of ten-by-ten-foot platforms held up by four stout wooden pillars and connected by a short flight of stairs between each one. The highest platform was level with the roof of the bed-and-breakfast, and a couple of pillars were in place on top. Looked like it was going to be built up even taller.

"What's that?" I asked.

Tate cleared his throat. "I guess that all depends on who's doing the asking."

"What does that mean?"

"Well, if it's your grandma asking, then that thing is a fire escape. For the safety and well-being of her valued customers." Tate took the soggy toothpick out of his mouth and pointed up at the structure with it. "See how each platform is flush with one of the windows? In case of a fire, or some other emergency requiring immediate evacuation"—Tate gave me a meaningful look at that one, and I knew he was thinking about the debacle last summer—"each guest can funnel right out one of them centrally located windows on their floor, step onto the platform, and then file down safely to the ground."

"Okay..." I looked up. It appeared to be well built, and the whole thing was actually a pretty good idea. "But what if *I'm* asking?"

Tate slid the toothpick back between his lips and chewed on it while he studied me. "You see, that depends, too. Can I trust you? On a man-to-man basis?"

I nodded. "Sure."

"Then that, boy, is my own personal watchtower."

"Watchtower?"

"Follow me."

Tate led me up the steps of the tower until we reached the top. I got a tighter grip on my quilted bundle and stayed near the middle of the platform. It made me a little dizzy to be up that high without any walls around me.

"We're gonna build it up another level or two, and then I'll be able to see almost everything." He pointed off in the direction of town. "Look there. I got a clear sight line all the way down the road, and I'll be able to see over the tops of all these trees right into downtown. Be able to tell if anyone is coming, or if there might be any problems with the guests." He turned and pointed in different directions. "And I'll be able to see right into the park...and down along the river there...and up the logging road there...and farther up the mountain a spell to that clearing by the lake." He stuck the toothpick back in his mouth and surveyed the scene before him.

"I guess this'll be pretty useful," I said.

"You bet it will. Running security for an operation like this, you need to eliminate as many surprises as possible. Have to be able to keep an eye on friend and foe alike, both comin' and goin'."

When he said "foe" I remembered why we came out here in the first place. "It looks good, Mr. Tate. But what does it have to do with Scratchull? And the weapon he was building?"

"Did someone call my name?" I flinched at hearing that deep voice unexpectedly. I looked over and there was Scratchull, walking along the sloped roof, holding a toolbox. His feet were only an inch or two from the gutter. But he looked straight at us instead of watching his step, seemingly unaware or unconcerned that one slightly misplaced foot could send him over the edge to splatter on the ground below.

He leaped off the roof a little too soon, sailing over open space before landing on the wooden floor. I instinctively took a step backward; it seemed like a tight fit on that platform with three people, especially with Tate being so big and Scratchull so creepy. "Whatever were you two discussing?"

Tate pointed at me. "This is a good one, Scratchull. The kid here thought you were building yourself a weapon."

My whole body flushed with anger. How could he just go and say something like that? I should have known better than to trust him.

"Is that right?" Scratchull said. "It would seem earthling children have such active imaginations that it's hard for them to distinguish between fantasy and reality. But I wonder what could have put the notion into his head in the first place."

"Says he saw you putting together your little flying contraption. Thought it was some kind of dangerous weapon." Tate rolled his eyes and made a *Can-you-believe-it?* face.

"Is that so?" Scratchull took a quick glance in my direction and sneered.

"Yeah." Tate chuckled. "I guess he thought you were planning to take over the Earth with just a tricked-out nail gun." His chuckle turned into a guffaw at his own joke.

Scratchull turned away from Tate and looked right at me with those dark eyes. "My, my. Take over the Earth?" A tiny pinprick of red light appeared in the center of each eye. "Whatever would I *do* with it?"

Scratchull moved toward me, and I took another step backward.

"Whoa, there," Tate said. The big man grabbed me by the elbow. "Watch your step, boy."

I looked behind me and saw that my heels were only a few inches away from the edge of the platform. My stomach went funny and I almost threw up. I lurched forward but also sideways, trying to get clear of the edge and stay away from Scratchull at the same time.

Tate motioned to Scratchull. "Let's show him how your new toy works, so he doesn't have any nightmares. Give the kid a demonstration."

"Gladly." Scratchull stepped right off the edge of the platform and dropped out of sight.

My heart skipped a couple of beats and I got the throw-up feeling again. The shock must have been pretty plain on my face because Tate looked at me and grinned. "Spooked me, too, first time I saw him do that. Doesn't hurt him or nothing, though. It's like he's got bones made of rubber."

Tate stepped to the ledge and looked over. I carefully did the same. Scratchull was kneeling far below, hooking up his contraption to a generator. Suddenly the flying nail gun was zipping through the air. It whirled around the entire wooden structure, circling upward, and when it reached the joints between platform and pillar, it fired off a quick burst of nails. It only took a few minutes to get to every joint, hovering for a moment to spit out nails before it moved to the next one.

"Pretty slick, huh?" said Tate. "It would have taken a four-man crew a couple of weeks to build something like this. With Scratchull and his homemade toys, it's taken the both of us just two days to get this thing up. And we're nearly finished." Tate clapped me on the shoulder. "I told you he was all right. A real straight shooter. No pun intended."

Tate chuckled to himself as the nail gun rose higher into the air. It nailed the joints below the platform we were standing on, and then it popped up into view just in front of us. Just in front of *me*, actually. It hovered there, the barrel of the gun pointed straight at me. I had seen how hard the nails slammed into the wood, and I got chills imagining one of them shooting out and hitting me in the forehead.

I stepped to the side, and the thing followed. I ducked down, and it lowered. "Tell him to get that thing away from me," I said.

"You can tell me yourself." Scratchull walked up the stairs to stand beside us. He flicked lightly at the remote control, and the flying nail gun floated right over into his hands, where the blades stopped whirring and fell silent. "In fact, the next time you have any kind of problem with me whatsoever, I suggest you come to me directly before prattling on to someone else. I'm sure we can settle any misunderstandings ourselves."

I looked at Tate for support, but he just cleared his throat and said, "Good advice, kid. Part of growing up."

I took a few deep breaths, trying to get my anger under control. Clearly, no one was on my side right now.

I forced myself to look right at Scratchull. "Fine," I said. "I'll do that. Just the two of us."

I was hoping it wouldn't come to that. But if it did, I wanted him to be sorry that he had ever suggested it.

7

Snarffle woke me up the next morning (that creepy white alien said he was called a snarffle, so I guessed that was as good a name as any). He was balanced on his hind legs, that purple beach ball of a body pressed against the door, while his other four paws scrabbled at the wood.

Despite being groggy from the too-early wake-up call, I had to smile a little. As crazy as the circumstances always were at Grandma's house, some things remained comfortably familiar all over the universe: pets had to go to the bathroom in the morning.

But I couldn't let him run around outside and risk him

tearing off toward town. "Just give me a minute, buddy." I pulled on some sweats and squeezed out the door.

When I returned from Grandma's storage sheds, Snarffle was whistle-whining and hopping up and down. "Okay, this shouldn't take too long," I told him, dumping an armload of materials on the bed: a couple of old dog leashes, a Johnny Jump Up baby bouncer, and a bunch of bungee cords.

Even though he was anxious to get out, the little guy was actually a pretty good sport about sitting still and letting me try things on him for size. I managed to rig up a harness that fit over him, snug but not suffocating. I slipped the bungee cords around his two front legs, and then attached the whole thing to the leashes, which I tied together to give him some room to run. It wasn't pretty, but now I could take him outside without worrying about him escaping. So we left the room and trotted down the hall, just a boy and his loyal companion from space.

Most of the Tourists were early risers, and there was already a lot of activity around the Intergalactic Bed & Breakfast. I had to stifle a laugh as we walked down the back-porch steps and encountered an alien family having a picnic breakfast on the lawn.

Now, I'm sure Amy did a great job with the new *Welcome to Earth!* tutorial . . . but that didn't mean aliens had any grasp of earthling fashions. The mom looked straight out of *Little House on the Prairie*, wearing a plain pioneer dress and an old-fashioned bonnet; the kid seemed like he had stepped out of a silent movie with his knickers, sweater-vest, and flat tam-o'-shanter cap; and the dad was impersonating a disco king with tight bell-bottom jeans, a puffy Afro wig, and a

yellow polyester shirt with lapels big enough to serve as aux-
iliary wings. Sure, they could pass for human, but it looked
like they had all gotten dressed in a short-circuiting time
machine. Might be time for Grandma to update her trunks
full of thrift-store clothes.

I was so focused on trying not to crack up that I didn't
notice Snarffle had stopped moving until his leash grew
taut and yanked me to a halt a few yards from the family's
picnic blanket. I looked back at the purple alien and saw
him staring intently at the food. That little cave opened
underneath his eyes, and a few wispy tendrils snaked out
to sniff at the air.

Breakfast. Of course. After a bathroom pit stop and a
quick walk through the woods to get his energy out, I would
find him something to—

But Snarffle wasn't interested in waiting. His mouth gaped
wide—and I mean *really* wide, over half of his body seemed
to open up—and made a loud whistling-groaning noise that
sounded kind of like a vacuum.

The alien mom gasped. I turned to see whole plates of food
sliding off the picnic blanket and across the grass, headed
straight for us. Snarffle was sucking them in like the Death
Star's tractor beam. I lunged for Snarffle, but not before he
had inhaled a plate piled high with cinnamon rolls.

"How rude!" the mom said. "You should watch over your
pet more closely."

But I was already racing toward the edge of the forest,
cradling the alien in my arms as he happily chomped away.
"Sorry!" I called over my shoulder.

I didn't set him down until we were well away from

Grandma's lawn and safely in the woods. "Man, you must be really hungry."

Snarffle whistled at me and wriggled all over in agreement. I scanned the trees. "Hey, follow me. I think I can find something to tide you over until we get back to the kitchen." After all, the forest provided plenty of meals for the wild animals out here. And I remembered where there was a huge patch of blackberry brambles from last summer.

We hiked through the forest for a few minutes, Snarffle literally bouncing along in his excitement to be outside. When we reached the right spot, I saw another Tourist had had the same idea; he was picking berries and filling up a big Tupperware container.

"Good morning." I smiled and he waved back. His disguise was normal—sweatshirt, jeans, and a baseball cap—and he looked so humanoid that I would have been worried he was an earthling if I hadn't recognized him from Grandma's sitting room the evening before.

I plucked a handful of berries, careful not to slice myself on the thorns, and tossed them to Snarffle. He slurped them down and did a happy dance that involved chasing his tail in a circle until he became a purple blur. "I think maybe he liked those," the Tourist said. We both laughed.

I turned to collect more berries and quickly noticed that this area had been picked pretty clean already. I got up on my tiptoes to try to grab a few fat ones above my head, but the brambles were so thick and thorny that it was hard to get access to them.

"The best ones are always just out of reach, aren't they?" I said to the alien.

"Oh, I don't know," he said. Then he took off his baseball cap. A dozen or so snakelike growths on his head unfolded and stretched over the top of the thicket. They whirred in a frenzy of activity while the alien calmly stood there, and when the growths coiled back, I saw that each one ended in a little pincer that held a few berries each. The tendrils dropped their cargo into the Tupperware and returned to his head.

I nodded, trying to look nonchalant. "That's one way to do it."

The alien grinned. "So is that." He inclined his head to indicate something behind me.

I turned. Snarffle was ripping through the brambles like a buzz saw, leaving wide swaths of bare earth in his wake. It only took him half a minute to clear out an area the size of a basketball court. He ran back, licked his lips, and dog-grinned at me.

"Um . . . wow." I looked at the new clearing and then back at Snarffle. "Is that going to take care of breakfast for you?" Snarffle turned to face the remaining blackberry bushes, clearly ready for round two.

I bent down and scooped him up. "Okay, you, let's head back to the kitchen and find something else. Probably not a good idea to throw the forest's ecosystem too out of whack on your first full day." I grinned sheepishly at the Tourist. "I hope you enjoy your stay." He nodded and waved as we hustled back to Grandma's house.

When we got back to the kitchen I grabbed a garbage sack and filled it with random food items. Sure enough, he liked everything. Back in my room he ate a huge mixing bowl full of fruit salad, four bags of potato chips, two frozen pizzas, a loaf of bread, three cans of tuna, a bag of pretzels, and a jumbo-sized box of Froot Loops. Pretty much all of the normal food that Grandma had bought for my arrival.

I couldn't help but wonder when Snarffle's family would show up to claim him. And what their grocery bill must be like.

After he ate everything I had brought, Snarffle curled up at the foot of my bed and fell into a nap. Only when my stomach rumbled did I realize that I had forgotten to grab anything for my own breakfast. I eased out the door, hoping Snarffle would stay asleep and let me head to the kitchen for a few minutes to grab a bite. I definitely wanted to be back by the time he woke up.

Something told me that taking care of Snarffle was going to be a full-time job.

When I pushed through the swinging kitchen door, I found
Amy standing at the counter. There was an entire loaf of
bread spread out before her, along with several jars of peanut
butter and jelly. She looked up. "Oh. Hi, David."

"Hey."

We just stood there. Amy could have used her butter knife
to slice through the heavy silence.

Finally she said, "It's nice to see you," although it sounded
like an automatic response. Then she dipped the knife into a
jar of peanut butter and spread it on several pieces of bread.

This was nothing at all like the easy interaction we had fallen into last summer, and that was back when I was desperately trying to hide Grandma's secret from her. How could things be so weird between us, especially now that we were on the same team? Unless I was right about her having met someone else. . . .

I took a deep breath and stepped into the kitchen. "Amy?"

"Mmmm-hmmmm?" She didn't look up from the counter.

"Are you, I don't know, like, avoiding me or something?"

Amy shook her head, but still no eye contact. "Of course not. I've just been busy. You remember how it gets around here."

I chewed on my lip. "I guess." I just stood there for a while. Finally I said, "I've got a little time now. Wanna hang out?"

"I'd love that, David, but I'm actually in the middle of something really important."

I crossed my arms over my chest. "Really? It looks like you're just making a bunch of PB and J sandwiches." No response from Amy. "Seriously? That's more important than talking to me?"

"David, please don't be mad."

"I'm not mad. I just . . . I'd like you to tell me if anything is going on." Why couldn't I just ask what I wanted to know? "So . . . is anything going on?"

Amy lifted her head. I'm no good at reading people, especially girls, but even I could tell there was something off about her expression. The wrinkled brow, the distant look in her eyes. Finally something cleared and she really looked at me, maybe for the first time since I had arrived. "David ...can I trust you?"

What??? Okay, now I was maybe getting a little mad. "Can you *trust* me?" I spread my hands out to indicate the entire bed-and-breakfast. "We're sharing the biggest secret on Earth. What do you think?"

"I didn't mean it like that."

"How else could you mean it?"

"I just..." She studied the knife in her hands. "If I show you something, do you promise not to tell anyone?"

Who was I supposed to tell? It's not like I had a regular lunch meeting with the mayor of Forest Grove. I opened my mouth to say just that when she looked up at me again. She was genuinely worried, I could tell. So I just nodded. "Sure. Of course."

Amy moved to the kitchen table, where there was a platter stacked with cheese and crackers and a pitcher of lemonade. There was also a little pot with some fake flowers poking out. She grabbed the silk petals, lifted the flowers, and set them on the table. Then she reached back into the pot and slowly pulled out something that looked like a—

"Is that a baby monitor?"

Amy put a finger to her lips and nodded. "But not just any baby monitor," she whispered. She carefully pried the plastic casing from the back and held up the device to show me its exposed electrical innards. I stepped closer for a better look and she pointed to something inside. "See that little metallic square? It's tiny. Right there, by the circuit board."

I leaned forward and squinted. "I think so."

Amy nodded and snapped the plastic casing back in place. "It's a translator."

My eyes opened wide. "You mean . . . ?"

"Yep. Just like the ones that the aliens use to understand good old earthling English."

"But aren't those—"

This time Amy put her finger to my lips. "Yes, David," she whispered. "You can skip the lecture. I know that it's illegal—highly illegal—to bring any advanced off-world technology to a primitive planet like Earth. And especially to use it here."

"So how did you get your hands on something like this? And what are you doing with it?"

Amy wrapped the monitor in a dish towel and stuck it in a drawer. "It has a recorder function. You know, like a bug? I'm not taking any chances." She shut the drawer and motioned me back to the counter and continued making her sandwiches. "Let's talk and work at the same time. I want to get out there right away."

We made sandwiches and arranged them in wedges on the platter. "Getting the translator was the easy part. A lot of aliens our age come here on vacation with their parents. I've been able to make some friends. They're way more inter-esting than anybody at school, obviously." She got sort of a faraway look in her eye. "It's definitely been one of the best parts about working here."

Oh, great. Here I had been worried about Amy meeting someone she liked while I was gone all year. My one comfort was that I figured at least the odds were in my favor—I mean, how many cool guys could there really be in a place as small as Forest Grove Middle School?

But now I guess I would have to compete with every teenage life form in the universe. Perfect.

"David? Are you okay?"

"Huh? Oh, yeah."

"Looked like I lost you there for a second." Amy wiped her hands on a paper towel. "Anyway, I met this one Tourist who was really into gadgets. Just like teens on Earth, I suppose, but alien toys are way cooler. So one day he showed me—"

"*He?*"

"Yes, *he*. Are you sure you're okay, David? You're giving me kind of a weird look."

"No, I'm not. I mean, no, I'm fine. Whatever. Keep telling your story." I shuffled the sandwich wedges around on the platter to give me somewhere else to look.

"Anyway, the aliens have the translator chips inserted right into their brains, you know? We had this long conversation once about how they worked, and I think he could tell that I was really interested, so the second time this teen alien visited, he brought me—"

"The *second* time he visited? How many times has he been here?"

"I don't know, maybe three or four. His parents are botanists. They travel all over to study plant life on different planets. But would you stop interrupting? I need to get out to the backyard soon."

"Fine. Go ahead."

Amy grabbed a stack of plastic cups from the cupboard and placed them on the platter. "So he brought me an external

chip—I guess it was an older model or something—and helped me rig it up to the baby monitor. Now, whenever someone speaks an alien language and it's picked up here" —Amy retrieved the monitor from the drawer and dropped it back into the flowerpot—"then I can listen to the translated English version here." She pulled the thin baby monitor speaker from the front pocket of her cutoff denim jeans and held it up. "Isn't that cool?"

"Okay." I shrugged. "But what do you need to listen to?"

"Grab that extra pitcher of lemonade and follow me."

Amy picked up the platter with both hands and walked through the swinging kitchen door. I got the lemonade and followed her down the hall and onto the back porch.

It was a rare hot day around here. The sun lit up Grandma's huge backyard, which was surrounded on all sides by the dense wilderness that extended all the way up the foothills to Mount Baker. Sports and game equipment was scattered across the lawn, as usual, but it was rarely used in a way you could recognize. As we made our way across the backyard, a group of aliens was using the materials for croquet, badminton, and lawn darts to play something that looked like it might be capture the flag, except for the fact that hovering in midair and using your tentacles as a lasso were both legal in this version.

Some Tourists ate out of picnic baskets while their little alien offspring climbed trees. A few guests were sprawled out on beach towels, and I think they might have actually been sunbathing. Man, if they traveled to the Pacific Northwest for the sunshine, they must be from an ice-encrusted planet with no discernible heat source.

I followed Amy toward the back of the yard. A dozen or

so aliens sat in a circle in lawn chairs, having an animated conversation. Their varied shapes, sizes, and colors indicated that they were from different planets, but they all wore similar clothing: a silvery one-piece jumpsuit thingy that had the look of some kind of uniform.

As we got closer it became apparent that they were all speaking in their different native tongues, creating a wall of unintelligible sounds all jumbled up on top of each other.

When Amy and I reached the gathering, the noise stopped as suddenly as if she had flipped a switch. A skinny alien with a long, yellowish face turned toward Amy. "Thank you, dear," he said. "You can just leave those here, if you don't mind." He indicated the middle of the circle with elongated fingers.

Spread out on the aliens' laps and on the surrounding grass were a variety of magazines and newspapers—*Time, Newsweek,* the *Wall Street Journal.* Some were in languages that I didn't understand, but they all looked to be Earth publications.

Amy stepped in between the chairs and set the platter on the lawn. The flowerpot wobbled and nearly fell over. My breath caught in my throat, but Amy grabbed the pot and set it upright. I put the pitcher of lemonade beside the platter. The aliens were all silent, watching us.

Amy gave them a little wave, and we stepped back out of the circle of lawn chairs. As soon as we got a few steps away, the buzz of conversation started up again. I didn't understand any of it, of course, but the tone suggested this wasn't idle vacation chatter. There was something urgent about it, with a not-quite-friendly edge.

"Just keep walking. Don't look back," Amy whispered out of the side of her mouth. "Pretend like everything's normal."

I cocked one eyebrow and stared at her. "You know what I mean—as normal as a house full of aliens ever gets." She smiled broadly and waved to the Tourists we passed as we made our way back to the house.

Amy led me through the back door, down the hall, and into the room she used for the kids' movie night. She closed the door and pushed a big reclining chair firmly up against it.

"All right, secret agent, are you going to explain what's going on?" I said.

"I first saw them a little bit after you left last summer. I asked your grandma and she said they've been meeting here about every five years ever since she opened the place up." Amy knelt in front of a window and pulled a corner of the curtain aside, giving us a view of the backyard. "But lately it's been way more often than that. Every month or so. I could tell they weren't here just for a vacation."

I knelt beside her, my shoulder brushing against hers while we watched the circle of aliens. "So, who are they?"

"From what I can tell, they're all xenoplanetologists. They're trying to—"

"Zee-no-what's?"

"Xenoplanetologists. They're scientists from all over. Apparently they've been doing research on the Earth."

"Okay. So these are, like, some of the best and brightest minds in the universe?"

Amy nodded.

"And you're doing undercover wiretap surveillance on them . . . with a modified baby monitor?"

Amy bit her lip and studied my facial expression. She nodded again, slowly.

"I knew there was a reason I liked you so much, Amy."

She broke into a grin, a big one that crinkled up the freckle patch on her nose, and I returned it. For a moment, it was just like last summer again.

Amy fished the listening device out of her pocket and set it on the windowsill. "Based on what I've gathered so far, they're trying to decide whether or not to allow Earth to join the Collective. But some of them think—"

"Whoa, slow down. What exactly is the Collective, again? Some of us haven't spent all year spying on the interstellar scientific community, you know."

"I'm not *spying*."

"Right. Of course not."

"I'm . . . doing research. Besides, most of the stuff I've learned about the Collective I heard from the alien who helped me build this." She tapped the speaker for the baby monitor.

I sighed. *Him* again? Great.

"So what is it?"

"The Collective is a group of affiliated planets from all over the universe. One of the requirements for joining is that a native population has to figure out how to reach another planet on its own, with no outside help." She indicated the group of aliens on the lawn with a nod. "One of the things they argue about is whether our moon should count."

I rested my arms on the windowsill and placed my forehead on the cool glass, studying the aliens. "What would Earth get out of that arrangement? You know, if they let us into their big Collective?"

"Oh, it would be the best!" I glanced over at Amy, and her

eyes were flashing with excitement. "We could share philosophy and art and technology with millions of advanced civilizations. It would be the next great leap in our social evolution."

"I suppose that would be—"

"And we'd be so much better protected," Amy rushed on. "Members of the Collective offer aid to each other in a planetary crisis—a worldwide epidemic of disease, maybe, or some catastrophic natural disaster like a huge meteor headed right for the planet's orbital path."

"I guess that sounds pretty—"

"And don't you see? This place wouldn't have to be a secret anymore! Your grandma wouldn't have to waste half her time hiding everything. She would become humanity's first ambassador to the universe."

I smiled. Amy's excitement was contagious. "She *would* be great at that job."

Amy's expression slowly soured. "But I don't know if it's going to happen."

"Why not?"

Amy grabbed the little plastic speaker. "Here, listen. That's all they've been talking about during the last few meetings."

She flipped the ON switch. A burst of scratchy static settled into a persistent hiss, and then voices cut across the white noise.

". . . you imagine if one of these barbarians got loose in the transporter system? It'd be like the proverbial Garggadin in the pottery shop."

"Come now, they're not all barbarians. Witness the peaceful creatures we have met around here. They are lovely, are they not?"

"Lovely? Have you taken the time to read this . . . ?"

I watched the group on the lawn as one of the aliens grabbed some newspapers and held them over his head, gesticulating wildly.

". . . Or this one? Or how about this? Or any of these? Lovely, indeed. The reports are war, murder, and mayhem, each and every time we visit. It never changes!"

"Oh, please. They are not the first species to endure a violent phase, nor shall they be the last. The humans have progressed much in a short time, using reason to triumph over some of their basest tribal instincts."

"Reason? Hah! The only thing they use their reason for is to make bigger and better killing machines! You would scream until your scales fell off if a human barbarian showed up unexpectedly at your front door."

"That is simply not true. How many times—"

The discussion devolved into a garbled shouting match that melded in with the static of the monitor. "This is pretty much how it goes every time," Amy said. "Half of them think humans should be officially contacted and brought into the intergalactic community. They say that we're 'citizens of the universe' just like everyone else."

I gestured toward the lawn. "And the other half reads our newspapers?"

"Something like that."

More garbled shouting. Amy turned the volume down to a buzz.

"And they think we're the ones who have trouble getting along?"

Amy rolled her eyes. "I know. But they are right about one thing—they never get violent."

"Why's that, do you think?"

"Simple cost-benefit analysis, I guess. Any planet that resorts to violence to solve problems is kicked out of the Collective. The aftereffects would be equally devastating for everyone living there."

"So they're forced to figure out some way to get along?"

"Sounds like it. But I guess it works."

The buzzing sound from the monitor got quieter. Out on the lawn, the aliens had all taken their seats and calmed down some. "Turn it back up," I said.

". . . perhaps if the humans could be nudged in the right direction, they could—"

"Absolutely not. You know what the studies show about the deleterious effects of nudging. *It throws the whole development of the species off-kilter. And often the* nudgers *don't have any idea when to stop."*

"I'm not a fool. I don't advise handing out photon-processors to a clan of cavemen. Why must you always—"

"Gentlemen, please. Let's cut right to the pertinent question: what will be our process for deciding whether or not the earthlings are ready to be invited into the Collective?"

"Yes!" Amy's face lit up and she grabbed my arm. "They might actually make a decision this time!" Her voice was breathy with excitement.

"Um, okay, so when will—"

"Shhhh!"

"This would be the perfect time for a period of close monitoring. Now that we have installed one of our own, a being of higher intelligence, at this transporter establishment, couldn't we make his time here less punitive and more scientifically valuable? Perhaps request a detailed weekly report concerning Earth?"

"Are you sure he can be trusted? Remember why we sent him here in the first pl—"

Amy's fingers dug painfully into my skin. "They must be talking about Scratchull!" she whispered.

"I know, but they're saying he can't be trusted to—"

"Shhhh!"

The sound of the Collective scientists laughing burbled through the speaker.

"Oh, he wouldn't like that a bit, would he?"

"No, but he is not on vacation here. He will do as we command. And with someone residing here full-time, we will receive a much clearer picture of the earthlings' readiness for full inclusion than we do with our sporadic visits. Are we agreed?"

Murmurs of assent came from the group. Amy flicked off the monitor and shoved it into her pocket. "This is amazing! I *knew* that Scratchull had to be more than just some traveling interstellar handyman." She let go of me and paced around the room. "He's just so smart, and so amazingly articulate. And think about it—he will be the one who influences whether or not Earth joins the Collective!" It sounded more like she was talking to herself than to me.

I cleared my throat. "I guess so, Amy. But did you hear them say he 'wouldn't like it'? I'd be careful about—"

"Do you realize the position this puts us in? We actually have the chance to influence the most important decision in the history of the planet!" She stopped at the window and surveyed all of the Tourists, hands on her hips. "I'm going to make sure Scratchull hears all the best parts about Earth. That's my new job around here, as far as I'm concerned." She turned to look at me. "Oh, you'll help me, won't you, David?"

Ummmm...no. But before I could try to talk her out of it, she threw her arms around my neck and hugged me fiercely. "How will I ever be able to thank you for getting me a job here?"

Good question, but I couldn't afford to think about that right now. I managed to disentangle myself from her arms. "Are you planning to tell Grandma about all of this? *Any* of this?"

Amy slowly exhaled. She sat on the edge of the couch, looking at the floor. "No. I don't want to worry her unless they come to a concrete decision. It's not like there's anything she could really do. I mean, she's already a shining example of the goodness of humanity, right?"

"Sure...and if you told her, it would also mean you'd have to confess about this highly illegal alien technology that you're hiding inside her house."

"...Yeah. There's that." We were quiet for several moments. "Look, David, I know it's sneaky. Your grandma

has been so nice to me, and I owe her everything. I just..."
Amy shook her head slowly.

"You felt like you had to do everything you could," I said.
"For something you thought was really important. I get it."

When she exhaled it sounded like a sigh of relief. "Thank
you, David." She looked up to meet my gaze. "There've been
times I felt so alone this school year, not having a human I
could talk to about this stuff. And when you got here I was
worried maybe you'd be mad at me for spying on them."

"As long as you don't get caught," I said. "Trust me, that's
not very fun."

She gave me a quick kiss on the cheek. "You're the best,
David."

We looked at each other. Amy's eyes were so happy, they
glistened. I suddenly realized we were alone, for the first time
since I showed up, and the door was blocked from the inside—

"Whoops, there they go!" Amy pulled away and pointed
through the window at the group of scientists as they stood,
apparently wrapping up their meeting. "I have to go pick up
that platter of food before they knock over the flowerpot."
She shoved the recliner out of the way, pulled open the door,
and took off down the hall. "Thanks again, David!" she called
over her shoulder.

Oh, well. At least maybe there would be sandwiches
left over. This was the second time today I had forgotten
breakfast. If I hadn't been so busy taking care of—

Snarffle! How long had I been down here with Amy?
Could it have been an hour? More?

I ran through the halls and up the stairs to my room,
hoping his nap had been a long one.

9

When I flung open the door to my room I found a very happy, very awake purple alien. Shredded bits of candy wrapper were stuck to his face, and a chocolate-mixed-with-space-drool slurry dripped down his cheeks. He whistled happily and twirled his little tail like crazy when he saw me.

He was sitting on top of a pile of my scattered clothes. There was a huge hole in my suitcase.

"Please tell me that you did not just eat through my suitcase to get at my candy stash." I sighed. "Why would you do something like that?"

Snarffle tilted his head and gave me a look that seemed

to say, *I don't know...maybe because I don't have opposable thumbs?*

Oh, well. It's not like I could get that mad. I was the one who left him up here on his own, after all.

I knelt and sorted my clothes into separate piles of "wearable" and "way too slobbery." Snarffle watched me, looking like he really hoped I wouldn't be too angry.

"So, my man, you ever have any troubles with the female snarffles where you're from?" Snarffle took this as his cue to creep forward and nuzzle under my arm. "You know, maybe you have no clue what they're thinking about half the time or what you should say to them?" Snarffle snuggled closer, panting and bobbing up and down. He definitely knew where I was coming from.

When the clothes were all sorted, I picked up the suitcase to set it on the dresser...and I noticed there wasn't any dresser. What? Could someone have taken it? I looked in the closet and even the transporter. No dresser. Man, that sucker was heavy. And big. It would have taken some serious weight lifting to get that thing out of the room.

And where was the wooden rocking chair that had been beside the bed? And the old-timey coat stand in the corner? Did they just disappear? Even for an Intergalactic Bed & Breakfast, that was pretty weird.

I cupped my chin in my hand and scanned the room, trying to remember where—

Snarffle burped.

He used that long tongue to lick the chocolate off his face. I bent down and looked closer. Was there some sawdust mixed in there?

Oops. Looks like I had some explaining to do to Grandma, not to mention some flea-market shopping.

And I was going to have to be much more careful about keeping track of Snarffle's mealtimes. I wondered if Grandma had access to any intergalactic libraries, because I could sure use a copy of *Proper-Care-and-Feeding Tips for When You're Snarfflesitting.*

Oh, well, I'd have to do the best I could. I wasn't about to let him out of my sight again, so we hung out together for the rest of the day. We tried to play fetch, but instead of retrieving the sticks, he always ate them. We ended up either hiking around or trying to find the end of his bottomless appetite. When it got dark we finally headed back to my room. I yawned and glanced at the clock: 10:17 p.m. Time for bed.

I was in a pretty good mood as I drifted off to sleep. I had made some progress with Amy (even if I did have to worry about extraterrestrial competition), and I felt like I was better equipped to handle any potential Snarffle disasters. As long as I could find enough for him to eat, tomorrow was going to be awesome.

I was back home in Tampa, lying on the beach. The warm surf washed over my face, and I could taste the salt in the seawater. It felt so good to be able to lie there and not have to worry about the challenges that went with a houseful of aliens. I just stretched out and soaked it all up.

Slorch! Slurp!

What was that noise? Something tickled my ear. When I reached up to scratch, there was so much slimy liquid in there that my finger made a squelching sound as I dug around inside.

Another slurping sound pulled me fully out of sleep. The purple alien pet was crouched right by my head, licking me over and over with that long tongue. "Gross!" I sat up and pushed him away, then grabbed an extra pillow to dry my face off. No matter how hard I scrubbed, there always seemed to be a slick film still left on my cheeks and forehead.

I looked at the clock: 1:17 a.m. Ugh.

The alien pressed closer, twirling his tail. I pushed him farther down on the bed. "Snarffle, get away from me."

The round alien hopped back up. He lowered his head and nudged me in the side, over and over, like he was trying to push me out of the bed.

Again? I had taken him out to go to the bathroom right before bed. Did the creatures on his planet have microscopic bladders or something? I really hoped this wasn't going to be a nightly ritual. Or, worse, a several-times-a-night ritual.

But I guess it was easy to understand: four meals, three snacks, my entire stash of candy, a roomful of furniture, a half acre of blackberry brambles . . . It was going to take some time to get all of that out of his system. "Okay, okay, I get it," I mumbled. "Let me pull on some sweats." I was not looking forward to standing out in the cold and waiting for this little guy to do his business in the woods.

I kicked off the blankets and shuffled to the door, motioning for him to follow. But instead he jumped off the opposite side of the bed and looked at the window.

"No, we have to go out this way," I said. Snarffle just stared

at me. "Come on, I really don't want this to take all night."
But he stayed where he was, still staring at me.

I made a show of opening the door and stepping out
into the hall, watching the little alien the whole time. He
remained by the window, eyes fixed on me. He nestled right
up against the wall, then hunkered down on all six of his little
legs until his round belly rested on the floor.

Suddenly his legs uncoiled and he shot straight up. At the
peak of his jump, about six feet in the air, he threw himself
sideways and bumped into the closed blinds. He landed for
a split-second and then bounced back up, nudging the blinds
again with his beach ball body.

What was he doing? I finally walked over to pick him
up. When I got close he stopped bouncing and glanced at
me, then up at the window, then back to me again, making
a series of little whimpering whistles.

"The window? You want to look out the window?"

His little tail twirled like a propeller. I sighed and twid-
dled the handle that opened the blinds. "See? Nothing to
look at out there. It's dark. And if you want to go outside,
then we need to walk downstairs and use the—"

Then I heard it, too. A muffled thump and some scratching. I turned off my lamp and eased the window open as
quietly as I could and stuck my head out.

I quickly found what Snarffle had heard. Scratchull was
sitting on the edge of the roof, three stories up, his legs dan-
gling over the gutter. It would have been nearly impossible
to see him with those dark coveralls blending in with the
night, but his head and hands picked up the moonlight and
gave off an eerie glow.

I ducked down below the windowsill, out of sight. Had he been looking at me? Watching my window in the middle of the night? That was beyond creepy.

Snarffle nuzzled up next to me and let out a few growly whistles. I patted him on the head. "I know how you feel, fella."

Slowly, I took a deep breath and eased my head out the window again. I squinted, trying to make out what he was doing up there.

Scratchull's chalky hands disappeared into something sitting on the roof by his side. A toolbox. He pulled out a device the size of a screwdriver, with a long silver handle and little green lights flashing along the side.

The skull-faced alien got up on his knees. He reached out for something attached to the roof and grabbed at the ...little TV satellite dish? I can't believe Grandma got one of those. It was definitely not here last summer.

Scratchull fiddled around for a few minutes. When he finally closed up his toolbox, the little mechanism with the flashing lights was attached to the top of the satellite dish. Then he stood up and walked along the roof, in the direction of my room.

I dropped my head below the windowsill again. The sound of his footsteps above grew very faint, and then disappeared altogether. I held my breath. Next to me, Snarffle was shivering slightly but totally silent.

I finally convinced myself that Scratchull wasn't going to come crashing through the window with an alien war whoop to punish me for spying on him. But I still closed the blinds and checked the lock on my door. Twice.

10

Every time I came close to falling asleep, I would half-dream/
half-remember something disturbing about Scratchull. The
way he was crawling around on the roof in the dead of the
night. The pinpricks of fiery red light that sprouted in the
middle of his black eyes when he got mad. The eerie glow of
his chalky face.

So when I saw that face again, jammed right up in front
of my nose, my groggy brain must have figured I was still
dreaming. But then I felt bony fingers dig painfully into my
shoulders. I noticed the sunlight shining through the blinds.
And then he started shaking me, my head flopping back and

forth before it smacked into the headboard and snapped me
mostly awake.

"Aaaaaghh! Wha—whazzat?" I tried to sit up, but
Scratchull pinned me to the bed. Adrenaline-fueled panic
flooded my brain. Was he trying to kill me? My fists acted
on reflex and battered against Scratchull's arms, but it had no
effect on the white alien. It felt like I was smashing against
a pair of two-by-fours.

Scratchull's so-purple-they-were-almost-black lips peeled
back from his teeth, and he leaned in, grimacing. Was he
going to *eat* me? I should have done something cool and heroic
then, head-butted him right in the nose like a tied-up action-
movie hero. But I'm ashamed to say that I slammed my eyes
closed tight and drew my head back into my scrunched-up
shoulders. My whole body cringed as I waited for the horrible end.

But nothing happened, except that Scratchull gave me one
last shake before releasing me. "Your presence is required
downstairs."

"Huh?" I cracked one eye open. Scratchull towered over
my bed, arms crossed over his chest. It didn't look like he
was in attack mode.

I woke up a little more and remembered him on the roof
in the middle of the night. So what was he doing here now?
"Don't you ever sleep?"

Scratchull scoffed. "No being of true intelligence *sleeps*.
Shedding that useless habit is the first baby step to cognitive evolution." He made a dismissive gesture toward my
bed. "You humans have the life span of a sick fruit fly, and

then choose to spend a third of that precious little time in a comatose state."

"I don't want you in my room," I said. I pushed myself farther up in bed and flipped on the lamp. The light made me squint. "Get out of here."

"Oh, I don't require an invitation for leaving. The smell alone would be incentive enough." Scratchull took a step backward and threw the door open wide. "But duty calls me to inform you that your grandmother needs your help. Urgently."

I tried to fight through the haze of sleep deprivation to make sense of all of this. "Why should I trust you?" I said.

"This is no time for petty grievances." The white alien gestured to the open door. "There is an emergency. Your presence is needed downstairs immediately."

"What?" I kicked off a tangle of blankets and reached for a pair of sweats on the floor, my body working faster than my brain. "Is—is everything okay?"

"It might be if you manage to make it down there in time. Your expertise is required out front. Quickly."

When I stood up to pull my sweats on I saw that Snarffle was at the alien's heels, his mouth clamped onto the bottom of those dark coveralls. A low, whistling growl came from deep in his chest, and he shook his head back and forth, just waiting for my signal to eat the coverall pants right off the white alien's legs.

"Come here, boy." I knelt down and snapped my fingers at the floor. "Come on. Let go."

"There is no time for that." Scratchull waved me away.

"You are needed at the front door. An important job awaits you. I will watch the beast until your return."

Something about that offer didn't sound quite right, but my mind was still foggy after such a restless night. Plus, I was more concerned with finally having an *important job* around here again. I took a few steps toward the door, grabbed the knob, then turned to face Scratchull. "What's going on down there?"

"A pair of off-world guests is leaving the premises, but they have not been through the proper procedures. Their arrival went unnoticed by the rest of the human staff." Scratchull motioned toward the door and down the hallway, making a shooing gesture.

"Wait. Why are you the one telling me this?"

Scratchull sighed heavily. "I admit that I remain highly skeptical of your abilities. But your grandmother and the head of security are away presently, leaving you as the only human who can keep two uninitiated extraterrestrial visitors from strolling into the Earth village. As an employee I have a vested interest in keeping this place safe from outside scrutiny."

I dashed out of the room and took the stairs two at a time. Finally, a real job. My specialty last summer had been GRADE assignments. I would meet the aliens as they stepped out of the transporter, welcome them to our planet, and make sure they looked passable for their vacation. Usually they needed some help to perfect that earthling look—a fake beard to cover up some purple scales or an extra mouth, or maybe a reminder that we button our shirts down the front instead of the back, that kind of thing.

I reached the bottom of the staircase and found the sitting room completely empty. And I realized that I hadn't seen anyone in the halls. That was a little weird for this time of day. But it didn't totally register since I was more worried about the fact that it looked like the uninspected aliens had already left.

I lunged toward the door and pulled it open. There! A couple of Tourists walking down the steps of the front porch. Phew. I was just barely in time.

"Just a moment, please," I called. I trotted down the stairs past them and turned at the bottom of the steps. I was now blocking their way down the path that led to the road, but in what I hoped would be seen as a casual, nonthreatening manner. "Hi, folks. Welcome to Earth!" I was proud of how easily I slipped back into customer service mode. Friendly and composed but definitely in control of the situation.

"Ummm . . . okay," the male said.

These two looked a little wary of me. Sometimes new visitors were like that at first, which is understandable after traveling millions of light-years for a weekend getaway. You never know—maybe it was their first time doing any sort of off-world travel at all. As an experienced GRADE consultant, it was my job to make them feel comfortable while I did my inspection. I gave them a big smile and served up some friendly small talk. "We're so glad you could visit with us. I hope you find our planet's weather patterns to be, you know, suitable to your needs. It's actually supposed to get pretty warm here today."

The male and female looked at each other and raised their eyebrows, then glanced back at me. They didn't say anything, so I tried to lighten the mood. "Yep, supposed to get pretty warm. Although," I gestured at the sky, "we do just have the one sun around here." I rolled my eyes and made a *Can-you-believe-this-planet?* face.

The couple looked at each other again, then up at the space decorations all over Grandma's place, and then back at me. Still didn't say anything, though. Oh, well. Better get right down to business, then. Some alien guests wanted to skip the small talk and get started on their vacation. Time to inspect their disguises.

I cupped my chin in one hand and tilted my head, sizing them up. They must have studied the *Vacation on Earth* brochure very closely back on their home planet, because they looked pretty realistic. Sometimes GRADE jobs were easy like that.

But after getting so much on-the-job experience last summer, I had learned to notice the small details that might get them detected. The male alien had a big, round torso underneath his Hawaiian-style shirt, but really skinny legs poking out of his shorts. He looked way out of proportion, a common telltale sign of extraterrestrial origin. I took a step forward and poked at his soft midsection. "Are you sure you're not hiding any extra limbs under there, sir? If so, you better keep that shirt buttoned up tight. We wouldn't want a third arm to pop out and scare the people of Earth." That had actually happened during my very first GRADE job last summer.

"What?" He stepped backward and nearly tripped on the stair behind him.

I turned my attention to the female. "You look great, ma'am. Although your wig is sitting a little bit lopsided, and the women on this planet try not to get the lipstick on their teeth." I pointed helpfully at her mouth.

The female's eyes went wide. She made a face like a fish trying to breathe on dry land.

The male patted her on the arm and pulled her away from me. "There, there, dear. I'm sure there must be an explanation for—"

"I've never been so insulted!" the female finally spluttered. "What kind of an establishment is this, anyway?"

Tate burst out of the front door. "Boy, what in the Sam Hill are you doing?" He stood at the top of the steps, arms crossed over his belly, glaring down at me.

What was he so mad about? "I was just . . . I was trying to help." I gestured weakly to the Tourists. "They haven't been GRADEd yet. I thought that . . ."

Tate jerked his head at the couple and glared even harder at me. Clearly he was trying to send me a message, but I had no idea what it might be.

Grandma glided out of the front door then, followed by Amy. Grandma walked halfway down the steps and put her hand on the male guest's shoulder. "I'm so terribly sorry if there was any confusion, sir. Why don't we—"

"We're leaving. Now." The male brushed off Grandma's hand, put his arm around the female, and marched down the steps and along the walkway to the front gate. Amy's eyes went wide and she glanced from the couple to me and back again.

Grandma moved to follow them down the front path, but Tate stopped her.

"Just let 'em go," he said softly. "The damage has been done. You'd only make it worse."

Grandma sighed. We all watched the couple climb into a red convertible. The female grabbed the rearview mirror and grimaced, rubbing furiously at her teeth with her index finger. The male fired up the engine and the car took off.

"Wait . . . They drove here?" I said.

Tate scoffed. "He *still* doesn't get it."

Grandma wrung her hands and avoided eye contact. "David . . . even though I always tell anyone who calls for a reservation that all of our rooms are filled up . . . occasionally people just stop by out of curiosity. . . ."

Oh, no. No, no, no.

"You mean . . . those were humans?"

Grandma nodded.

Amy started to laugh, then clapped her hand over her mouth. She saw me watching her and tried to compose herself. "Oh, David. I'm sorry," she said. "That must have been . . . awkward for you."

"Awkward for him? What about that couple?" said Tate. "They stop by a little roadside inn on a Sunday drive, and David welcomes 'em to the planet with some advice on how to dress up like earthlings." Tate made a show of craning his neck to look down the road. "We should look on the bright side, though. He did a bang-up job." Tate nudged his daughter with his elbow. "I don't think anyone in Forest Grove will suspect a thing."

A choked laugh escaped from behind Amy's hand. Then another. Tate joined her, just a little at first, but pretty soon his jowls were shaking as he chuckled and pointed at me. Grandma put up a good fight to keep a straight face, but after a few moments she couldn't resist laughing along with them.

I tried to smile so I didn't look like a total jerk, but there's no worse feeling than being laughed at. Especially when you deserve it.

They went on and on. I turned my head away, silently willing my face to stop getting so hot, when a flicker of movement caught my eye. There, in my bedroom window on the second floor, was Scratchull, filling up the frame. His purple lips were stretched into a hideous grin. He gave me a little wave with his chalk-white hand, grotesquely mimicking the dainty movements of a parade princess acknowledging the crowd.

I looked away. My embarrassment turned to anger. I considered telling them about Scratchull setting me up, but quickly decided against it. I was already the boy who cried space-wolf after the misunderstanding with the flying nail gun. I would have to settle this between the white alien and me.

Finally the guffaws from Grandma, Amy, and Tate quieted down to giggles and died out. After a few hiccupy relapses, they all dried their eyes and composed themselves.

"Now, even though we're laughing, this is really no laughing matter," Tate said. "You're gonna need to be a lot more careful around here this summer. I had a perfectly good Code Green going there, and you blundered right into the middle of it."

"Code Green?"

"Evasive tactics, boy, like I been telling ya." Tate lumbered down the steps to stand in front of me.

"Come on, Dad." Amy followed Tate down the steps. "David hasn't been here all year. You can't expect him to know all of your new rules."

"When a human couple shows up unexpected-like, I sound the alarm for a Code Green." Tate jabbed a thick finger at the house for emphasis. "All of the Tourists return to their rooms and shut the doors. Your grandma greets the humans, apologizes for not having any vacant rooms, and excuses herself to the kitchen. The humans mill around for a couple of minutes, get bored, and then leave, none the wiser." Tate shook his head and spat on the lawn. "No telling what that couple will be thinking now. Or what they might say to other folks."

"Now, Tate, there's no reason to worry," Grandma said. "There was no real harm done."

"Yeah," Amy said. "That couple will just think that the kooky folks up at the Intergalactic place were taking themselves a little too seriously."

"And great galaxies, I can hardly remember your rainbow of code situations, and I live here full-time," Grandma said. "Let's see, Code Blue is for when an off-world guest doesn't return at the appointed time in the evening, and I think Code Red is when—"

"It's okay, Grandma. I know you're trying to make me feel better. But Tate's right. I should've been more careful." I was learning there were lots of things I would have to be careful about from now on.

Tate checked his watch. "All right, then. If we sit around all morning we won't be any better than those lollygagging aliens," he said. "Time to get to work."

"I'm off to perfect my recipe for the baking contest," Grandma said. "Now, I know that David has been looking for a job." She looked at Amy. "Maybe he could help you out with—"

"I got a job for him," Tate said. "This place needs a good disinfecting."

"Now, wait just one minute," Grandma said. "I always—"

"I know, I know." Tate held up his hand to stop her. "You wash the linens and mop the floors and keep everything ship-shape and spic-and-span."

Grandma arched her eyebrows and gave him a look. "So what are you saying?"

"I know you don't believe me about alien germs and microbes and whatnot, but I think we'd be better off safe than sorry." Tate gestured at me. "Come on, boy. I picked up some industrial-strength cleaner. You can give the floors and walls a proper scrub-down."

Grandma looked at me, a question in her eyes. I knew she would let me get out of it if I tried.

But having a job that I could do alone sounded pretty good. It was going to take a while before the sting of my humiliation wore off. And besides, I needed some time alone to plot out my next move concerning Scratchull. "Sure, I can help you out."

Grandma smiled, and her tone was a little too bright when she spoke. "Okay, everybody. Let's have a wonderful day!" She walked into the bed-and-breakfast.

Tate gestured toward the door. "I'll get you the supplies, boy. You can start on the bottom floor and work your way up."

He walked into the house, but I hung back when Amy pulled on my sleeve. "I'll be right there," I called after him. Then I turned to Amy. "What's up?"

"I have something I want to show you," she whispered. "Stay right there." She ducked into the house and quickly returned with an overflowing double armful of books and magazines.

"What's all that?"

"I got these at the library." She gestured at individual books with her chin as she spoke. "This one's about how the major religions of Earth focus on peace and harmony among all people . . . That one explains how all of the annual charitable contributions in this country dwarf the defense budget . . . and this is about the green movement and the rise of environmentally conscious jobs . . ."

A book tumbled off the pile and fell on the porch. I stooped to pick it up. *"Ten Steps to an Earth-Friendly Existence?"*

"Aren't they great?" Amy lowered her voice again and gave me a conspiratorial wink. "I think they're really going to help, don't you?"

"Help with what?"

Amy gave me a funny look. "What do you think? I'm going to leave them lying around in places where Scratchull will come across them."

I must have made a face, because she was quick to add, "The bad news gets all the headlines, but when he reads stuff like this he'll know it's time for Earth to finally be invited to join the Collective. I was thinking I'd leave some of them by the seat where he usually eats his meals, and a couple in the bathroom in his hallway, and maybe a few out in the sheds where he likes to tinker with machinery. What do you think?"

What could I say? Her face got so animated when she was excited about something. I couldn't just shoot her down entirely. Especially when I didn't have any proof that

Scratchull was up to something worse than the prank he had just pulled on me.

I set the book back on top of Amy's pile. "I think that if I had to pick anyone to speak up for the Earth, it would be you," I said truthfully.

"Thanks, David." She beamed. "Hey, do you want to hang out tonight? I don't have any activities. We could take a hike by the river—there's something I've been wanting to show you out there since last summer."

"Sounds good."

"Great. Okay, wish me luck. I'm off to place these books in strategic positions." She dashed through the door.

I sighed and looked back up at my bedroom window, but it was empty and dark. I wasn't sure which was worse—seeing that creepy alien's gruesome face as he mocked me, or not knowing exactly where he was or what he was doing. And if he even tried to lay one of those pale fingers on Snarffle...

I marched up the front steps. If Scratchull was actually going to be performing surveillance on the Earth, then maybe it was time somebody started keeping better tabs on *him*.

11

I spent the day either hunched over on all fours or balancing on a stepladder, scrubbing the floors and walls. I'm not sure I eliminated any dangerous outer-space bacteria, but I had to admit the place at least looked better.

Snarffle hung out with me, tethered to his new leash, as I made my way from room to room. I considered fixing brushes to his feet and letting him race up and down the walls, but with my luck today, that would turn into some unforeseen disaster. Plus, Tate would probably think he was spreading more harmful alien germs than he was cleaning up.

Still, it was nice to have the little guy around for company. He never laughed at me. And as long as I fed him every couple of hours he didn't spaz out too bad.

At about five o'clock I decided to call it a day. I headed for the bathroom to take a shower before my hike with Amy. I figured since I was a total dork in front of her this morning and she was a way better employee than I would ever be, the least I could do is smell good.

As I passed the kitchen, Grandma poked her head out from behind the swinging door. "David? Could you come in here?" She held the door open and Snarffle trotted in ahead of me. He dashed to the communal dining table and hopped on top. Grandma whisked away a platter of baked goods just before he could inhale them.

"Still working on your contest entry?" I nodded toward the platter.

"These scones have a layer of fresh Kerntaberry preserves baked right into the center. Try one."

I grabbed one and inclined my head toward Snarffle, eyebrows raised. "All right," Grandma said. "He can have one, as well." I tossed the scone into the air, and the alien's tongue shot out and lassoed the flying snack. He was like a frog with superpowers. Grandma grinned. "His manners need some work, but I suppose I should be flattered that he likes my cooking so much."

I tossed Snarffle another scone, and then grabbed one for myself. It was still warm, and I closed my eyes when I bit into it, savoring the otherworldly goodness.

"Grandma, you seriously need to think bigger than the Pioneer Day baking contest. With recipes this good—that no one else in the world has ever tasted—you should host your own show on the Food Network."

"Wouldn't that be a hoot?" She spread her hands out in front of her, highlighting an imaginary marquee. "I could call it *Baking Tips from Beyond the Asteroid Belt*."

"Sounds good. Or maybe *Secret Recipes of the Stars*. I'm sure it would be a hit."

Grandma placed the platter on top of the fridge, hopefully out of Snarffle's tongue range. "As soon as this planet is ready to handle our little secret, perhaps I'll do just that." I couldn't help but think of the Collective scientists for a moment.

I popped the last bit of scone into my mouth and licked the jam filling off my fingers. "So, you need me for something? Or did you just want a couple of taste testers?"

Grandma walked over to the swinging door and peeked out into the hallway, then checked to make sure no one was listening outside the window. Finally she stepped close to me. "Actually, yes," she whispered. "I have a rather urgent job for you."

"Yeah?" That sounded good. Anything to try to erase the memory of my big screwup from this morning.

"Our friend Sasquatch should have returned by now. Normally I wouldn't be such a worrier, but he's always on time, that one." She glanced out the window again. "Plus, Tate made such a big deal out of his visit. And I really don't have time to put up with a lot of his Code Blue nonsense. If Sasquatch is missing for too long, Tate will want to evacuate the premises, close down the transporters, and generally mess up everyone's vacation plans. I'd feel a lot better if Sasquatch returned and got safely back into his transporter before that man starts asking a bunch of nosy questions."

"Okay." Snarffle nuzzled up against my feet, and I reached down to pat him. "But how can I help you with that?"

"I was hoping you could hike up the logging road this evening." Grandma watched me hopefully. "Poke around a little bit, see if you can find our guest?"

I was a lot more comfortable in the woods after my camping adventures last summer, but I didn't exactly see how that was going to help in this situation. "Grandma, you know I'd do anything you asked . . . but I don't think I'd have much of a realistic chance of finding him. I mean, haven't thousands of people gone out there looking for him? Haven't they been searching for years and years?" It was nice to know she still had some confidence in me, but having messed up so badly made me hesitant to put an impossible task on my to-do list.

Grandma waved away my objections. "Oh, sure, but they go about it entirely the wrong way. Those weekend warriors tromp through the woods and set clumsy traps baited with half-rotten food. Then they sit around drinking beer in some abandoned deer hunter's blind. The only thing they ever catch doing that is a cold." Grandma gave me a wry smile and shook her head. "Sasquatch finds them hilarious. After they fall asleep, he usually leaves a couple of footprints for them to find in the morning. But don't tell Tate that," she added.

"So what do you want me to do?"

"Just walk down the middle of the logging road and call his name." Grandma swept her hands down an imaginary path for emphasis. "Trust me, nobody ever tries that technique."

I guess she had a point. My facial expression must have still been pretty skeptical, though, because Grandma pressed on. "And most people, of course, have no idea when he's in town. They're lurking up there in the forest while he's back on his home planet. Plus, we have a couple of other factors in our favor. We know approximately where he's staying, and best of all, he's already met you. If he hears someone calling his name and spots you, he'll just pop out from his hiding spot and say hello. He has excellent hearing."

I nodded. "Sure, I can do that for you. I'd like to."

"Oh, bless you, David." She put her arm around my shoulders and led me out of the kitchen and down the back hall.

Suddenly I remembered something else from this morning. "I was supposed to hang out with Amy tonight. You mind if I invite her along?"

Grandma opened the back door. "Actually, dear, I don't think that would be a very good idea."

My spirits sank. "Really?"

"Amy's wonderful, and if it ever came right down to it, I trust her not to mention anything to Tate. But I just don't like putting her in a situation where she might have to lie to her father if he asked her anything. Not if I don't absolutely have to."

I dropped my head a little. "Yeah. I see what you mean."

Grandma shut the door and squeezed my shoulders. "You know what? I'm sure everything's fine with Sasquatch. It always has been before. You can head up there in the morning."

"No, it's okay." This was the first time she had really needed me since I showed up, so I couldn't turn her down. Especially

after this morning. "I'll go now. Just let me reschedule with Amy first."

"She's running an errand in town with Tate. I'll fill her in when she gets back." Grandma studied my face for a moment. "Don't worry. I'll tell her I insisted that you go. And that you were terribly disappointed."

I really hoped Amy wouldn't be mad. But I had to admit, it felt good to actually have something real to do. I looked down at the purple alien nuzzling up against my shins. "I think I will take Snarffle, though. Let him stretch those little legs before bed." Snarffle bobbed and wriggled. He thought that was a great idea.

A few minutes later Snarffle was strapped into his new harness and dragging me up the logging road. Pretty soon sweat was pouring down my forehead. Fortunately, I got a little break whenever he stopped to make a snack of the clusters of pale mushrooms that sprouted from rotting logs, or to chew on long wisps of moss hanging from tree branches.

It didn't take long to put civilization completely behind us. The old logging road narrowed and became more of a hiking trail with a pair of fading wheel ruts. No houses or buildings, no car noises, no people.

As peaceful as the whole scene was, the forest was still a busy place. Families of deer smashed through thickets of undergrowth as the little purple alien bounced and scampered from one side of the road to the other, making mini-excursions into the woods as far as his leash would allow. Squirrels raced circles around the big evergreen trees and chattered at him,

while birds squawked from the branches overhead. Snarffle whistled happily back at all of them.

Now, I knew they were just animals...so why was I so embarrassed to be calling out "Sasss—qua-atch? Sassssss—qua-aa-atch!" at the top of my lungs every couple of minutes? I hoped we'd find him soon.

Walking through the forest, with the surrounding trees forming hundred-foot walls and a canopy of branches knotting themselves into a ceiling, your mind could be tricked into thinking you were still indoors. So when we came upon a huge, barren clearing, it definitely surprised me. Snarffle, too. We both stopped and stared.

The clear area off to our right was enormous, about as long and wide as a city block. It didn't look like any of the clearings I had seen while hiking last summer, those peaceful mountain meadows covered with wildflowers. Places like that made you wish you had brought a picnic lunch and a blanket to lie on while you looked at the sky.

This was different. It looked unnatural, like a huge scar slashed across the landscape. The whole area was featureless and flat; no vegetation, no rocks or logs, no little ponds.

And the surface seemed to be shifting and moving, even though there was no wind, not even a breeze.

Snarffle nuzzled his purple body up against my leg, making little whistle-whimpers deep in his throat. The sound was so persistent, I almost didn't notice the noise just underneath. I dropped down to one knee and patted him on the back. "Shhh, it's okay, boy," I whispered soothingly. "It's okay. Just be quiet for a minute. Shhhhhh."

Snarffle's whining simmered down, and the other noise became more noticeable.

Bloop...slllshh...bloopbloop...

What *was* that? It sounded like...well, like a pot of soup boiling on the stove. But that was ridiculous.

I watched the landscape, trying to make some sense out of that eerie, shifting movement.

A flash of motion caught my eye. It was halfway across the clearing and off to our left; something rising out of the ground, only to disappear after a few seconds. What the...?

I let my eyes drift over the clearing, not really focusing on any one section, watching for another flicker of movement.

There! Only ten yards away and right in front of us. Coming up out of the ground, it was a series of...dirt bubbles?

It happened again, out in the middle of the clearing. And there were more over on the right-hand side, close to the edge where the trees started growing again. Little splashes that threw up brown bubbles of dirt. These rose out of the ground, hung ponderously in the air for a couple of seconds, then popped, sending dirt drops splattering down to be reabsorbed into the ground. It was like the surface of an enormous cauldron as a thick stew boiled and bubbled.

I scooped up a rock and threw it out in the middle of the clearing. *Blorp!* It sent up a brown splash of dirt and then disappeared below the surface.

"You ever see anything like that where you're from, fella?" I whispered to Snarffle. He responded by nuzzling up even closer, and I patted him on the back. His whistle-whimpers increased in volume and intensity. "It's okay. It'll be just fine,"

I told him, even though I wasn't sure how much I believed my own words.

We kept staring, frozen by the strange scene in front of us. Then one of the enormous Douglas fir trees at the edge of the clearing, about half a football-field length away from us, started wobbling back and forth. For a split second I worried that maybe a bear was at the base of the tree, shaking it to dislodge a woodland creature that he had trapped, but the trunk was way too massive for that.

The top of the enormous tree swayed in larger and larger arcs, smashing right through the branches of the surrounding firs. The tree dipped even farther in the direction of the clearing, hung suspended in the air for a few moments like the Leaning Tower of Pisa, then tipped past the point of no return and fell all the way over with a majestic slowness.

You know that old riddle about whether or not a falling tree makes a sound if there's no one there to hear it? Well, I sure wish I wasn't the one around to hear this tree fall. Because it landed with a horribly unnatural squelching sound, sending up a shower of dirt spray. The whole thing just looked *wrong*. The tree bobbed on the bubbling surface of wilderness-stew, and then with a sickening sucking sound it disappeared into the earth, like the clearing was a greedy mouth slurping it up.

The strength went out of my legs. I dropped to the dirt and just stared. Snarffle crawled into my lap, and I wrapped both of my arms around him. I'm not sure how long we stayed huddled there, but it was enough time to see three more hundred-foot trees surrender themselves to the hungry ground below.

The clearing was spreading.

I had to get back to the B&B, fast, and tell somebody. I was trying to rouse myself out of this stupor when Snarffle leaped off my lap and charged toward the clearing. He moved so swiftly that his leash burned right through my palm, and I lost my grip on it.

"Snarffle, no!" I jumped up and ran after him.

It looked as though he was going to plunge right into the clearing, but he veered off at the last second and headed for the tree line. I raced after him and finally saw what had him so excited—a mama deer and her baby fawn, leaping nimbly through the trees.

Snarffle crashed into the brush near the deer, startling them and flushing the pair out of the woods and onto the logging road ahead of us.

He scampered along the road after them, that long tongue wagging. Snarffle placed himself between the two deer and the soupy clearing. It took me a few moments to figure out that he was trying to save them by herding the pair away from this new danger.

The doe bounded away in smooth, powerful leaps, all four hooves hitting the ground at once and rebounding like rubber to send them ricocheting back into the air. The fawn lagged behind. It was a tiny thing, hardly bigger than a golden retriever, and still had a pattern of white spots on its side.

The fawn veered toward the clearing, and Snarffle dashed nearer to remain in a protective position but got a bit too close, running up under the baby deer's heels. The fawn got skittish and shot off of the road—

Right into the soupy ground.

It vanished beneath the forest floor, which was far more surreal to see than watching the trees sink below the earth. I lunged for Snarffle's leash and managed to grab hold of it, stopping the little purple alien before he could splash in after the baby deer. He stood at the very edge of the shifting ground of the clearing, his little tail twirling like a ceiling fan and his eyes darting back and forth.

Suddenly the fawn's head broke the surface of the earth, streaming rivulets of brown dirt juice. Its eyes rolled wildly in their sockets. The front hooves emerged for a moment and scrabbled in a frantic dog paddle, but then it was slowly sucked back underneath.

Snarffle strained at his leash. "No! I'll do it!" I shouted. I wrapped the end of the leash around a nearby branch, tethering Snarffle to the tree, then moved along the edge of that swampy mess like a tightrope walker.

There was a roiling whirlpool of activity as the fawn thrashed around just beneath ground level. I reached out and stuck my hand into the earth, shuddering at the texture. It wasn't like mud—it was both smoother and heavier, like jamming your hand into semi-wet concrete.

I grabbed one of the fawn's struggling legs and pulled as hard as I could. The hoof rose slowly above the surface, followed by the leg, then the deer's head. That's when it opened its mouth and screamed, an eerily human sound. It really did a number on my last good nerve.

The fawn tried to rip its leg out of my hand, but I held on in a death grip, my heart pounding in my ears. The animal wriggled around some more and pulled me off balance. I fell headfirst into the boiling, soupy mess.

Everything went black. I tried to pop back up above ground, but it didn't work. In a swimming pool you feel light and buoyant; this was the opposite. I felt buried in sludge, the weight of the earth pressing in on me from all angles. My arms flailed uselessly.

The fawn struggled, its hooves thudding into my chest, but I couldn't see anything.

The fierce need to breathe consumed me. I tried to pull all my confused thoughts together, knowing I didn't have much time.

Instead of trying to "swim," I shot my hand straight up above my head. It broke the surface; I splayed my fingers and felt the cool evening air. I did the same with my other hand and then, keeping my elbows locked, pushed down with all my might until my arms were at my sides. I couldn't be sure, but I thought maybe I had lifted myself up a bit. I struggled to do it again. And again.

Finally, my head poked up through the liquid earth. The light reminded me that I was still alive. I gasped painfully. Snarffle was racing back and forth at the edge of the clearing as far as the leash would allow, whistling shrilly.

I tried to make my way over to him, but my natural swimming motion was worthless. I started to slip under again, the sludge lapping at my chin.

Snarffle turned his back on me and scaled the trunk of the tree as easily as he climbed the walls of my bedroom back at Grandma's place. What—he wanted to play *now*? My head slipped below the muck, back into that suffocating blackness, but I managed to propel myself back up by working my arms through the earth again.

I came up spluttering and spitting out dirt juice, but quickly slipped back down. Sludge oozed back into both of my nostrils, choking me. I desperately needed more oxygen. My arms were tired, and I was in a battle with gravity that I had no chance of winning.

I spied a purple streak of motion. Snarffle had shinned out onto a tree branch directly above me. He flipped upside down on the branch, then spun himself back upright. He did it again and again, a blur of purple.

The muck pooled around my temples, flooding my vision. This was it. I knew that if I went under again, I wouldn't be coming back up. They say your life flashes before your eyes at the end, but that wasn't true for me. I just saw a clear image of Amy's face, smiling her lopsided smile at me, and I remember hoping that she would miss me.

Just before the ground covered my remaining eye, I saw Snarffle leap off of the branch. His purple beach ball body plummeted straight toward me—

And stopped short, a few inches in front of my eyeball. He bounced back up, then dropped down again, bobbing in the air like a bungee jumper on the end of his leash.

My head slipped back underground, but something warm and slimy wrapped itself around my wrist. My downward slide was halted. The grip on my wrist stabilized me, and I was able to work my other hand up through the muck. Waving my arm around, I blindly found one of Snarffle's feet and clamped on.

Using the last bit of my strength I pulled on the alien's foot. The slimy grip on my other hand matched my effort. Gradually my body rose.

My head broke the surface and I shook the sludge off my face like a wet dog, spitting out the liquid earth. With my good eye I saw Snarffle above me, hanging upside down by the leash attached to the tree branch. His tongue was wrapped around my wrist.

I heaved mightily on his foot and raised myself inch by inch out of the earth stew. Snarffle unraveled his tongue and freed my hand to reach above him and grab onto the leash. I let go of his foot and climbed the leash hand over hand like it was one of those big ropes in gym class. When my legs came out, the soupy ground sucked the shoes right off my feet.

Finally I was able to grab the branch, panting and wheezing with exhaustion. I hooked my armpits over the tree limb and prayed it wouldn't snap and send both of us crashing back into that mess. I unwound Snarffle's leash with my free hand. He jumped onto my shoulder, gripping fiercely with all six of his little feet. I pulled myself up until I could throw my leg over the branch, then I worked us along the length of it, scrunching up and expanding like an upside-down centipede. We reached the trunk and slid down until my shoeless feet hit the firm ground at the edge of the clearing.

I didn't think I had any strength left, but Snarffle started whistle-whimpering and pacing back and forth, and I knew I was still going to have to try to save that fawn.

I slipped the harness off of Snarffle and looped it over another branch, tugging on the leash to make sure it was secure. With a good grip on the leash this time, I leaned out over the clearing.

When my hand plunged below the surface it was hard to fight off the panicky feeling of being trapped down there.

I raked through the sludge until I finally found one of the fawn's legs. There was no struggle in it anymore.

Bracing myself against the leash, I lowered myself into a squat and heaved. Slowly, a back leg emerged, followed by another, and then the fawn's hindquarters. After several minutes of concentrated effort, the entire body of the little deer was up on solid ground.

He wasn't moving, just lying there on his side with his legs curled up underneath him. Snarffle hunkered down near the fawn's head and sniffed at it with his little nose tendrils. He kept looking back up at me, clearly wanting me to do something.

"I'm sorry, Snarffle. I just think this little guy might have been under for too long."

But after a few moments the fawn made a choking sound, and drops of dirt juice splattered out of his mouth and nose. His legs twitched and he made a feeble attempt to lift his head, but he was just too exhausted.

I could relate. The energy to stay upright drained from my body, and I sank to the ground. I slumped backward, my head resting on a bed of pine needles. Snarffle nuzzled up on my right side while the fawn stretched out on my left. We just lay there, panting heavily in the middle of the forest, the strangest hiking trio on Earth—a boy, his pet alien, and their fawn friend.

I was hoping that Grandma wouldn't be too upset that I didn't find Sasquatch when an even worse thought occurred to me.... What if he was buried under all of that sludge?

Off in the distance, another massive tree surrendered and splashed into the ever-expanding clearing.

The daylight faded until everything appeared to be wrapped in gray.

Something shifted on the road behind me. My thoughts immediately flew to Scratchull. I had a clear vision of him creeping up and shoving me back into the soupy clearing.

But when I turned my head I saw the mama deer watching us. She took a couple of shuffling steps forward. I kept my body still but tightened my grip on Snarffle, petting him to keep him calm.

The mama deer worked her way toward us a few steps at a time. She finally got close enough to crane her long neck and lick the top of the fawn's head. The baby deer stirred, then opened its eyes. Our heads were only about a foot apart. For a moment it just watched me sleepily, but as soon as it realized that we were from very different species, it lurched upright and stumbled away behind its mother.

"Good-bye," I said softly. "Stay away from this place. Tell your friends."

The mama deer held my gaze for a few seconds, then turned and bounded away into the woods, followed closely by her fawn.

I eased myself upright and stretched my tired arms. "I think I owe you a few treats for saving my life, fella." I scratched at the smattering of blue dots on Snarffle's back, and he wriggled with happiness. "You can have anything you want in the kitchen, how about that?" I looked out over the murky, boiling clearing and shuddered. "Heck, you can belly up to the all-you-can-eat furniture buffet if you like."

Snarffle whistled happily and licked my face as if to say, *I didn't do it for the treats . . . but I'll take some if you're offering.*

I sighed. "Well, boy, we better get back to Grandma's place and tell her about all of this."

His little tail twirled in agreement. I climbed up on sore legs—pulling that fawn out of the muck had strained my entire body—and slipped the harness back over Snarffle. We set out on the old logging road.

It was slow going with no shoes. Even using my flashlight, I couldn't seem to avoid all of the rocks and fallen branches and exposed tree roots that nature put in my path.

By the time we stumbled onto the little trail that led to

Grandma's backyard, it was the full dark of night. Snarffle flopped down underneath a rocking chair on the porch and was whistle-snoring away in just a few seconds. I know it's lame, but I envied him. How nice it would be to just block out all of this craziness.

No chance of that. My feet ached as I climbed the steps of the porch and staggered through the back door and into the kitchen.

Grandma and Tate were sharing one of the benches at the communal dining table. Sasquatch sat opposite them, his massive frame taking up two chairs. He raised a hairy paw in greeting as I entered. I waved back, but I wasn't entirely sure whether I was happy or angry to see him sitting there all cozy and dry. If it wasn't for him I wouldn't be—

"David!" Grandma called. "It's good to see you. We were starting to get a little worried." She gestured to Sasquatch while giving me a sheepish look. "As you can see, our friend returned safe and sound. He's been telling us all about his trip."

"Whoa, boy. How'd you get so dirty? And what're you doing walking around barefoot out there?" Tate made a sour face. "You're worse than those aliens, tracking all that muck through here. Looks like you didn't get your fill of scrubbing the floors this morning, 'cuz you're just going to have to do it again."

I looked down. My skin and clothes were coated with a film of soupy dirt juice, but here in the glare of electric lighting it looked more normal, just like dried mud.

Grandma swatted at Tate's shoulder. "Leave David alone. He looks exhausted."

Tate harrumphed. "At least it's good old Earth dirt and not a bunch of germs from outer space."

I remembered the murky bubbling of the clearing, definitely not how good old Earth dirt behaved. "There's something I need to show you guys. Up the logging road."

"What were you doing up there?" Tate said.

"Oh, you know. Just letting Snarffle stretch his legs. He's been pretty restless all day," I said, glancing at Grandma. She looked from me to Sasquatch and back to me again, smiling a little apology at me. "I guess I lost track of time."

"I know how that goes," Sasquatch said. "I stayed an extra day myself. The weather was fantastic."

I was about to ask him if he saw anything weird along the way when Grandma said, "Why don't you sit and rest, David?" Grandma patted the bench. "Relax with a nice cup of tea."

I noticed they all had cups and saucers in front of them. Well, except for Sasquatch. The dainty cups were way too small for his huge paws, so he was drinking straight out of the teapot. But he did lift one furry pinky as he slurped his tea—trying to fit in, I guess.

It was maddening to watch them all just sitting there so calmly—and cleanly—after my near-death experience. "But I really need to show you something. It's important," I said. "I think we should all get in the Jeep and drive up there. Right away."

Tate leaned forward and studied my face. "What's got you so riled up tonight, boy?"

Grandma stood and crossed the room to me. "What is it, David? Is one of the guests in trouble up there?"

"No, it's nothing like that. It's ... well, there was this ... I guess it was kind of, sort of, a *swamp*, but not really." I tried to recapture the creeping horror of the spectacle—the eerie movement and that boiling noise—coupled with the terror of being sucked underground. But here in the safe warm glow of the kitchen, the intensity of the experience was slipping away. "Only it was more than that. There was—"

Scratchull pushed his way through the swinging kitchen door. He stopped short and gaped at me for a second, taking in my wet socks and gritty hair, but quickly recovered himself. He directed his attention toward Grandma and Tate. "I was checking to see if you needed anything further before I retired for the evening."

"Actually, we might need you to stay up a while longer and keep an eye on the place while we drive up the old logging road," Tate said.

Scratchull's eyes narrowed slightly. "Whatever for?"

"Apparently the boy ran across some kinda swamp up there." Tate stood and fished the Jeep keys out of his pocket. "Not entirely sure what he's talking about, but it seems like it might be worth checking out."

Those red pinpricks of light flared up in Scratchull's eyes, but quickly faded. "David is from a very different part of the planet, climate-wise. Has someone informed him that in a rainy, temperate climate such as the Pacific Northwest, the ground tends to get wet? Which can lead directly to swampy conditions?"

Sasquatch nodded in agreement.

"It was more than that!" I blurted out. "The clearing was huge, and it was sucking trees right down into the middle of it. And there were these…bubbles…" Even I could tell how lame that sounded. "I don't know, these dirt bubbles, and they were—"

"Dirt bubbles?" Scratchull said, barely containing a hideous little smirk. He turned his attention to Tate. "David is certainly leaping to all sorts of interesting conclusions today, isn't he? Wasn't it just this morning that he accosted a pair of humans, mistaking them for off-world guests?"

My face flashed hot in anger and embarrassment. "That has nothing to do with—"

"Simmer down, now, David. I'm sure you saw something up in those woods. Nobody's disputing that," Tate said.

"Scratchull does have a point," Sasquatch interjected. "The rainwater and glacial melt run down those foothills something fierce, and water gets trapped in all sorts of unusual places. Mud slides can rip trees right up by their roots. Why, I've seen sinkholes open up wide enough to swallow…well, *me*."

"Exactly," Scratchull said, still addressing Tate. "And I ask you: are those really the best conditions for driving around in your Jeep in the dark of night?"

Tate shoved his keys back into his pocket. He sat down and cleared his throat. "Scratchull's right. Seems like an unnecessary risk. Especially for something that's not exactly of an emergency nature."

Scratchull smiled and inclined his head at Tate. "Always the voice of reason, Officer Tate. We are all fortunate that you are in the proprietor's employ here. I agree that waiting until morning would be best. Now, if you will excuse me, I should go."

Everyone except me bid the white alien good night. I just glared at him as he made his way to the door. And was it just my imagination, or did he leave in much more of a hurry than he came in?

"You know, maybe we should drive up there and have a look tonight after all," Grandma said. I glanced up to find her studying my face. "I know David doesn't spook easily."

"Hold on, now. I know David's a brave fella," Tate said. "But walking around in the woods after dark can be unsettling sometimes. Especially if you come across a patch of wetlands unexpectedly and stumble headlong into a big mud puddle."

My face got hot; he made me sound like a toddler. "It was more than that," I mumbled, trying to preserve at least a piece of my dignity.

"I know what you mean, kid," Sasquatch chimed in. "Like I said, I've seen the hillsides out there after a mud slide. Looks like a big eraser came along and just wiped out a chunk of the forest."

That description came closer to describing the soupy clearing. Is it possible there was a simple, natural explanation for what I had seen...? Could I be really making too much out of it?

"Sometimes the ground gets downright unstable out there, especially when it's oversaturated," said Tate. "You get your foot caught in that muck, and it can feel durn close to quicksand. That how it was for you, David?"

I nodded. "Quicksand, yeah. Felt like I was being sucked under. I lost my shoes...." I stopped before I started crying. Now I felt like a toddler. My words sounded lame —completely failing to capture the life-or-death aspect of my struggle in that mess.

"Well, we'll tool up there after we wake up in the morning." Tate held up his hand to cut off Grandma's objection. "I have no doubt that David came across something, okay? But Scratchull was right: if the ground is that unstable near the road, we don't want to go poking around in the pitch black. Get the Jeep stuck, and we'll be there all night."

Grandma pressed her lips together and looked hard at Tate, but finally nodded. "All right. In the morning. But you need to let me make you a good breakfast first."

Tate mimed having his arm twisted behind his back. "All right, you win. We'll let you cook breakfast."

Tate kept up the arm-twisting routine, mock pain contorting his face, until a little smile broke through Grandma's tight expression and she swatted playfully at him. It was sickening.

"I'm afraid I'll have to pass," Sasquatch said, putting down the teapot and stretching his huge arms over his head. "It's been a great little getaway, but it's time for me to get home."

"Will you at least stay for breakfast?" Grandma said.

"I better hit the transporter tonight, sleep in my own bed. Big shoe sale tomorrow. Too bad I don't have any in your size," he said to me with a wink.

"All right. Well, I'm sorry we didn't have more of a chance to visit," Grandma said. "You must let me pamper you a bit more next time."

"You got it. And let me know if anything comes of this mystery-swamp sighting."

Part of me wanted to scream, to wake them all up, to make them feel a fraction of the terror I had just experienced. But that part of me was getting smaller. Most of me just wanted to shower and go to bed.

Once I got under the covers, though, I spent most of the night lying awake, trying to decide if it was possible I had seen something that occurs naturally around here. It seemed hard to believe, but I had to admit I didn't know much about old-growth forests in the Pacific Northwest.

I sighed and stared at the ceiling. Then I started thinking about Scratchull. He was somewhere out there, right now. What was he doing, or thinking? Knowing that he never slept made it very hard to keep my eyes closed.

I wondered if I was going to get a single good night's sleep this summer.

"Nice kicks." Amy didn't even try to hide her smirk.

I looked down at the pink Converse high-tops with the blue stars all over them. They were the only shoes that fit me in Grandma's stash of thrift store clothing that we used for alien disguises.

"Just trying to fit in with the customers." The Jeep jounced over the rocks in the logging road.

"How much farther, boy?" Tate was hunched over the steering wheel, scanning the forest.

"Almost there." We were making much better time than

I had last night. I turned back to Amy. "Sorry I missed our hike. It would have been a lot more fun than what I was doing, trust me."

"No problem. I ended up taking a group of Tourists to a little outdoor concert at the park." Amy gave me a wink. "Besides, there's still a lot of summer left to hang out."

The clearing popped hideously into view. "Here it is," I called out.

"Whoa," Tate said. "That *is* a big clearing, all right."

"What happened to all of the trees?" Amy said.

"Scratchull was right—a mud slide must've swept through here at some point," Tate said.

Amy was on the side of the Jeep nearest to the clearing. She hopped out of her seat and took a couple of steps toward it.

"Look out!" I yelled. I yanked off my seat belt and scrambled across her seat. I lunged out of the Jeep and grabbed her arm. "Don't get too close."

Tate walked around the Jeep and surveyed the ground. "This is the place you saw last night, huh?"

I thought so . . . but it sure didn't feel the same. No dirt bubbles popped on the surface, and it was no longer shifting or moving at all.

Slowly, carefully, I approached the edge of the clearing with Amy and Tate watching. There was the proof—a few threads from Snarffle's leash, wound around a low-hanging branch. "Yep," I said. "This is the place." But it certainly didn't look like I had described it last night.

I bent down and scooped up a few rocks. I threw one out

into the middle of the clearing and it bounced once before thudding to a rest on top of the ground. I fired rocks in all directions and got the same result everywhere. No splash and burble, no rocks sinking below the surface, no liquid earth.

Tate walked out to the clearing, right on top of the spot where I nearly drowned. He stamped his feet in a wide circle. "Ground's a bit soft, but it looks okay to me, boy."

Amy looked at me sadly. "Sorry, David."

"It was different last night. I swear!"

"I believe you," she said. "Sometimes the ground drains really fast up here, you know? All of that water funnels into creeks and heads down the mountain to the river."

I nodded, but I didn't buy any of that. No way did this place dry out in one night. And no way was it natural for the ground to bubble like that, ever. This whole clearing had been as eerie and unnatural as—

Scratchull. Of course! His eyes had glowed red when he heard I was coming back from a swamp up in the woods. And then he had been so firm about the fact that they shouldn't go check it out last night. I'd been too tired and shaken up by my near-death experience to think about it then, but why would Scratchull care if they drove the Jeep in the dark? Why would he automatically argue that the whole thing was perfectly normal?

Because he was trying to cover something up.

I looked at my watch. Since Scratchull didn't sleep, he had had almost ten hours to get up here. Had he fixed it somehow? I had no idea how he could do that, but I was sure he was behind all of this.

And suddenly I knew what I had to do.

I didn't say anything to Tate or Amy. Just marched to the Jeep.

"Let's go," I said.

"Are you sure?" said Amy. "You don't want to look around, see if maybe the marshy ground shifted into the surrounding woods or something?"

"It doesn't matter," I said. "Let's go."

Tate walked out of the clearing and back to the Jeep, shaking his head and muttering, "Crazy kid. Wasting my time . . ."

"Sorry, Mr. Tate," I said. "I guess it wasn't as bad as I thought. What do you need to get done today?"

"Lots of odd jobs, this and that," Tate said. "First I need to take Scratchull into town for a supply run at the hardware store. He says there's lots of stuff he needs to finish up our projects."

Perfect. Scratchull's room would be empty. That would give me the opportunity I needed.

"Do you want to hang out today, David?" Amy said, interrupting my plotting. "I can probably postpone a few of my jobs until tomorrow." She looked at me hopefully. "We could make up for our lost outing last night. Besides, it might be good to have a chance to talk about . . . things."

Part of me wanted to say yes. Most of me, actually. Amy would be the perfect ally.

But she had all of her hopes for the future of the planet pinned on Scratchull. As much as I hated to admit it to myself, Amy might not be entirely on my side right now.

This was something I was going to have to do alone.

"Sorry, I'm going to be busy today." It didn't sound nearly as nice as I wanted it to. "Maybe later," I offered.

"Yeah," she said, her eyes cold now. "We'll have to check our schedules."

The rest of the ride back down to Grandma's house was quiet.

I watched from behind a spaceship sculpture as Tate and Scratchull walked through the gate in the picket fence to Tate's Jeep. Scratchull refused to wear makeup, but he did put on a hat, sunglasses, and gloves to cover up most of his glaring white skin. As soon as they headed toward town, I raced to the back of the house, pulling Snarffle along behind me.

Scratchull kept his room locked; I had already tested that out this morning. Snarffle and I climbed Tate's watchtower to the platform that was level with the top floor of Grandma's place.

I dropped to one knee and looped Snarffle's leash around a railing, then placed my hands on either side of his purple head. The little alien gazed up at me with those wide green eyes. "I need you to stay here, okay? And if that creepy old Skull-Face comes back, you need to let me know. You got me?"

Snarffle panted and bobbed up and down. Now, I wasn't one of those people who really believed that pets could understand what I was saying. But Snarffle made the same whistling-growling noise every time he saw Scratchull, so I figured that would be as good an alarm system as I was going to get. If Snarffle tipped me off to the white alien's arrival, I could dash out the front door of his room. Besides, I should only need a minute or two in there, tops.

I tightened the straps on my backpack. Scratchull's room was three windows down. I moved quickly, knowing if I stopped to think, I would chicken out.

I braced myself against one of the watchtower pillars and slowly slid my foot off the platform. It dangled out in the open air, above the terrifying drop-off, before I managed to place the tip of my shoe on the nearest window ledge. I jounced my foot up and down to test how securely it was attached—sometimes the wood on old houses gets pretty soft, especially in a climate like this. But the windowsill held firm.

I grabbed the gutter, then eased my other foot onto the sill, and finally let go of the watchtower altogether. The gutter was good for balance, but if my feet slipped, there was no way it would support my entire body weight. I wondered fleetingly whether the drop would be enough to kill me, or just break both of my legs. Then I decided I'd be better off not thinking about it at all.

I worked myself sideways, sliding feet and hands inches at a time. The boy who looked back at me from the reflection in the window appeared to be terrified.

I got to the very edge of the first windowsill, then had to lift my foot and seek out the next one with my sneakered toes. I extended my grip farther along the gutter until I was leaning far enough to be able to bring my other foot to the new ledge.

My legs were shaky and my head light from the exertion of maintaining perfect balance. I tightened my grip on the gutter and the plastic creaked and groaned. I froze in position and held my breath for a very long time.

A little alien stared up at me from inside the guest room. His tiny green hands grabbed the bottom of the window and yanked it up.

"What are you doing out there?" he said.

"Ummm . . . exercise," I said. "House climbing. It's very popular on this planet."

The alien slammed the window shut and ran out of sight. "Mom!" I heard him call. "Earthlings are weird!"

I sidestepped as quickly as I dared, then lunged over so I was standing in front of Scratchull's window. If I could just get one minute in there, I would be able to set the stage to reveal Scratchull to be the liar that he was. At least that's what I was gambling on doing.

But how was I going to get the window open now? It's not like I could let go of the gutter.

I slowly lifted one foot and placed the tip against the window. I pressed in, not hard enough to break it, but enough so the rubber gripped the glass. I pulled upward; my shoe squeaked along the surface, and the window budged a little. Maybe a quarter of an inch.

I repeated this until there was enough space to jam my foot in under the window. I lifted my knee with a grunt and the window slid most of the way open.

I dropped down and stepped inside the room. Ugh—what was that smell? I quickly found the source of the odor: a huge aquarium in the corner. There was no water, but it was filled with a writhing, squirming pile of *something.*

I crept closer. Gross! The aquarium was crawling with slugs. I have met life forms from all over the universe, and I have to say that regular old Earth slugs are the most disgusting.

If you've never seen one up close, a slug basically looks like a four-inch-long, squirming, pulsating booger. They come in classic booger colors: green, yellow, and brownish-black. They are sort of fascinating in their grossness. I mean, one of the cool parts about meeting all of the aliens was seeing how their bodies developed in an environment totally different from Earth's. But how could you even start to explain the existence of slugs? In school they told us that the law of nature favors the survival of the fittest. So aren't species supposed to get stronger, faster, and smarter over time? If so, it's strange that billions of years of natural selection would come up with a defenseless snot creature that moves about as fast as continental drift.

The hallway floorboards creaked outside the door.

Footsteps. I froze, but whoever it was tromped right on by. I realized I was studying the slugs to avoid the terror of being in Scratchull's room. Time to put my plan into action.

I slipped off my backpack, unzipped it, and withdrew Amy's enhanced baby monitor. Feeling the heft of its plastic case, I instantly felt guilty. She probably would have let me borrow it, but then she would have asked what I was going to do with it.

I would explain everything to her after I found some incriminating evidence. I mean, that creepy alien *had* to be responsible for the disturbing, bubbling, man-eating mud. I figured it shouldn't take me too long to pin it on him if I could keep him under constant surveillance.

Still, sneaking into Amy's room to find the baby monitor had not been my finest hour. She had hidden it in one of her drawers, and I'd had to dig through some of her . . . um, dainty things . . . to find it. Okay, enough about that.

I also felt guilty because I had sort of looked at some pictures she had on her dresser. I couldn't help it—they were right there, out in the open. The one I couldn't get out of my mind showed her with a big group in the snow, surrounded by sleds and inner tubes, probably up near the top of Mount Baker. Everyone had their arms thrown around one another's shoulders as they posed for the camera, their breath fogging the air.

They were all bundled up, but I could tell from the flashes of multicolored and scaly skin underneath hoods and scarves that this was no middle-school ski trip—Amy had taken a group of aliens up to go sledding. She was standing between two tall Tourists and had that lopsided grin on her face. Was one of those her teen alien friend, the one who set her up with the translator? The one who had visited three or four times (or more?) since I had been here last time? The one who she probably wanted to see again because he was so—

The transporter in the corner started humming. The circular light in the middle glowed blue, and a thin layer of steam floated out from underneath the door.

Not good.

The light pulsated in rhythm with the humming, getting faster and faster and louder and louder until finally it stopped altogether with a *Whoosh!*

The door would open any second. No time to get back out the window or even fiddle with the lock on the front door. Crap! What was I going to do?

The transporter door swung open. I lunged into Scratchull's closet and pulled the door closed behind me, leaving a small slit to peek through.

The alien that came out of the transporter stood about four feet tall, and his coloring was bright greenish-yellow. His face sort of melted into his torso without any neck. There were three black ovals near the top of his head that I figured were his eyes, and below these a fat, round, snoutish-looking thing stuck out. I couldn't decide whether it was a nose or a mouth.

And his legs. He didn't have any. The bottom half of his body was . . . it's kind of hard to describe, but from the waist region down he looked like a jellyfish. Sort of a mushy blob that shook when he moved.

There was no way that Grandma would be able to disguise something like that enough for him to mingle, undetected, with the citizens of Earth. But I had a feeling this alien was not here for a vacation.

Even without legs, he moved really fast. He shot out of the transporter and zipped around the room as if he were looking for something—glancing out the window, peeking under the bed—and then he was moving straight toward the closet, reaching for the doorknob. He had too many fingers to count, the tips hollow circles that opened and closed with a squelching sound.

It was all happening so fast, I hardly had time to be terri-fied. I searched for an excuse that would explain why I might be crouching in Scratchull's closet and came up empty. The green alien's fingers closed around the doorknob and every muscle in my body tensed up. I was so nervous I even closed my eyes, like a little kid does when he wants to disappear. Great move on my part. I could hear the closet door start to creak, but just then the door to the bedroom burst inward and slammed against the wall.

My eyes snapped open. Scratchull stormed into the room. When he saw Mr. Green Jellyfish-Legs, he pulled himself up to his full height, nearly scraping his gleaming white skull head against the ceiling.

Then Scratchull started talking and the most hideous noise came out. It was scratchy and hissy, with an undercur-rent of unbearable screeching, like when your dad is cutting his steak, but then something monumental happens in the football game he's watching on TV, and he gets so agitated that he doesn't realize he has cut right through his steak, and now he's scraping his knife against the bare plate—like fingernails on a chalkboard, only way worse—and the TV keeps showing the slow-motion replay over and over, and your dad keeps getting madder and madder and just keeps scraping that blade against the china in frustration. His voice sounded just like that.

Greenie cowered before Scratchull, covering his head with his arms. He opened his mouth and strange sounds came out, but these were softer and rounder, like the *blub-blub-blub* of bubbles in a water cooler. I finally figured out they were talking to each other in their native languages.

Moving as slowly as I could to avoid making any sound, I flipped on the baby monitor, keeping the volume low. I pressed the listening end against my ear.

"...have you been? Do you suppose I am enjoying my forced exile on this desolate rock?" Scratchull hissed.

"I am sorry, Master, so, so sorry. I have spent every moment trying to find what you requested, never thinking to stop for food or rest. You must believe me, Master."

Scratchull loomed over Greenie, those gray spiderweb lines creeping out of his collar and spreading across his neck as if his skin was about to crack into a thousand pieces. Greenie shrank before the white alien, putting his hands out before him and scrunching his head down into his rounded shoulders.

"Oh, please, Master. Please. I have had to smuggle bits and pieces past transporter security on a dozen different planets." Scratchull took another step forward. Greenie shivered all over, his gelatinous body quivering. "And these things you ask for...they are highly illegal. I am at great risk everywhere I go, and it takes me longer to—"

Fwap! Scratchull backhanded Greenie, and it sounded like

he had slapped a bowlful of Jell-O. *Splorsh!* The effect was about the same, too, as little greenish-yellow blobs of the alien's body broke off and splattered around the room.

"Enough excuses!" roared Scratchull, the fissures in his skin growing darker, spreading above the jawline and across his face. "Tell me you have brought the new device."

"Yes, yes indeed," Greenie said. He zipped along the wooden floor, scooping up the scattered bits of himself and pressing them back into his body. "Of course, Master. You know I never leave you wanting for anything." Greenie slithered closer to the closet, and I did another full-body cringe. But instead of opening the door, he scraped a few more mushy blobs from where they were stuck to the wood and patted them back onto his head, smoothing them over like a sculptor working with clay. He slipped away again, and I let out a long, shaky breath.

"Well? Where is it?" Scratchull said.

"Right here, tucked away. Safely hidden from those who would do harm to Master." Greenie jammed both hands inside the lower half of his body, the jellyfish part, and pulled them out again with a suction-y slurping sound. He held a sleek black device about the size of a deck of playing cards. "Do you see? I have assembled the whole thing from a smuggled piece here and a borrowed bit there, always according to your instructions. And I brought it for you, just as I promised. Do you see how—*aaahhhh!*"

A thin stream of white lightning shot out of the device and sizzled as it struck the bed. Instantly the big four-poster dissolved into a...well, into a *puddle* of bed. A viscous fluid seeped across the floor, the bright colors of the bedspread swirling around on the surface, mixed in with the darker wood tones of the headboard.

"Fool!" The lines on Scratchull's face were pitch black now and extended all the way to the top of his head. He wrenched the device out of Greenie's hands and then delivered another backhanded blow.

Greenie slipped around the room, collecting bits of himself and mashing them back into his body.

"This is not a toy!"

"I know, Master, I know. Of course not. It was an accident, Great One. A slip of my clumsy fingers. Please forgive me." Greenie smoothed his head back into shape, looking up at Scratchull as the tall, white alien delicately turned the device this way and that, studying it from all angles. "But at least this way you can see that it works, yes? Master is pleased, correct?"

The spiderweb lines covering Scratchull's face slowly faded. "Perhaps. The bed, of course, was merely for the sake of appearance." Scratchull sneered and made a dismissive gesture at the bed puddle with a long-fingered white hand. "But what kind of assurance do I have that this will work any better than the last one you brought me?"

"Ah, yes, assure you I can and assure you I will, Exalted Being. I took the power cells from the research facility on Balderbahn." Greenie sidled closer to Scratchull, gazing up at his skull face. "The work they are doing with the storage of regenerative energy is the best in the—"

"I know it's the best. It's *mine*. They poached the formula from me without any regard for proper compensation when the Collective mandated the sharing of knowledge within the scientific community." The dark-purple circles under Scratchull's eyes smoldered. "Shortsighted cretins."

The thick gel of the bed puddle oozed across the floor, and Greenie slithered out of its path. He studied the melted mess for a few moments. "What do you call your invention, Master?"

Scratchull held up the little black device, admiring it. "It's a Molecular Destabilizer. It breaks down matter at the cellular level, reconfigures it into a different state. Leaves it vulnerable to further manipulation and enhancement...." When Scratchull smiled it looked like a facial expression that he had read about but never tried. "Or, if left unattended, complete entropy."

"Manipulation and enhancement?"

Scratchull sneered. "Destruction and devastation, mostly. But some enhancement, yes."

"And for this they banish Master? Coerce him into exile on a primitive planet? Force him to do menial jobs for the humans and not return home?" Greenie glanced at the bed sludge on the floor again. "Surely they are not worried that Master will launch an attack on all of the furniture in the universe?"

Scratchull's spiderweb lines flashed gray for a moment across his face, like a passing shadow. "Was that an attempt at humor? At a time like this?"

"No, Most Glorious Leader. Of course not." Greenie quivered all over again and ducked his head. "I only meant that it seems a trifling matter for the Collective scientists to be so concerned about. For them to banish their best and brightest mind is shortsighted, indeed. Just like you said, just exactly as you said."

Scratchull nodded. "The Collective scientists have no authority, legal or moral, to do what they have done to me, it is true. Forced exile on a primitive planet is far worse than a prison sentence for a being of such superior mental facility." He held up the black mechanism again where it caught the sunlight streaming through the window. "But you're wrong about one thing. This is no trifling matter."

"Why is that, Master?"

"Let us just say we are lucky that you hit the bed and not the wall with your little accident."

Greenie leaned forward, nodding. "Yes? Go on."

"The liquefaction of the molecules would have been far more impressive. Since the wall is connected to every other part of the house, the entire structure would have come melting down around us."

"Really?"

"Yes, *really*. Now close your mouth—you look like one of the wide-eyed cavemen around here." Scratchull clicked something on the machine, and the top of the black case opened smoothly. He peered into the inner workings and fiddled around in there. "Ah, yes. And we were quite lucky that this is on the lowest possible setting." Scratchull pressed on the casing and closed the machine again. "Now if I were to use the highest setting—and if the thieving Balderbahnians have used my formula for the power cells properly—then this device should be capable of altering the molecules on a much grander scale. All interconnected matter would become a malleable mush in my hands."

"Meaning?"

Scratchull's lips stretched into another hideous grin. "Meaning that I hold in my hand enough power to destroy an entire planet."

15

The strength went out of my cramped legs, and I almost tumbled over backward. *Destroy a planet?* As I watched the viscous bed sludge ooze across the floorboards, my mind flashed back to the unnatural boiling of the soupy clearing. The sense memory of being sucked under that mess came back so strong, it was hard to breathe for a few moments.

"An entire planet, Master? Are . . . are you certain?"

"Quite certain. I practiced with the old device—the prototype—in the forest near here, but I had to abandon the experiments after an earthling child meddled in my affairs."

My hands balled into fists. *I'm just getting started, pal.*

Scratchull sneered. "No matter. The whole thing was taking too long, anyway. Spreading far too slowly. Even these feebleminded humans would have stumbled upon some sort of solution by the time it took to do any real planetary damage." Scratchull held up the little black machine, admiring it. "But this piece of ingenious engineering will serve my purposes much more boldly."

"Right..." Greenie scooched away from Scratchull, fidgeting with his hands. The holes on the tips of his fingers opened and shut furiously with that wet squelching sound. "And so you feel that the Earth must actually be *destroyed*, Grand One? Quickly and boldly? This serves Master's purposes... somehow?"

"All in good time," Scratchull said. "It's 'first things first,' as the humans like to say. They're quite fond of stating the glaringly obvious, you know."

"Pardon?" Greenie fidgeted some more. "I mean, I thought you said it was working too slowly for you?" Greenie scooted backward a little more, settling into a protective cringe. When Scratchull failed to smack him, Greenie continued. "Forgive me, sir, but your plan is far too cunning for one such as me to comprehend."

"It is very simple. I want to *escape* from this planet first, and *then* annihilate it, you graxx-for-brains."

"Yes, yes, of course... but... I thought you said..."

"Pay attention!" Scratchull took one long stride toward Greenie and—*splat!*—smacked him in the head again. "My first priority remains getting off this forgotten space island."

"But you can't use the transporters, right?" Greenie rounded up bits of his body again to replace the new gaping hole in his neck. "I remember that part, Master, I surely do. And you can't use them because . . ." Greenie stopped slithering around and scrunched up his jelly face in concentration.

"Because those imbeciles from the Collective embedded my DNA into the Not Authorized to Travel transporter filter." Scratchull indicated the transporter door with a jerk of his head. "If I step inside there and hit the button, my entire being will be vaporized and flushed across the vacuum of space."

"But can't you just fix—"

"No, I *cannot* just fix it." *Smack! Splorsh!* Green jelly blobs splattered against the wall. "There is no way to conduct proper scientific experiments unless I use myself as a test case. And that, of course, would be far too risky. If something went wrong, the universe would be deprived of this magnificent mind forever."

"That would be devastating, Master."

"I know. So the transporters are definitely out." Scratchull made a steeple with his fingers and placed his chin on top. He looked down at Greenie, who cringed in reflex. "That is where you come in."

"Y-y-yes, Esteemed Leader? What must—*may*—I do for you now?"

"Return to your home planet immediately to await further communication."

Greenie nodded so vigorously that his whole body shook. "Of course, Master. I can do that. I'm good at going home. Very good."

Scratchull sighed and rolled his eyes. "How reassuring." The tall alien brandished the sleek black device. "Now, listen. When the time is right—and that will be very soon, I warrant you—I will unleash the devastating powers of my invention on this pathetic little planet."

My whole body went cold. It took all of my willpower to stop myself from kicking open the closet door, grabbing that gadget, and cramming it right up his gleaming white—

"And what will happen then, Master?" Greenie's voice was hushed. It sounded like he wasn't sure he wanted to hear the answer. I could relate.

"Chaos." Scratchull licked his dark lips as if savoring the word. "Complete chaos on a planet-encompassing scale. Widespread instability in the structure of the Earth's crust will cause massive sinkholes to open up and swallow entire cities. The water cycle will be knocked off kilter, causing overwhelming storms and floods in some areas, complete drought in others. Crops will no longer grow. Any form of Earth travel will become too dangerous to attempt; the ability to transport goods and resources will be eradicated, along with the lines of communication." Scratchull stared dreamily off into the distance as he described the scenes of destruction. "Earth will be entirely at my mercy."

"And while all of this is happening... I will be on my home planet, yes? My safe and quiet home planet?"

Scratchull rolled his eyes again. "Yes, yes. But stay close to your satellite interface. When I get in touch, you will immediately go to the Collective headquarters on your planet and sound an alarm. Tell them you just transported from a primitive planet where natural disasters were ripping the place apart. Convince them to urgently notify the team in charge of Earth research."

"Right. Of course. A most masterful plan, Master." There was a long silence as Greenie fidgeted and studied the floor. "And...why will I be doing that...exactly?"

"So that the Collective scientists visit Earth again. Immediately."

"...R-iii-ght." More fidgeting. More staring at the floor. "But I thought...that is to say, I thought that you...*hated* the Collective scientists? The ones who have done this to you? So why would you want them to visit—"

Scratchull brought his hand back in a sweeping motion, but before he could deliver the blow, Greenie shivered all over so badly that little bits and blobs shook off from his body all by themselves. Scratchull grinned and let his hand drop.

The white alien spoke slowly. "To review: I cannot use the transporters to get off this planet. Are you with me so far, or shall I draw up some sort of diagram to aid your comprehension?"

"I remember that part, Master."

"Good. It means the only way off this planet is by ship. But no ships ever come to Earth, do they?"

"No, sir."

"And why not?"

Greenie opened his mouth, but nothing came out. He scratched at his head in thought so vigorously that he dug a furrow in his jelly skin. "Because...hmmmm..."

Scratchull sighed. "Because it would be a colossal misuse of time, space fuel, and common sense."

"Right. I was just about to say that, Master."

"Of course you were. Now, when the Collective scientists come here for their talky little tea parties, they use the transporters. But if something major is going wrong with their pet planet, they'll bring a ship. Several ships, as a point of fact. They'll need to bring loads of equipment to study what has gone wrong, and the softies running that committee will want to bring emergency aid supplies for the poor little earthlings." Scratchull spread his hands before him, palms out, setting the entire scene. "And with a fleet of spaceships coming here in the middle of all the mayhem, and the Collective scientists distracted with trying to help the earthlings, it will be the perfect opportunity for me to..."

Scratchull nodded expectantly and made a *carry on* gesture at Greenie, waiting for the little alien to finish his thought for him. Greenie looked back up at him just as expectantly. When he finally figured out that Scratchull wanted him to say something, he stalled for time. "R-iii-ght...so many ships...all that mayhem...the perfect opportunity...and, er, whatnot..."

Fwap! "THEN I WILL TAKE ONE OF THE SHIPS AND FINALLY GET OUT OF HERE!"

"Yes! Yes, I see now. You will hijack a ship and escape. Brilliant!"

"I know it's brilliant. But *hijack* is such a crass way to put it. I will merely be requisitioning the necessary materials. I figure at least that much is owed to me in punitive damages for what those idiots have done in making me suffer needlessly here."

The oozing sludge of the bed puddle lapped up against Greenie's jellyfish body, and he slithered away again. Studying the mess, he said, "But, Master, will you be safe here? On a planet that is crumbling away? Will you be safe until the Collective scientists arrive with their ships?"

Scratchull flipped open the black top of the device, twisted something in there, and then pointed it at the bed puddle. A red stream of lightning shot out and buried itself in the muck. Instantly the puddle expanded and then stiffened. The wood regained its solidity, and the bedspread its fluffiness ... but it was still all jumbled up in a swirl of colors and materials. A mound that looked nothing like the original bed, it was more of a lumpy, mixed-up bed boulder now.

Scratchull sniffed. "It's not exactly the original structure, of course. But I can create a little oasis of land that is stable enough to allow me to ride out the storm of destruction. And I have already seen to it that there will be plenty of food provisions, as well."

"Brilliant," Greenie said. He patted the multicolored mound. "And so ... when you leave in the ship ... then you can use the device to halt the cycle of planetary destruction? Make things solid enough again for the humans to rebuild?"

Scratchull cupped his chin in his hand and cocked his head to the side thoughtfully. "And why would you assume I desired to do something like that?"

"Well ... I mean ... that is to say ..."

"Yes?"

"Is it really necessary to destroy the planet, Master? *After* you have already escaped?"

"Do not look at me in that insolent way. Having the humans die so that I may continue my valuable work is a small price to pay. If you spent any time here at all it would be plain enough for even you to see: a single one of me is worth billions of these earthlings. Indeed, an entire planet of them."

I realized my fingernails were digging trenches into my palms. I wanted so badly to burst into the room and throw myself at the white alien in a full-body tackle. But I knew that wouldn't do anything other than alert Scratchull to the fact that I knew what he was up to. I was going to have to put a serious plan together to stop him.

"Besides, it will serve my purpose. After the destruction of an entire planet, everyone in the universe will know of my dominance," Scratchull continued. "Whoever controls that kind of power will control the Collective. Which will be of great benefit to the universe, when you think about it. As it is, those fools are buried in their own bureaucracy. They can't make a decision to go to the bathroom without passing it through three subcommittees first." He gazed at the device, running his hands lovingly along its sides. "But with one undisputed leader, the Collective will be a much more efficient organization."

"I suppose you'll have to change the name, though. Right, Master?"

"What?"

Greenie cowered. "Well...it won't exactly be a *collective* anymore, will it, Most Illustrious Being?"

Scratchull's lips spread wide and a series of scratchy sounds hissed out. I think they might have been what his real laughter sounds like. It made me cold all over.

"Very amusing. Well done."

Greenie straightened himself back up to his full four-foot height. "Thank you, Master."

"And you have done well in bringing me this device. It is a comfort as well as a strategic coup to be reunited with my life's work." Scratchull tucked the little machine into his coveralls pocket and patted it. "You should have a reward. Please join me in a delicious meal before you leave."

"I would be honored, Master. Most honored."

"These fool humans let the greatest delicacy on their planet go to waste, completely unharvested." Scratchull walked over to the aquarium and plucked out a yellow-and-black slug that writhed between his fingers. He held it up to his nose, inhaled deeply, and smacked his lips.

"It looks a bit like those chewy grennbuleen creatures from the Haverny system," Greenie said.

"Indeed. But these taste twice as good." Scratchull bit through the meaty middle of the slug's body. Half of the slug disappeared into his mouth, while the other half continued to squirm and contort itself around his fingers. The slime on its body glistened in the summer sunshine filtering in through the window.

Scratchull chewed slowly, swallowed, and closed his eyes in appreciation. "Oh, and the texture is sublime. Your teeth need to work through a somewhat rubbery exterior, but the juicy filling makes it well worth it." Scratchull popped the other half of the slug into his mouth and chomped it down.

After swallowing, he licked a trail of slug slime from the corner of his lips. "Exquisite."

Scratchull dipped his hand back into the aquarium and offered a dozen or so writhing slugs to Greenie, then got a handful for himself. They tossed the small ones in their mouth like popcorn, one after the other. My stomach tried to force breakfast back up my throat, but I gritted my teeth and held it down. I tried closing my eyes, but it didn't help—I could still hear their loud smacking sounds.

"These are delicious!" Greenie said.

"They have been an absolute lifesaver for me. They help to drown out the horrible taste of that human woman's grotesque cooking." A slug wriggled out of Scratchull's mouth and slimed its way across his chin before the white alien slurped it back up like spaghetti; I had to bite my lips and clamp my hand over my mouth to keep from spewing everywhere. "When I finally leave this planet, these delicious creatures will be the only things worth taking with me."

Oh, no. Just then I heard Snarffle's whistle-growl and the thumping of all his feet coming from behind the hallway door. How had he gotten out there?

If Scratchull found me in here now, I had no doubt that my corpse would end up buried on some desolate desert planet three galaxies over. I held my breath and prayed that Snarffle would go away and wait for me somewhere else. Anywhere else.

The sound of hurried footsteps tromping down the hallway cut over Snarffle's noise.

"You must leave at once," Scratchull said, herding Greenie

153

toward the transporter with his long arms. The wobbly alien slid quickly along the floor. Scratchull grabbed a smooshy green arm just before his accomplice entered the transporter and spun him around. "Remember. Never leave your satellite interface. Be ready to respond as soon as I call you."

"Of course, Master."

The sounds in the hallway grew louder. "Snarffle, what has gotten into you?" (Grandma's muffled voice.)

Greenie glanced at the lumpy bed boulder, then up at Scratchull. "Master, how will you hide this—"

His voice cut out as Scratchull shoved him inside the transporter. "I'll take care of it," he whispered, and slammed the door shut.

Grandma's voice got louder. "What in the universe are you so agitated about?" She was clearly struggling with the purple alien out in the hall. "Scratchull?" she called. "I'm sorry to bother you, but are you in there?"

"Just a moment, my dear woman," he said.

He fished the little black device out of his pocket, flipped it open, and messed around with the controls. Then he pointed it at the mound of bed. A stream of white lightning shot out, and the bed dissolved back into a gluey mess.

Scratchull knelt, pried up the corner of a loose board, and tucked the device underneath the floor. After fixing the board back in place, he stood, crossed to the door, and cracked it open. "Yes?"

"I'm sorry to bother you," Grandma said. "But this creature has been making such a racket." Grandma was holding Snarffle's harness as the purple alien struggled to get into the room. "I can't find David anywhere. I think he tied this little guy up somewhere, but Snarffle chewed right through his leash, and I've been chasing him all over the house. He's been frantic about leading me right to your door."

"I must say that I'm not too happy with that creature at the moment, either."

"Oh? Why is that?"

"A little while ago I left my door open while I went to use the restroom facilities. I was only gone for a minute or two when David's pet ran in and did *that*." Scratchull swung the door open wide and gestured toward the puddle of bed.

"Oh my stars and comets!" Grandma laid her hand across her chest, and her mouth dropped open. Snarffle stared at Scratchull and whistle-growled. "Whatever happened in here?"

"This . . . *beast*," Scratchull said, gesturing toward Snarffle, "dashed in, ate my bed in its entirety, and then regurgitated it all over the floor when he found that it did not agree with his digestive system."

"Are you sure?" Grandma said.

"Quite sure. I returned in time to see him finish the unpleasant deed. I was just about to come and find you when you knocked on the door."

Snarffle growled even louder now, the sound coming from deep within his throat.

Grandma said, "I just . . . I don't know what to say. I'm truly sorry. This is so unexpected."

"Not precisely. At least not when you take recent events into account."

"What do you mean?"

"Well, the creature has been eating furniture in David's room. Were you not aware of this?"

How did he know about that?

Grandma's brow got wrinkly and the corners of her mouth turned down. "No. I wasn't."

I was going to tell her. Really. I just didn't want her to be mad at me or Snarffle—it took me a couple of days to learn his food needs, that's all. It wasn't going to happen again or anything. And it's not like I was really using the stupid coat stand or rocking chair anyway.

"I don't blame this creature," Scratchull said. "He's just an ignorant animal. But David seems like a bright young man. It would appear that he should know better, yes? That he should be taking his duties around here a little more seriously?"

Grandma nodded absently, staring off into the middle distance. "I see your point, Scratchull. I'm sorry this happened in your room."

"Now, I assure you that I am not upset. Adolescents on all planets go through phases like this. But maybe having David clean up this mess would be the first step in teaching him a valuable lesson. It would be such a shame if you were forced to send him back to his home prematurely." Snarffle glared at the white alien, and his growling became even more intense. "And it might be prudent to keep this little creature penned in, perhaps tied up, until he learns to be a little less rambunctious. Clearly David cannot be trusted if he is just going to run off and let the creature fend for itself."

"I will take care of this, Scratchull," Grandma said. "You

have my word. David is a wonderful boy, but I may need to talk to him. At the very least, I will have him clean up your room."

"Excellent. Together, I think we can mold him into a responsible young man." Scratchull held the door open and indicated the hallway with a sweep of his hand. "I will accompany you. I would also be interested in David's whereabouts while his pet got into all of this mischief."

That little cave opened up underneath Snarffle's eyes, and his sniffing tendrils snaked out and tested the air. Then he looked right at the closet. His little tail started twirling like crazy and he strained even harder at the harness.

Not good. I had to act.

Scratchull was looking at Grandma, in the hall. I nudged open the closet door for half a second, gave Snarffle a quick headshake and put my finger over my lips.

He instantly settled down, turned, and followed Grandma into the hall. Scratchull walked out and closed the door behind them.

Phew. The relief was so strong, my bones felt as mushy as Mr. Greenie's quivering body.

I counted to ten after the sound of footsteps faded. Then I stood up, my stiff legs cramping in protest, and moved from the closet into the bedroom.

I jammed the listening end of the baby monitor into my pocket, then carefully hid the monitor itself behind some paperback novels on a shelf. It wasn't likely that Scratchull had much interest in what some human fiction writer had to say.

Then I knelt down and pried up the loose floorboard. When I picked up the black device, I did so very carefully, making sure not to press any buttons accidentally. Then I slipped it into the pocket of my shorts.

I felt a little bit better now that I had it on me. Earthlings might be as stupid as Scratchull said, but he was going to learn that we knew how to fight back.

16

I found Amy in the backyard, setting up a croquet course.
Probably another one of her Senior Night activities.

I slipped into the woods for cover and skirted the lawn,
slowly making my way toward her. I hid behind a tree and
whistled to get her attention.

"David?" Amy stood and wiped the grass from her knees.
She started walking toward me. "Your grandma was looking
for you a few—"

I held up my hand as a stop sign and put a finger to my
lips. Amy tilted her head, studying me, then looked up at
the house.

"Can you meet me up on the logging road?" I whispered. "Five minutes?"

"I don't know." She glanced back at her equipment on the lawn, and then down at her shoes. "I kind of have some things to do right now."

"Please? It's really important."

She lifted her head and crinkled her eyebrows. "Important how?"

I took a deep breath and tried to make a Very Serious face. "Amy, the future of the planet is at stake." Man, how do you say something like that and not sound like a delusional idiot? Even if it *is* the truth.

But her eyes lit up. "Is it about the Collective? And their decision?"

"Sort of. But look, it's even bigger than that. Just come and talk, okay?"

Amy chewed on her lip, and then nodded. She started walking toward me again.

I shook my head fiercely until she stopped. "I'll go through the woods. You go around the front of the house and head into the forest where the main road cuts out. I'll meet you up there. If you run into anyone, you never saw me."

A few minutes later Amy walked up the logging road, and I stepped out from where I was kneeling behind a huge fern patch.

"David! You startled me."

"Sorry."

"Why are you being so weird? What is so top secret?"

I glanced back in the direction of the house, even though it was hidden by trees. "I really need to talk to you."

"Right. That's why I'm here. Let's talk."

"In private."

Amy laughed, looking all around. "More private than this?"

I checked over my shoulder again. "I just want to get farther away first."

She crossed her arms over her chest. "Come on, just tell me what this is all about."

I scanned the trees. "It's about Scratchull," I whispered.

"Really?" She sighed. "You're worried about him again?"

"Shhh!" I waved her off. That creepy guy could be anywhere. "Look, just trust me, okay? I need a really private place to tell you this. No one else can find out."

Amy shrugged. "Fine. I'll play along." She slipped her arm through mine and pulled me off the logging road, deeper into the forest. "Besides, it's a nice day for a hike, whether the planet is ending tomorrow or not." She was kidding, but I felt a chill go down my spine. "I know the perfect spot."

We waded through fern patches and climbed over rotting logs. I was intensely aware of Scratchull's device in my pocket. Amy led the way while my brain whirred on autopilot, my concerns multiplying with each step we took.

Was it possible that the device had some kind of tracking system that would tell Scratchull where it was at any given moment? Or could he have a way to operate it from a distance by remote control? Worse still, was it possible that the thing would self-destruct and melt me into a David puddle if I didn't handle it properly?

"You okay?" Amy asked. She stopped and reached out to touch my shoulder.

I nodded. She studied my face for a moment before continuing her march through the forest.

But I was far from okay. Any of my concerns could be possible. And I'm sure there were some things I didn't even know I had to worry about. Lots of things.

Hiking along, watching Amy's back, I tried to think of how I was going to tell her . . . and fully realized how disappointed she was going to be. She was counting on Scratchull to deliver Earth to some glorious new future.

Wait—would she even believe me? The sudden realization that I might not be able to convince her knotted my stomach up even more.

I traced the outline of the machine in my pocket. Scratchull had told his wobbly green lackey that it was on the lowest setting. Maybe I could give her a little demonstration? I would have to pick something that wasn't connected to anything else—a river stone, maybe—and prop it up on a dead log. If I could melt something like that, maybe then Amy would believe me.

I was still mulling over the idea when I heard the roar of the Nooksack River up ahead. Amy faced me. "We're close now." She grabbed my hand and hauled me toward the sound of the white water.

After fighting our way through some thick tangles of undergrowth, we finally emerged near the riverbank. "There it is," she called, pointing.

We were standing at the edge of a little creek that split off from the Nooksack, separated from the main river by a long sandbar covered in tall grass. I followed the line of

Amy's pointing finger and saw it: a big dam, piled high with logs and rocks and mud. The jumbled wall stretched across the entire creek, causing a pool of water to form behind it.

"Isn't it awesome?" Amy said. "Some guys from the high school build one every summer. Makes for the perfect swimming hole."

We both just sort of stood and stared at it for a few moments. The spot was so beautiful, and it was so nice to be here alone with Amy, that I was able to forget for just a minute about why we had come out here in the first place.

Amy pulled me toward the pool.

"Is it safe?" I asked.

"Sure. I've been swimming here since I was a kid." Amy gave me a look. "Just don't, you know, tell my dad or anything."

"Oh, so he doesn't think it's safe?"

Amy rolled her eyes. "My dad has spent his life in law enforcement. Something is safe for his daughter only after the county council has approved it, three independent agencies have tested it, and the insurance premiums are all paid up. Relax, okay?"

We picked our way over scattered bits of driftwood and a field of river stones to the edge of the swimming hole. The surface was surprisingly calm, especially compared to the turbulent white water of the main river roaring on the other side of the sandbar.

Amy dipped her toe, stirring up a series of circles that expanded across the still water. "I *have* to jump in. It's kind of a ritual when I come out here."

"Amy...look, before we go swimming or anything, we should really talk about—"

"I know. But we've got all afternoon to talk. And it feels like it's going to be one of the hottest days of the summer."

She had a point. But, still...

"Come on, David. I love your grandma's place, obviously. But we both work too hard. You know that, right?"

"I guess, but I really need to—"

And then she yanked her tank top over her head. She was wearing a pink bathing suit underneath. She pulled her denim shorts off and dropped them on a shelf of rock beside the water. More pink bathing suit underneath...but not a lot more.

Okay, so I'm not saying I forgot all about the destruction of the planet and the end of human existence as we know it or anything...I just suddenly realized that maybe it could wait for the tiniest bit. An hour, tops. I mean it's not like Scratchull was going to charge down here, rip the device out of my hands, and destroy the Earth right this second. Not so early in the day, anyway.

Amy kicked off her shoes with a little too much force, and one of them sailed over her head and landed on top of the dam. "Whoops." She looked up at the stranded shoe. "I'll grab that later." She turned and studied the pool for a moment. "It's kind of cold at first, so you just have to plunge right in. Get it over with." Amy reached up and untangled a piece of rope tied to an overhead branch. "This helps."

Then she climbed up onto a low-hanging branch, got a two-handed grip on the rope, and jumped off. She swung out over the pool, yelling out an excited *"Whoooo!"* She waited until the apex of her flight, just before the rope was about to swing her back to the tree, and let go. Her pink-bathing-suited body splashed down into the water.

Circles rippled across the pool, their rims glinting with reflected sunshine. Amy stayed under for a minute and then popped up right in front me. She pulled herself out and twisted her body around in one smooth motion, so that she was sitting on the rock with her legs in the pool.

"How's the water?"

"Refreshing."

"Does 'refreshing' mean totally cold?"

"It's glacial runoff, David. So, yeah. But it gets better, trust me."

She reached back and grabbed her hair with both hands, squeezing the water out in that way that girls do until it was beaded up all over her bare skin. Even though the wilderness around us was vast, it felt as if I suddenly had no idea where to direct my gaze. Everywhere I looked, there she was. How was that possible?

She grabbed my calf with a wet hand and pulled me toward the pool, almost knocking me off balance. "Come on, Mr. Florida. You'll get used to it."

"Whoa! Okay, okay, let go. I'll get in." I stepped away from the pool and stripped off my shirt and shoes. As Amy dove back underwater, I slipped Scratchull's black device out of my shorts pocket, wrapped it up in my shirt, and carefully tucked it into one of my shoes.

When I let go of the rope swing and my whole body was submerged in the pool, my heart stopped. It didn't just feel freezing, it *hurt*. I scrambled to the edge of the pool, half dog-paddling and half trying to run across the surface of the water like a frantic cartoon character. I tucked my hands into my armpits, my whole body huddling into itself for life-conserving warmth. "R-r-refreshing, h-huh?"

Amy burst out laughing, then clapped her hands over her mouth. "I'm sorry, David. That was very good for a first try. Especially for someone who's used to swimming in the Gulf of Mexico." She was treading water in the middle of the pool. "It feels warmer the second time you jump in. I promise. Your body gets used to it."

Some parts of my body would *never* get used to it, but I didn't say that. To be honest, I really didn't feel like jumping in there again. Ever. But she was out there, clearly enjoying herself, so I couldn't wuss out.

I jumped back in. And while it was still chilly, she was right—it wasn't nearly as bad as that first time. As we swam around together it got better and better. Of course, that was probably just the early effects of full-body hypothermia, but still. At least I was finally getting the chance to hang out with Amy.

We had a who-could-do-the-coolest-jump-off-the-rope-swing? contest, which I won by swinging over the pool upside down and then diving in headfirst. We had a who-could-stay-underwater-the-longest? contest, which Amy won by a mile. We stacked river stones into a funky little sculpture thing on the rock ledge lining the pool.

But the best part was stretching across that sun-warmed shelf of rock after we were done swimming, just lying there and letting the rare Pacific Northwest sunshine dry us. It was way better than hanging out at the community pool back home, because we were the only two out here. Surrounded by nothing but blue sky and mile after mile of uninterrupted wilderness, it was easy to believe that we were the only two people who had *ever* been out here. And when you're with someone like Amy, that's a pretty cool feeling.

"A day like today is just so perfect," Amy said, one finger tracing a circle in the still water of the swimming hole.

"Mmmm-hmmmm." I didn't want it to end.

"I've been thinking. I bet if he took a little time off from work and just spent an afternoon like this one with us, our problem would be solved. He'd see what a beautiful, peaceful planet this is and put in a good word for us, for sure."

"Huh?" Her words didn't register at first. I certainly wasn't in the mood to be thinking about anyone else. "Who are you talking about?"

"Scratchull, of course. Part of my plan to convince him to rave about Earth to the Collective." She sat up and swatted at my arm. "And you're supposed to be helping me, remember?"

Scratchull. I sat up and tried to gauge how long we'd been out here. Good lord, how could I have wasted so much time?

"I really need to talk to you about that secret now." After hopping down off the rock ledge, I carefully unraveled Scratchull's black device from my bundle of clothes, then pulled the shirt over my head and shoulders.

"All right, I'm listening." Amy stretched. "But it was nice to just hang out and get a little break from our top secret summer jobs."

She would probably think I was just being paranoid about Scratchull again. I was going to have to convince her.

"I have to show you something, too."

"Okay, you win." Amy sighed. "Just let me put my clothes on first." She pulled her shirt on. After she got one shoe on, she started tiptoeing around the edge of the pool toward the dam. "Just need to grab my other shoe."

"That looks kind of dangerous," I said. "Want me to try it?"

Amy glanced at me over her shoulder. "That's sweet, David. Really. But I'm the one who's been coming out here for years, remember? I know all the tricks."

She approached the dam slowly, jouncing a log with her foot to test how firmly it was fixed into the overall structure. When it didn't give, she stepped up on it with both feet. She made her way along the dam, moving cautiously across the uneven surface of logs and rocks with her arms held straight out at her sides like a tightrope walker. She treated each step carefully, making sure the new foothold was stable before putting all of her weight on it. I probably should have been more worried about her, but instead I was too busy watching the muscles on her legs grow taut as she shifted her center of balance with each step. I could have watched that all day.

The spell was broken when Amy reached her shoe and tried to grab it. As she bent down to pick it up, she lost her balance and fell to one knee, dislodging a rock that had been embedded in the mud. The football-sized stone tumbled over the side of the dam and fell in the dry creek bed with a heavy thud.

"You okay?" I yelled. I ran around the pool and down into the creek bed, stopping at the base of the dam, where I could look straight up at Amy. I wanted to be in place to try to catch her in case she fell off the top.

"Yeah, I'm fine." She stood up and wiped mud from her leg. "Just scraped up my knee, is all. It's a little bloody, but not too bad." She balanced on one leg while she pulled the shoe on to her other foot. "I should probably wash it off in the river when we—*aaaah!*"

Amy lost her one-legged balance, and the shoe she had just put on came down heavily on top of the dam. The log underneath her rolled and she fell backward. She thumped down heavily in a sitting position with a startled *guh!* sound.

Three more stones dislodged from the top of the dam and tumbled down the side—I quickly sidestepped out of the way before they hit the ground. Then a huge clump of logs shifted crazily, and a rush of water streamed out of the side of the dam, hard, like someone had turned on a fire hose. The next second, more hoses spurted from three different spots.

Then the *entire structure* started moving.

It was all going to come crashing down.

There was a chance that I could have dived out of the way, saved myself. But Amy froze me to the spot with her eyes. They were looking right at me, stretched wide, filled with pure, animal terror.

Even worse, they were silently pleading with me, begging me to do something.

But what could I do? My mind's eye showed me, in terrible detail, what would happen in the next few seconds. The tremendous pent-up force of the water would be unleashed. The dam would collapse. And the power behind thousands of gallons of rushing water would grind those massive logs and rocks together like they were in a blender.

And Amy would be caught in the middle of it all.

So would I, if I stayed here. But how could I possibly leave her?

I was still frozen to the spot, still staring up at Amy and her haunted eyes, when the dam burst. The whole thing suddenly moved forward as if pushed by a giant hand. Just a second or two until impact.

I acted on pure reflex. I whipped Scratchull's black device out from behind my back, tapped open the top of the case, and jammed it into the tumbling wreck of a dam.

My thumb found a button, and I pushed it.

leaving the unthinkable unsaid. She leaned forward slowly, gripping a log with both hands, and looked down to where I stood with one hand still jammed into the middle of the dam. "David . . . did you *do* something?"

"Maybe. I don't know. I mean, I tried to do something, but . . . I don't know."

She stood up carefully. "I'm going to swim back to the other side. I don't want to try to climb down this dam."

"Good idea. Looks like it could fall at anytime."

"It looks half-fallen already. But that doesn't make any sense." She scanned the face of the dam and shook her head. "You should get away from there, too. Right now."

"Another good idea." But when I turned to step away, my hand remained stuck in the dam. I pulled, but it wouldn't budge. And as the panic partially wore off, I realized that my hand was very, very cold.

"What in the . . . ?" Amy said from atop the dam. She was turned away from me, facing the water. "The pool," she said. "It's . . . it's *frozen*."

"What?" I called. I couldn't see the water at all from the base of the dam.

"It's frozen," Amy said. "And not just a little crust on the top, either. It looks like it's frozen solid all the way through to—oh, no!"

"*What?*"

"It's not just the pool—it's the entire creek!"

I tried to pull away again, but my hand didn't move at all. And it was going numb now. Freezing.

Using my free hand, I gripped a smallish rock from the side of the dam and pulled. It stuck firm for a minute but

17

Nothing happened.

The logs didn't melt into wood puddles. The rocks stayed as hard as...rocks.

I cringed. That meant that in less than a second—

Wait. *Nothing* happened. Amy still sat safely on top of the dam, a very confused look on her face. Even though the dam was tilting at an impossible angle, it stayed in place, completely motionless.

"What happened?" Amy said. It came out in a whisper that was swallowed by the vastness of the forest. "I thought the dam was going...that I was about to..." She trailed off, finally popped free. The place where it had just been was solid ice, now with a concave rock-sized indentation in it.

Suddenly Amy was standing by my side. "David, do you know why this is happening?"

"Maybe. Just help me get free first, okay?"

Together we dislodged the dam debris surrounding my forearm. My hand was encased in a wall of ice up to my wrist.

Amy and I used sharp rocks to chip away at the ice, until finally I could pull my hand free. My fingers were so red with cold they were almost purple. But they were still clutching at Scratchull's little black device.

"What's that thing?" said Amy.

I switched it to my other hand and stuck my frozen one into my pocket, trying to warm it up. "This is what I need to talk to you about," I said. How to start? "About Scratchull. Look, I know you're going to be disappointed, but he's not what he seems to be. At all. In fact, he's—"

"I know that," Amy said. "He's just pretending to be some transporter repairman, but he's actually here to report on Earth for the Collective and tell them—"

"No. *Listen*. The Collective sent him here for a punishment. Earth is, like, his prison."

"What?" Amy's face scrunched up in confusion. "Why would they do that?"

"Because he invented this." I held up the device. "It has enough power to destroy the entire planet."

"*What?*" She took a couple of steps backward, away from the device. Away from me. "Wait—how do you know all of this?"

"I was hiding in his closet, and this little green dude

popped out of the transporter, and he was all 'Master, this' and 'Master, that' and 'I brought you the device you requested,' and then he—"

I stopped. Amy was giving me a strange look. "What were you doing in Scratchull's closet?"

I took a deep breath. This was going to be a long story, and I could tell it was one that part of her didn't want to believe.

I looked past her, at the dam, where the wall of logs and rocks tilted crazily but stayed suspended in midair, held motionless by the grip of the ice. All of a sudden I felt intensely uneasy. We were so exposed out here. Even though it was a secluded area, it seemed like any minute someone could come hiking through the woods and see that frozen creek.

What would we say then? What if someone called the forest ranger, or the police? And then we got linked to this craziness? Oh, man, what if it was a repeat of last summer, with the town storming the B&B and me the cause of it all?

"Look, Amy, I can explain everything later, when we have more time. I promise. But right now we have to figure out what we're going to do about this." I gestured at the dam. "We need to make a plan."

"But I don't understand anything that's going on."

"I know, I know," I said, as we jogged around the side of the dam. "I don't either, really." It felt like the whole world was closing in on us, and I was running out of time to stop it.

Back up at the pool, we looked down the length of the creek. The entire surface was a sheet of ice.

"I saw Scratchull use this machine to melt the bed in his room. It turned into mush. I was trying to do the same thing with the dam," I said.

Amy looked bewildered and horrified at the same time.

"There was no time," I went on. "I didn't want all those logs to, you know...crush you..." I left the words *to death* unspoken.

Amy shuddered. "But you didn't know what it could do..." Her eyes kept going from my face to the black device in my hand and back again. "You risked the potential destruction of the Earth..."

"Well, I didn't think it..." She was making me realize how stupid I had been in that split-second of panic. "It was on the lowest setting," I said lamely.

Amy stared at me. "Are you telling me you actually gambled on the welfare of the entire planet just to save me?"

It sounded so reckless when she said it like that. But I guess there was no other way to put it. "Yeah," I said. "I'm really sorry if—"

"David, that's the sweetest thing ever!" Amy threw her arms around me and hugged me fiercely. I almost dropped the device, but managed to hold on, and even had the presence of mind to put my arms around her, too.

Then Amy broke off the hug and immediately reverted to her scientific self, pointing to the watering hole, now a frozen pond. "The device must've touched the water instead of the dam," she said. "And instead of converting a solid to a liquid—"

"—it was the other way around," I finished the sentence for her. "But look." I bent down and ran my hand over the icy surface. I held my fingers up to show her that they were wet. "It's melting already. Maybe—*hopefully*—it will just go back to normal. To the way it was before."

"Yeah, but it's going to take a long time for all of this to melt. Even if it stays sunny." She frowned as her eyes scanned the length of the creek. "A couple of days, at least. Maybe a week?"

I nodded. "At least. I hope no one comes out here before then. What would someone do if they saw this in the middle of summer?"

Neither one of us had an answer to that question. We just stood there in silence, studying the long stretch of solid ice.

And then I noticed something about the silence. It was complete, and not just because we weren't talking. It felt eerie, but I couldn't put my finger on it. I cocked my head and listened to . . . nothing.

I suddenly realized what was missing. There was no roar of the—

"Oh, no. No, no, no."

"What now?" Amy said.

"Follow me."

I grabbed her hand and we walked straight across the pool, something that felt very strange since we had been swimming in there just a few minutes ago. I walked slowly —the surface was slick with that thin layer of melted ice on top—but when we hit the sandbar on the other side, we ran, half stumbling through the thick clumps of wild grass, then stopping short when we reached the riverbank.

The Nooksack River was frozen. The whole thing. It must have happened as quickly as it had with the creek, because it looked like a photograph of a raging river: completely still, with the white water surf frozen exactly in place.

I looked upriver, and the Nooksack was sheer ice as far

as the eye could see until it went around the bend toward Mount Baker.

Then I looked downriver. Worse—*much* worse—was the fact that the river was frozen as it made its way toward Forest Grove.

"Oh, David." Amy's face had gone nearly as pale as Scratchull's. "What have you done?"

18

It's hard to have a conversation while you're sprinting through the forest, exposed tree roots tripping you up, and thorny brambles ripping at your skin, but Amy and I were trying.

"What are we"—*huff, huff*—"going to do?"

"How can we possibly"—*pant, wheeze*—"explain something like this?"

Snap! Crunch! "What are we going to tell your grandma?"

Crash! "Ouch! Or your dad?"

I guess it wasn't really a conversation. Just a series of questions without any good answers.

When we finally burst through the forest at the edge of Riverside Park, I felt like all of the wind had been knocked out of me. Then I saw what was going on at the park, and I almost threw up.

A huge mass of people was gathered along the edge of the river.

The crowd stretched throughout the whole park. Every person in Forest Grove must have been out there.

Parents herded small children away from the ice while teenagers heaved rocks that bounced and skidded across the surface of the river. People pointed and shook their heads. Cameras clicked all over the place. Some folks lingered by the playground equipment, fifty yards away from the edge of the river, expressions of undisguised fear on their faces.

Amy and I were doubled over, hands on our knees, as we watched the crowd and tried to catch our breath.

"This is not good. Not good at all." Amy wiped a clump of sweaty hair out of her eyes. "This is terrible. This is the worst thing that—"

"I get it."

"Oh, David. What are we going to *do*?"

"We have to get to the B-and-B. Right away." I knew what we had to do, even though it was the very last thing in the world I wanted to do. "We need to talk to Grandma."

Neither of us moved.

"I'm really worried," Amy whispered. "And scared."

"Me too." I wasn't ashamed to admit it, either. The alien brothers who got loose in the forest last summer were seen only by a few people, almost all of them kids. And the picture that had made the front page of the newspaper was grainy and barely in focus, easily explained away.

But this—everyone in town was seeing this. A crystal-clear, high-definition, 3-D image.

"Come on," I said. We could have walked through the park to get back to Grandma's. It would have been easier, and it's not like anyone would connect us with what had happened to the river. At least not yet. But a deep sense of shame caused me to turn and sneak back through the forest, hiding behind the screen of trees from all of those people.

There was nobody out front at the B&B. We made our way around the side of the house to the backyard and then stopped short. A group of aliens—maybe two dozen or so—was huddled together at the base of the porch steps. They were all different shapes and sizes, but they shared the same facial expression: confusion mixed with fear. They looked a lot like the group of humans we had just seen at the park.

Grandma worked her way through the crowd, offering a comforting hug here and a reassuring pat on the back there. "No need to worry. We'll get this all figured out in no time." She spoke slowly, in soothing tones. "No reason to be distressed."

A tall alien took off the thrift store fedora he had gotten from Grandma's trunk of disguise clothing, and scratched at a ridge of bumps covered in green scales. "Then why do the natives seem so upset? They've formed a mob very close to here, you know. Those of us enjoying the park were quite anxious when they all converged."

"Well, that's not a *mob*, exactly," Grandma said. "More of a...peaceable assembly. Average folks banding together in a time of uncertainty. Temporary uncertainty. Nothing to be worried about." She managed to plaster a big smile on her face. No one returned it.

An elderly alien clutched her traveling partner. "I don't like mobs when I'm traveling off-world," she muttered. "I don't like them at all."

"The humans are just a little nervous right now," Grandma said. "Here on Earth we don't see water freeze like that so suddenly. Especially in such a large quantity. Humans don't know how to—"

"We never see anything like that, either! Especially when it's so warm out," another alien chimed in. "I realize this is a primitive planet, but shouldn't the basic laws of physics still apply?"

This set off a rumbling of muttered side conversations. Grandma kept trying to calm everyone down, but the aliens formed a rough semicircle around her, firing so many questions that she couldn't possibly keep up.

"All right, simmer down now. That means everyone!" Tate's shout cut through the crowd noise. The screen door banged behind him as he strode out onto the porch. Grandma looked up at him, and her face softened, clearly relieved.

Tate held up his meaty arms for silence and then addressed the crowd. "I appreciate everyone hustling to return and grouping up back here. Good work." He paced back and forth on the porch, a general addressing the troops. "Now this here situation calls for a Code...um, a Code...well, I don't think we have a code color set up for this exact set of circumstances. But that doesn't mean we need to—"

"Can you explain what's going on?" the alien with the bumpy head called out.

Tate stopped pacing and fixed him with a stare. "I don't rightly know, yet. But I aim to find out mighty soon."

A bundle of nerves, cold as that frozen river, bunched up in my stomach when he said that.

Tate paced across the wooden boards again. "Now, *as I was saying*, there's no need to panic. We simply ask that you return to your rooms for the time being. Sit tight for a bit. If you hear the alarm, then double-time it into your transporter and go home. If we—"

"In which case we would give you a full refund for your vacation, of course," Grandma interjected. "And offer you a free weekend stay anytime you'd like to return."

"Now we can all do this in a nice, orderly fashion," Tate said. "Folks staying on the third floor should—"

He stopped and scrunched his eyebrows together. He cocked his head, one ear turned toward the sky.

And then I heard it too. The unmistakable *chukka-chukka-chukka* of a helicopter propeller. Closing in fast.

"Move!" Tate shouted. "Move, move, move! Everyone into the house!" He bolted down off the porch and herded the aliens up the steps. The crowd squished together. A few aliens lost their footing and tripped up the stairs, getting smooshed in the rush of frenzied movement.

"Tate!" Grandma cried. "You don't need to—"

"No time! Move!" he yelled.

The crowd bottlenecked at the backdoor, the aliens muttering protests. Tate cursed and scanned the sky while the Tourists filtered through the doorway. He pushed the last one into the house a second or two before the helicopter zipped by. It was white with KING-TV on the side in big blue letters. A man leaned out the cockpit door with a video camera mounted on one shoulder. The helicopter skimmed the tops of the trees, flying so low I could make out the Seattle Seahawks logo on the cameraman's cap.

But he wasn't interested in the B&B. The helicopter cruised over the house, then came to a hovering midair halt over the park. The cameraman placed one foot on the landing skids and leaned even further out of the helicopter.

Great. The whole world was about to get a look at the frozen river. That pukey, panicked feeling rushed back, stronger than ever.

Grandma stepped back out of the house. "I realize the circumstances are dire, Tate, but that doesn't mean you need to strong-arm my customers."

Tate planted his hands on his hips. "Would you rather nurse a couple of bruised alien egos, or have your little business turn up on the evening news?" He jabbed a finger in the direction of the helicopter.

"Well, that doesn't excuse—"

"Please stop arguing, you guys," Amy said. "Please. I can't take it right now." She stepped out from the side of the house, where we had been watching, and wiped at her eyes.

"Kids!" Grandma and Tate rushed down the stairs. They hugged us hard enough to cut off the air supply, studied our faces with concerned eyes, and generally made a big fuss.

"We was mighty worried when we couldn't find you this morning and then—"

"—so unlike both of you to just disappear like—"

"—this crazy thing with the river spooked us when—"

"—the whole town is in a tizzy because of the—"

"Whoa, whoa, okay." I held up both hands to quiet them down.

"We're really sorry," Amy said. Her words tumbled out in a rush. "We didn't mean to freak you guys out or anything, but it was just such a nice day, and we haven't had much of a chance to hang out together yet, then the freaky thing happened with the river, and now everything's messed up." She caught her breath. "We're really sorry." Tate pulled Amy close and rubbed her back.

Grandma shook her head. "I don't understand any of this," she said. There were worry lines raked across her forehead and bunched up around her eyes. She looked way older.

Tate scowled and watched the helicopter. "I understand one thing. There's gonna be a lot of unwanted attention paid to this area. A whole dang heap of it, trust me."

My mouth went desert dry. This was going to be a very painful confession. But if I was going down, then I was taking a certain skull-faced alien with me. I opened up my mouth to launch into my story when—

The sound of helicopter blades chopping the air fired up again, much louder than before.

There were two this time, clearly military-grade, both of them bulky and painted in that nondescript armed-forces green. They buzzed right over the house, so close that the windows rattled in their frames. The choppers circled over the park twice, then zoomed upriver and out of sight.

"Oh, what next?" Tate muttered. Then he herded us up the stairs.

We filed into the house and sat at the dining table. Grandma sighed heavily and looked around at all of us. "Well, Team Intergalactic, looks like it's time for a powwow. We have some serious planning to do to get through this one undetected."

My heart sped up, and the queasiness washed through me again. "Actually, Grandma, I need to say something first." If I waited any longer it was just going to be tougher to spit it out.

"What is it, David?" Grandma said.

I looked at Amy. She grabbed my hand and squeezed.

"I know what happened to the river," I said.

"You do?" Tate moved close and stuck his face right in front of mine. His eyes were wide. "What was it? Why didn't you say something? How could you possibly—"

"Oh, for the Creator's sake, give him some air," Grandma said. She elbowed Tate out of the way and put her hands on my shoulders. "What is it, dear?"

"Well, I know what happened to the river...because I did it."

Grandma and Tate were shocked into silence. The door swung open, and we all turned to see Scratchull walk through and plant himself in the middle of the kitchen.

"Well, well. I would be most interested in hearing this little story."

19

My instincts told my entire body to get ready for a fight. The rational part of my brain was not invited to participate in the decision.

Every muscle in my body stiffened. My hands balled themselves up into fists.

My eyes flicked over to the steak knives on the counter, and I judged how many lunging steps it would take to be able to grab a few.

I sized up Tate as an ally. His bulky frame and pent-up aggression were going to be on my side once the alien-vs.-human battle started.

Finally, I mentally mapped out an escape route for Grandma and Amy. When Scratchull attacked, hopefully Tate and I could tie him up him long enough for them to dash out the back.

But what would they do then, call 9-1-1? What would they say?

I pushed that thought out of my mind. It was no longer time to worry about the consequences of anyone finding out we had aliens here. The only thing that mattered was protecting the Earth and everyone on it. If more humans had to get involved, then so be it.

I shifted my weight so I was standing on the balls of my feet, ready to lunge if needed.

"It's his fault!" I cried out. "He's the reason the river is frozen. Scratchull's responsible for the helicopters and the crowd at the park and all the rest of it!"

I braced myself for action. Now that Scratchull had been outed as a fiend and backed into a corner, I knew that things would get ugly. "It's his fault," I said again, pointing right at his chalky face.

But after I accused him...he just stood there. And was he smiling?

I noticed that Grandma and Tate were not paying the slightest bit of attention to Scratchull. They were staring at me, clearly confused.

"Whatever do you mean, David?" Grandma said.

Okay, so I guess I was going to have to do a little more to convince them. I probably should have thought of that before.

"He's trying to destroy the planet. Really. I heard him talking about it and everything." The adults were still staring at me, frowning thoughtfully. "He wants to, like, melt the entire thing down." Still staring. "You know, Earth. The whole planet."

"Boy, just what in the Sam Hill are you talking about?" Tate said.

"I can prove it. He built a machine that has the power to destroy an entire planet." I reached into my pocket and carefully withdrew the little black device, then held it up for all to see.

"That little thing?" Tate said.

"Okay, I know it doesn't look like much, but it works. Trust me. I just touched it to the river for one second, and it froze the whole thing."

"Where did you find that?" Grandma asked.

"And just why were you sticking it into the river, anyway?" Tate asked.

"Did you know it was that dangerous?" Grandma said.

"Wait—were *you* the one trying to destroy the planet?" Tate's face was going red.

I swallowed. Why were they still looking at me instead of Scratchull, asking all of these stupid questions? "I was trying to save Amy. We were swimming in a creek, and then she was on top of this dam, and I thought it was going to fall down, so I pulled..."

I noticed—too late—Amy shaking her head at me.

Tate turned to his daughter. "You were at that dang swimming hole? After who knows how many times I've told you to stay away from there?"

Amy opened her mouth to say something, then slowly closed it.

"That's not the point," I said, trying to deflect attention away from her. "We need to—"

"I'll tell you what the point is." Tate took his toothpick out of his mouth and jabbed it at me. "You're expecting us to believe some story about the transporter repairman destroying the Earth with a little plastic gizmo, when we can't trust either of you to even follow a simple rule. How can you expect us—"

"The real point is that we're all in danger!" I shouted. *Why could no one understand that?* I pointed at Scratchull again. "Terrible danger!"

We all looked at Scratchull, still just standing there on the white kitchen tile. He did not, I had to admit, look terribly dangerous at the moment. His hands were clasped formally together and his smile was actually getting bigger.

He covered his mouth with his fingertips in a dainty little gesture. And then he laughed—an imitation of a slightly amused human giggle, not the hideous steak-knife-screeching sound I knew was his real laugh.

"My apologies for the unseemly display of mirth. I realize you are all upset," he said. "But I must admit I find this very amusing."

"Oh yeah? What's so funny about it? Huh?" As soon as the words left my mouth I knew how stupid they sounded. Did I think I was on a kindergarten playground? Man, I was going to have to be way more on top of my game to go up against this guy.

Grandma gestured to the little black device in my hand. "Scratchull, does this belong to you? And is it really capable of freezing that entire river out there?"

189

Scratchull sighed heavily. "I had *so* wanted it to be a surprise. But it appears as if this eager young boy has forced my hand a bit."

He held out his smooth white palm for the device. I shook my head and pulled it closer to my chest. Scratchull chuckled. "Very well. You may hold on to it for the time being if that makes you feel better. But, please—for all of our sakes—be very careful. We wouldn't want you to cause any more disasters than you already have."

Scratchull stepped forward and walked through the middle of our little group. I instinctively recoiled and pressed myself against the wall, but the others just let him pass. He stepped through the doorway and onto the back porch, then looked at us over his shoulder. "If you would be good enough to follow me, please."

I exchanged a glance with Amy, but I couldn't read her facial expression at all. Tate and Grandma looked at me strangely, then they all filed out the back door. I had no choice but to go after them.

Scratchull led us down the steps and across the backyard, talking the whole way. "I realize that I have only been here a short time. But I am already so enamored of the human race." He nodded at Grandma. "You have been so welcoming and kind. And, Mr. Tate, you have provided a classic case study of competence and leadership as you manage your resources to protect this establishment." He spread his hands out and looked up at the blue sky and surrounding trees. "This is all the very definition of natural beauty. And the good citizens in town have been so hospitable." He took a deep breath and let it out in an *aaahhhh*. "You could say I've fallen in love with Earth and her people."

Oh, please. Where could he possibly be going with this?

We neared the place where the backyard ended and the forest began. Scratchull turned to face us, his back to the wilderness. "So, naturally, I was greatly distressed when I read about some of the struggles plaguing your planet. Particularly with food production and distribution. Droughts, floods, famine. Millions of humans going to bed hungry every night." He used a knuckle to dab at a nonexistent tear in the corner of his eye. "And the worst part was thinking about the children...so many human children in need...."

He actually bent his head and lifted one finger in the *Just-give-me-a-moment-to-compose-myself* gesture. Sickening.

Finally he cleared his throat and straightened up, smoothing his coveralls with both hands. "When I realized it was within my power to help the humans, I didn't hesitate.

"I asked a scientist friend of mine to bring me a mechanism that he has been working on." Scratchull gestured to the black device I was still clutching with both hands. "He had described its powers to transform planetary landscapes, and it sounded almost miraculous. I knew I must conduct experiments that might be useful to the humans." He made a sweeping gesture at the forest behind him. "If you would follow me, please, I would like to show you the results of those experiments." He ducked underneath some branches and disappeared into the woods.

The rest of us looked at each other. Grandma seemed very worried, but I couldn't tell if she was nervous about following Scratchull or upset because she was convinced her only grandson had gone crazy. "I don't think it's a good idea to go in there with him," I said.

"Horsefeathers," Tate said. He marched toward the trees and yanked aside a couple of branches.

"Well...be careful, at least."

Tate turned and sneered at me. "Sounds like you're the one who needs to be careful with that little gizmo." Then he walked into the forest and out of sight.

Grandma raised her eyebrows and tried to give me a sympathetic smile, but it just looked like pity. I thought she might say something, but she turned and followed Tate.

I looked at Amy. "You still believe me." No reaction. "Right?"

"Well, yeah, I guess. I just—I mean, I don't know what to think after everything that's happened today." She gestured toward the woods. "But we should probably go hear what he's telling them."

"In the wilderness? With no witnesses? I don't think so. What if he melts a big hole in the ground and pushes me in?"

"I don't think we have to worry about that. At least right now."

"See?" I said. "I *knew* you didn't believe me."

"No, I just meant I don't think he'll try anything in front of Dad or your grandma."

"Amy, *listen*. Didn't I tell you what he wants to do? Destroy. The. Planet. You think he cares about what those two think? He'll push them in the hole next!"

"You don't have to talk to me like I'm some confused first-grader. It's just that I thought maybe you misunderstood him or something. He's acting so normal and innocent, maybe this is all part of the report he's going to give to the Collective about—"

"He is *not* normal and innocent."

"Fine, but then why—"

Suddenly we heard Grandma, but her voice was very faint. "Oh my goodness!"

"Hey, now!" That was Tate, louder.

Amy and I shared a wide-eyed look before we plunged into the woods, pushing through a thicket of undergrowth.

The light was dimmer under the canopy of entwined branches, but I caught a colorful glimpse of Grandma's blouse, half hidden behind some trees. Amy and I sprinted toward her.

We rounded a patch of ferns and stopped short. I shook my head to clear the image, but when I looked again it was still there before me. No matter how many weird scenes I've come across at Grandma's place, that surreal quality of seeing something my brain refuses to believe always knocks the wind out of me a little.

"What is this?" Tate breathed.

Scratchull spread out his hands, capturing the entire scene. "I call it my Garden of Earthly Delights."

At first the huge, unnatural scar slashed into the landscape reminded me of the soupy mess that almost swallowed me whole. But this was different. The ground was firm, and running down the middle, in orderly rows, was a garden that looked like it belonged to a giant farmer in some fairy tale.

The corn stalks stretched all the way up to the midpoint of the surrounding hundred-foot cedar trees. The ears of corn were as long as broomsticks and very thick. Each kernel gleamed like a fat, golden marble.

The next row was strawberries, each one as big as a pumpkin, and a perfectly ripe red.

The far corner was given over to a watermelon patch. I would need a running start and a stepladder to be able to climb up on top of one of those things.

There were other enormous fruits and veggies—baseball bat bananas, basketball oranges—too many to take in all at once. I remembered what Scratchull had told Greenie: *I can create a little oasis of land that is stable enough to allow me to ride out the storm of destruction. And I have already seen to it that there will be plenty of food provisions, as well.*

All of us humans looked at each other, then back at the garden, and finally at Scratchull.

"But how can this...I mean, why did you..." It was pretty unusual for Grandma, who had definitely seen it all, to be speechless.

Scratchull smiled broadly. "You like it, then? I'm so pleased." He gestured toward the device I was still holding. "This mechanism has all sorts of wonderful properties." The white alien looked right at me, and I caught a glimpse of the fury he was hiding under that mask of friendliness. "When it's not being used rashly and improperly to freeze rivers, that is."

Scrathull's half-hidden rage disappeared, and he slapped another hideous smile on his face. He walked between the rows of monster fruit, and we followed in stunned silence. "This entire garden flourished in just a few days' time. If we picked it all right now, every last bit, the soil would yield another bumper crop before the week is up. And this is all in the deep shade of the forest. Imagine what could be produced under optimal sunlit conditions."

Scratchull used both hands to pluck a hefty raspberry from a bush. He handed it to Tate. "Enjoy a taste test, Mr. Chief of Security."

Tate glanced around at us humans. He was no doubt contemplating the effects of *alien germs and microbes and who-knows-whatnot.*

"It's perfectly natural, I assure you, my good man," Scratchull said. "The technology that enabled its growth is alien, to be certain, but isn't that just another way of saying 'slightly more advanced'? And of course the soil and its nutrients are purely Earthbound. They have merely been tweaked in order to operate more efficiently. No different, really, than the agricultural enhancements that humans have been making for the last several centuries."

Tate took a bite and chewed slowly, thoughtfully. After he swallowed he wiped dripping red juice from his mustache with the back of his hand. We watched him, all of us holding our breath. I more than half expected him to keel over dead.

"That's the finest thing I've ever put in my mouth," he said solemnly. Tate broke off round clusters of the fruit and handed them to Grandma and Amy.

Grandma took a bite and squealed like a little girl. "Great galaxies! That would win first prize in the Pioneer Day contest all by itself!"

And even though I couldn't believe it, Amy took a bite, too. She raised her eyebrows and gave her dad the thumbs-up. "You're right, that's really tasty."

The three of them dug into the raspberry. Tate held out a chunk to me, but I shook my head. He glared at me for a moment, then went back to licking the juice from his fingers.

"How wonderful," Scratchull said. "Do you realize how many earthlings could be fed in a year, just using this small plot of land alone?"

"Millions of satisfied human customers served," Tate said through a mouthful of raspberry. "Better'n McDonald's."

Grandma finished eating. "The possibilities are certainly exciting, Scratchull." Then her eyebrows bunched up. "But surely you know the rules concerning the use of sophisticated off-world technology on non-Collective planets? In fact," she said as she wiped the rest of the berry juice from her fingers, "now that my mind has cleared a bit, I have to say this all makes me more than a little nervous. My place could be closed down for good if anyone found out."

Scratchull stepped closer to Grandma and took both of her hands in his. I tensed up, that urge to fight and protect stronger than ever. "I would never let something like that happen, I assure you," Scratchull said. "I have many friends and colleagues in the Collective, and would take full responsibility for this enterprise." Scratchull looked around at his garden, taking in the rows of enormous food. "Setting this up has caused me to reinterpret a few rules, certainly. But I was only doing what I felt was morally right. I could not stand idly by while so many humans suffered."

Tate cleared his throat. "Well, sure, but that won't—"

"Did you know that slightly altering the soil in dry regions could turn the barren deserts of Earth into fertile cropland? From wasteland to breadbasket"—Scratchull snapped his

196

fingers—"overnight. Why, it would revolutionize the way the entire planet eats. Just think of it: no more hunger. Humans everywhere could concentrate on far more important endeavors than the mere day-to-day survival of their species." He glanced at Amy and dropped her a wink. "Important endeavors such as, say, petitioning the Collective for the inclusion of Earth."

Amy's expression was so hopeful that my heart broke a little. And then when she actually returned his smile, it was ripped out of my chest, put in a blender, and poured in a shallow grave.

Thankfully, Grandma still looked a little skeptical. "That may be...but don't the leaders of the Collective feel that planets should evolve at their own pace?" she said. "If a race of people gets access to important technology they don't fully understand, there is the danger they will become overly dependent on whoever supplies that technology. At least that's what I've heard."

"My dear woman," Scratchull said. "These are the types of ethical debates that the Collective leadership engages in all the time." I wondered what kind of effort it was taking him to pretend like he actually cared about any of this stuff. "Let me give you an example. When a natural disaster devastates an impoverished community, or a terrible drought wipes out the year's crops for a developing nation, and people are suffering on a most tragic scale...what do the rest of the earthlings do?"

"We all pitch in, of course," Grandma said.

"Sure," said Tate. "We send food, money, doctors. You name it."

"Exactly," said Scratchull. "You do not stand by and watch while innocents suffer needlessly, do you? Crossing your fingers and merely hoping that they might 'figure it out for themselves' over the course of the next hundreds—perhaps thousands—of years. You do what you know is right."

Scratchull reached up and plucked a kernel of corn from an ear on a nearby stalk. He took a bite out of it like it was an apple. "There is what's legally right, and there is what's morally right. Unfortunately, they are not always the same thing. There are a few misguided individuals in the Collective leadership who are solely interested in consolidating power. Exclusivity is the hammer they clumsily wield." He finished up the kernel of corn and brushed off his hands. "They care nothing for the human suffering that must take place in order for their arbitrary little rules to be followed."

"I know what you mean," Amy said. Hearing her agree with Scratchull felt like a hard punch to the spleen. "I definitely think the Collective should let Earth in so we can share ideas and stuff. Sure, other civilizations might be more advanced, but I think humans have a lot to offer the interstellar community."

"What a clever girl," Scratchull said. "I certainly could not have phrased it better myself."

I glared at Amy, but she wasn't looking at me. Instead she was focused on the white alien. "Do you mind if I try one of those? They're my favorite." Amy pointed to a tree with peaches so large it looked like James and his talking insect friends might come dancing out of one at any second.

"Of course."

"Thanks!" Amy said. Scratchull and Tate helped her get

a peach down from the tree, so she didn't end up crushed underneath it, and she scooped out handfuls of fresh fruit.

Grandma approached Scratchull. "Assuming we are able to produce all of this food safely and secretly, how could we possibly distribute it without letting the entire human race in on our little secret here at the Intergalactic Bed and Breakfast?"

Scratchull nodded. "An excellent question. I have been studying that challenge myself, madam. And while I would love to share my ideas with you, I think we have far more pressing matters to discuss at the moment."

Tate jerked his thumb in my direction and harrumphed. "You mean like David accusing you of global destruction?"

Scratchull smiled. "Well, yes, we should probably chat about that, shouldn't we? But I was thinking rather more of all the recent attention being paid to the area." He pointed at the sky and twirled his finger to indicate the helicopters.

Tate's face paled. "Good lord. I was so amazed by all this, I nearly forgot. Let's get back to the house." He grabbed Grandma by the hand and pulled her away from the garden and through the forest.

Amy tossed back the last few pieces of fruit and trotted after her dad.

That left Scratchull and me alone at the edge of the garden. I stared hard at him. I'm sure my fear was still there somewhere, but at the moment it was being suffocated by anger.

Scratchull swept his long arm in the direction of the house in an *after you* gesture. But I held my ground and glared at him.

Scratchull smiled. "Just look at you," he said. "Blood rushing to the cheeks, increased breathing rate, hands balled into fists—your body has chosen to revert to its animal state, and you just let it happen. I can practically watch you devolving right before my eyes."

"You won't get away with this," I said.

"Oh, but I already am getting away with it, my dear boy." His smile died. Those red pinpricks of light flared up in the middle of his eyes again. "Such a pity you won't be around to see how it all turns out."

The fear came flooding back. Was he going to try something now, right here? I turned and ran through the forest, but the only thing following was the screechy sound of alien laughter.

20

"These disturbing images are being brought to you live, courtesy of KING-TV of Seattle." The CNN anchorwoman's voice cut over the bird's-eye-view video of the frozen river snaking its way through the forest. "Confirmed details are scarce at the moment, but we do know that at around one p.m. today, Pacific Daylight Time, the entire length of the Nooksack River, located in the northwest corner of Washington State, froze solid. According to several eyewitness accounts, this unexplained phenomenon happened instantaneously. Apparently an unprecedented force of nature is at work here."

The scrolling banner underneath the video read CLIMATE CHANGE GONE CRAZY?

I was sweaty all over, my clothes clinging to my skin, but at the same time I felt so cold—almost like I was coming down with the flu. But instead of a virus, this was caused by all of the stress and worry about what I was going to do and what could possibly happen next.

I glanced up at Amy, Grandma, and Tate staring at the breaking news report, and their pale faces told me they were feeling the same way. Why did seeing something on TV make it seem more real?

"The river is frozen from its source, a series of glaciers in the Cascade mountain range near Mount Baker, all the way down to Bellingham Bay. The salt water there appears to be unaffected." The new video showed people lining the banks of the river. They were staring at the place where the frozen river ended in a block of ice at the edge of the calm water of the bay.

"We hope to provide more information soon. Our field reporters are gathering on site and efforting to obtain interviews with members of both the armed forces and the scientific community, who are converging on the area."

The video switched to a caravan of vehicles—plain white civilian trucks mixed in with military rigs—climbing up the mountain road. My throat constricted, making it harder to breathe. I swear I could *feel* all of those outside people and their prying eyes getting closer.

I leaned over to Amy, sitting on the other end of the couch, and whispered, "Don't tell me you actually believe him."

She answered quietly, out the side of her mouth. "1
going to hear him out, okay?" She turned her head slight
looked at me for the first time since we found the garden.
don't think it's at all possible you made some kind of mista

I bulged my eyes at her and mouthed *NO!* She turned
attention back to the TV.

The onscreen footage went back to the sweeping aer.
shot of the river as the helicopter flew toward Mount Bake
For a long stretch the icy Nooksack was surrounded on botl
sides by uninterrupted forest. But then the trees cleared and
the town of Forest Grove popped into view. The people in
the crowd at Riverside Park turned their faces up toward the
camera. Some of the kids waved.

And then the Intergalactic Bed & Breakfast appeared. It
wasn't much, just a blip in the corner of the screen as the
chopper passed over, but still... How many millions of people
were going to see this footage before the day was through?
How many of them would remember the day last summer
when the B&B made an appearance on the nightly news? How
many conspiracy theorists would it take to connect the dots?

CNN cut back to the studio to show the somber anchorwoman at her desk.

"There has been no official word from the White House,
but officials at the Pentagon have stated that the possibility
of terrorism has not been ruled out at this point. When they
determine exactly how this—"

Scratchull hit the power button, then stood in front of
the TV and faced us. "It would appear that we need to make
haste in deciding how to handle this."

Grandma held her head in both hands and let out a long, shaky sigh. "I hate to admit it, but I don't have the first notion about what we should do."

Scratchull inclined his head deferentially toward Tate. "Does our head of security have any ideas?"

Tate frowned and waved a hand at the dark TV screen. "Terrorism? Seriously?" He sounded exhausted. "If they're using the T-word, then this whole region will get the fine-tooth-comb treatment." He reached over and patted Grandma on the hand. "I know it'll pain you, but I think the best thing would be to shut 'er down. The whole operation. No guests until everything blows over for good." He shook his head slowly. "And I fear that might be one lo-o-ong time comin'."

Grandma took off her glasses and wiped at her eyes. Tate put an arm around her shoulder. Amy kept looking at the blank TV as if the pictures of my epic mistake were still dancing across the screen. I couldn't help but notice that no one would look in my direction.

This was so unfair.

"None of this would be happening if not for him," I said, leveling my finger at Scratchull. "He's the one trying to—"

"Oh, give it a rest, boy," Tate said. "We've already heard your little conspiracy theory."

"It's not a *theory*." My voice was rising now, but Tate just turned away, totally dismissing me. "And it's not *little*, either. I told you already, he wants to melt down the whole planet."

Tate, still facing away from me, just shook his head in disgust.

"You're the one who's always so suspicious around here

even when there's nothing to worry about." I gestured at Scratchull who was watching all of this from the corner of the room, a little grin on his face. "And you let the biggest threat of all walk around right under your nose."

Tate crossed his arms over his chest but still ignored me. I had never been so mad in my entire life. "No wonder you're not sheriff of this town anymore."

Tate slowly turned his head. The look he gave me would have been terrifying if I didn't have Scratchull's burning-eyed stare to compare it with. Amy faced me now too, and she was glaring. Grandma's head was buried in her hands.

Tate stood up slowly. He approached my chair and loomed over me.

"That's a mighty big accusation you're making against Scratchull." His kept his voice low. "Are you certain of these allegations, boy?"

I nodded quickly.

"One hundred percent?" he asked.

"A thousand," I said.

"Like you were certain about Scratchull's construction tool being some sort of a weapon?"

"No, that was—"

"Like you were certain that the human couple leaving the B-and-B were aliens in need of your guidance?"

"But he was the one who—"

"Like you were certain about all of that crazy quicksand destroying the trees? Some big forest-eating monstrosity that seemed to disappear overnight?"

I just looked at the floor.

205

Tate leaned in further and I could feel his breath on the top of my head. "Like you were certain that you knew how to use that device and not bring the scrutiny of the whole dang country down on our heads?"

"Tate," Grandma said, her voice thick with tears, "David did not do any of these things with a mean spirit. There must be some other explanation for everything."

Tate scoffed. "Scratchull's given me all the explanation I need." He finally moved away from me and sat on the armrest of his chair. "There's an old adage in police work: when faced with a mysterious set of circumstances, go with the most likely solution. Now what seems more likely here: that Scratchull was trying to destroy the entire planet, even though he still happens to be on it, *in case you hadn't noticed.*" Tate directed this last part straight at me. Then he turned back to the others. "Or that Scratchull had something else in mind, and David made a whopper of an error in judgment?" Silence from Grandma and Amy. "Pardon me, I meant *another* whopper of an error in judgment?"

More silence from the ladies. Tate plopped back down into his chair. "That's what I thought. You all saw that garden out there. Scratchull's been trying to help us."

Scratchull cleared his throat and stepped forward. "Take heart, friends. I believe I may be able to help you once more."

"How's that?" Tate said.

"I have become quite adept at using this helpful little gadget." He pointed to me. "And if David would stop grasping it as if it were a toddler's security blanket, I could put it to good use."

Tate tugged at his mustache. "What do you mean?"

"The device froze the river in an instant, correct?" Tate nodded. "Well, I could set it flowing again just as quickly."

"You could?" Grandma said, lifting her head. Seeing Scratchull bring a look of such renewed hope to her eyes twisted the knife of shame deeper into my belly.

"Of course. It's merely a reversal of the mechanism's basic function. I assure you, if it can produce the amazing garden you have recently witnessed, certainly I could coax it into returning the river to its natural state. Immediately."

"Well, why didn't you tell us that earlier?" Tate said.

"I was under serious accusations from David. He has been employed here longer than I have and is related by blood to the proprietor." Scratchull put out his hands, palms up, just an innocent alien in the wrong place at the wrong time. It was infuriating. "In all honesty, I felt like I needed to show you the garden in order to absolve myself first."

Tate nodded slowly. "Makes sense. But does unfreezing the river really solve the problem, though? You can't make all of those busybodies disappear with that thing, can you?" Tate said.

"That's *exactly* what he wants to do with that thing," I muttered. "Make them disappear forever."

Tate turned and pointed a thick finger at me. "Enough."

"My study of earthlings is admittedly incomplete," Scratchull continued as if I had not said anything at all. "But I have learned enough to know that when there is nothing left to take pictures of for the television, the humans will disperse."

Tate nodded. "You got a point there."

"A few of them may linger and poke around. But I don't

imagine that would last long when they come up empty. And I see no reason why they should come here. Especially if we get things cleared up forthwith."

"Oh, can you do it right now, Scratchull?" Grandma said. "The sooner this place quiets down, the better I'll feel."

"Certainly." Scratchull made a big show of turning his whole body and facing in my direction. "That is, of course, unless you would like David to try it first."

Tate grunted out what might've been considered a laugh under better circumstances. "I don't think so." He looked at me. "Hand over the contraption, son."

I shook my head. I tried to keep my body and face calm despite the fact that the adrenaline running through my body was making me all jittery. "Never."

"Boy, this is serious business," Tate said. He started to push himself out of his chair. "We need to move quickly if we want to—"

"Please remain seated, Mr. Tate." Scratchull motioned for the big man to get back into his recliner. "Let me say a few things first." Tate slowly settled back into his chair while keeping his eyes fixed on me.

Scratchull paced back and forth. "I realize that adolescents can sometimes make poor decisions. The same is true for societies on many, many planets—I suppose it's the nature of the beast, as they say. So I always strive to be as patient and understanding as possible with those of the younger generation." He rested his chin in one chalky-white hand as he paced.

"However, the events of the day have gone far beyond mere juvenile misbehavior. Now, I probably would have been able to overlook the fact that David broke into my room, where I keep that powerful device safely hidden. And I might have even been able to forgive him despite the fact that he then stole this mechanism from me and slandered me outrageously."

Scratchull paused and inclined his head toward Grandma. "I know you feel a great deal of affection for the boy. And, as I say, I might have been able to forgive a few of these youthful transgressions." He shook his skull head slowly, as if the words he was saying brought him great pain. I couldn't help but wonder whether they gave out Academy Awards on his home planet.

"But the fact that he used these stolen goods in such a reckless manner makes this far, far more serious. Not only has he put your business in danger, but if the device had been on a higher setting…" Scratchull trailed off, wiping a hand across his brow as if the mere thought of such a thing was giving him terror sweats. "If it had been on a higher setting … and the freezing effect had worked its way through the bay and out into the oceans of Earth…" Scratchull stopped pacing and turned to face us. "Well, David's tall tale about 'destroying the planet' may have had the potential to actually become fact. At the risk of being melodramatic, I fear that David came very close to truly endangering all life on Earth."

No one would look at me. The room was terribly silent for several moments. But what could I say? It was the one time Scratchull was actually telling the truth.

"Here is what I think should happen. For the good of everyone concerned." Scratchull took a deep breath. "First, David should hand over the device immediately. I will take

209

it and find a secluded spot on the river. It should only take a moment to set right what he has put so terribly out of joint."

He inclined his smooth white head toward Grandma. "Next, and I know this will cause you a measure of some distress, but I feel strongly that David should be sent home."

Grandma let out a little gasp. "Oh, do you really think that's necessary?"

"I do. Not only does he need to understand the severity of his actions, but I fear the rest of his summer would be most uncomfortable if he stayed. You humans employed here are keeping the planet's most important secret. The group dynamic would be seriously compromised now that he has lost your trust."

"You got that right," Tate said.

Grandma rubbed at her temples. She looked almost as miserable as I felt. "Oh, Scratchull, are you sure? He did such a fantastic job for me last summer. And he's such a wonderful young man. I'm not sure what has gotten into him."

Maybe the worst part of everything was that she couldn't bring herself to look at me when she said any of that.

"I do not doubt for a moment that what you say is true," Scratchull said. "And perhaps he could come back next summer. Get a fresh start, as it were."

I couldn't imagine leaving. I had to try one more time. "Look, I know I messed up, but why will no one believe me?" I said. "Grandma, does all of this sound like something that I would just make up? Do you think I would hurt you on purpose?"

"Of course not." Grandma wiped at her eyes.

She opened her mouth to say more, but Scratchull stepped in.

"Very well," he said, looking at me. "The floor is all yours. Regale us with the tale of how you came by this special knowledge of yours."

"I'd be quite interested to hear this," Grandma said.

The humans leaned forward in their chairs, but only Grandma looked like she still had some hope in her eyes. I should've told Amy the whole story when I had the chance, done whatever it took to convince her by the dam—I might at least have one ally—but that frozen river spooked me so bad, all I could think about was getting back here. Too late now.

This felt like my last chance to convince everyone. I had to phrase it carefully so Scratchull couldn't turn my own words against me again.

"Okay." I wiped my palms against my shorts. "Okay. I suspected that something was wrong with him. So, yes, I did sneak—"

"Why'd you think something was wrong with Scratchull, anyway?" Tate said.

"He's way different when he's not around you guys. I guess you'll just have to trust me on that one."

Tate grunted again. "Just how are we supposed to trust—"

"Dad, he saved my life," Amy said. "Whether or not you believe anything else he says, that is true. Please let him finish."

I was grateful for that much help, at least. "So, yeah, I did sneak into his room. I wanted to see if he was hiding anything in there. I felt like I needed to find something incriminating, or whatever, for you guys to believe me about him. Anyway, I had just gone in there when somebody came by transporter, a green alien I'd never seen before. I hid in the closet. Then Scratchull came in and the two of them started talking about—"

"Breaking into a private room? Skulking around? Eavesdropping?" Tate shook his head. "No wonder Scratchull's upset that—"

Grandma swatted at Tate's shoulder, and the big man fell silent.

"Anyway, the green alien brought him this." I held up the little black machine. "And they started talking about what it could do. And Scratchull said he was going to use it to destroy the planet. Or threaten to destroy it, at least at first. He said he wanted to get off the planet because the transporters wouldn't—"

"If I may interject here, for just one moment." Scratchull held up a long white finger. "An associate of mine did visit and bring me this device, as I have already informed you. But something puzzles me." Scratchull tapped his cheek with one finger, making a show of mulling something over. "When I speak to off-world friends, I always use their native language. Or mine, of course. No offense intended, but earthling English is not exactly the *lingua franca* of the universe."

I did not like where he was going with this. Not at all.

"So I'm wondering how, exactly, were you able to understand our conversation?" I just stared at him. "Perhaps, instead of Spanish or French, your school back home offers beginner courses in dialects from the Grunterian galaxy?" A smile played at the corner of his dark lips, and this time it looked very genuine.

I swallowed drily, the heat of everyone's stares turning

my cheeks red. What could I say? It's not like I could admit to using the baby monitor. No way. The technology in there was banned, too, and Grandma knew that I knew it. I would just look worse than I already did. And I hadn't even told Amy that I'd "borrowed" it from her underwear drawer. Or panties drawer. Whatever.

"Well, David?" Grandma said. The look on her face killed me. She was clearly anxious for something to come out of my mouth that would make me look better, get me out of this mess. "Were you able to understand what they were saying?"

Maybe that was it. Tell them I didn't understand every word, but I picked up the gist. Tone of voice, body movements, that sort of thing. Like charades. And the demonstration with the bed puddle! That's it. I'd tell them I saw that and figured out how—

"Perhaps this aided your comprehension?" Scratchull said. He reached into a pocket of his coveralls and pulled out the baby monitor.

No. No, no, no. I glanced at Amy. Her expression was wide-eyed and panic-stricken. I knew she was afraid of being caught. Then she turned to me and her face distorted, eyes getting narrow and mouth going all scowly. She might as well have had *How could you, you big jerk?* tattooed across her forehead. Then Grandma and Tate started muttering about what Scratchull was holding, and she went back to looking worried again.

"As I was saying, I consider myself to be quite forgiving. If this were the *first* time David had sneaked around behind everyone's back and used illegal technology, that would be one thing. . . ." Scratchull popped the top off the monitor, reached in, and withdrew the circuit board with the translator chip. "But it appears that he has been making quite a habit of the practice." He told them about finding the hidden baby monitor and then explained the alien technology.

"David?" Grandma said it so quietly. The oversized lenses of her glasses made her eyes appear huge, as if they could look right through me. And the worst part of everything was that there was *still* a little bit of hope in those eyes. "Is this true?"

What could I do at this point? I just nodded. That little light of hope flickered and went out. It was a clear and final indication that Scratchull had won.

"Just where did you find something like this?" Tate said.

I could feel Amy's stare like a laser-sighted scope from a sniper rifle.

I sighed. "I got it from an alien teenager, one of the kids in a Tourist family," I mumbled. "He set it up and showed me how to use it."

"Now you're dragging the *guests* into all of your sneaking around and illegal activity?" Tate said. "Guests who also happen to be minors? Really?"

All of the air leaked out of me, along with the fight. I glanced at Amy, who was watching the floor, a guilty expression on her face. But she stayed silent.

"I daresay this rather clears up all of David's confusion regarding my plans to destroy the planet," Scratchull said. "If he was huddling in the closet, furtively eavesdropping with this hastily mashed-together bit of outlawed machinery, it's no wonder he misheard a few things."

I wanted to say that I didn't "mishear" anything. Wanted to shout it, in fact. But Scratchull had me blocked at every turn.

"I did speak about altering the landscape of the Earth, of course, but in a good way," Scratchull said. "I'm sure it was an honest mistake. Well, as honest as David could muster, I suppose." A short burst of laughter escaped his dark lips. "Perhaps when I said I wanted to *feed* the planet, David thought he heard *defeat* the planet, and mistakenly assumed I was trying to take over!" No one laughed at Scratchull's lame joke, not even Tate. "In any case, I have seen some of the movies earthlings make about alien invaders and such. Pure propaganda, if you ask me. It's no wonder David has an active fantasy life. It's just unfortunate it had to have such a negative impact on the real world."

I chanced a peek over at Grandma. She was just staring into the middle distance, totally silent. I knew what I had to do. No other choice, really.

"Fine. I'll go," I said. This might sound terrible, but it almost felt like a relief at that point. I'd probably have to spend the rest of the summer at the Happy Camper Sleep-away Adventure in Lakeland, Florida, but at least there nobody would think I was a liar or a cheat or totally insane. Or a combo of all three.

"But on one condition," I added.

"Boy," Tate said, "you are in no position to—"

"Scratchull must destroy that device after he fixes the river. In front of all of us. Whether or not I was right about the rest of it, having something like that around here is dangerous. It's not like this little group can go up against the entire Collective."

Grandma still looked in a daze, but she said, "I have to admit, that would make me feel more comfortable."

"I humbly acquiesce." Scratchull smiled innocently. "Do you have any other demands?"

I just glared at him. It felt like a hollow victory, but if it ended up saving the Earth I guess it was the only one that mattered.

"Excellent. In that case, I will unfreeze the river and thereby put an end to the current crisis." Scratchull stuck his hand in my face, palm up, for the device. My whole arm felt numb. It lifted as if being operated by remote control, and I dropped the little black mechanism into his chalky-white palm.

"Thank you so much, young man. Now, after seeing to the river, I will raze the Garden of Earthly Delights, if that is indeed the will of the group. Regrettable, perhaps, but I understand your objections. When I am finished, there will be no trace of otherworldly influence. Are we agreed?"

Tate nodded, but he had eyes only for Grandma, who stared sullenly at the ground.

Scratchull walked toward the door, then stopped and turned to face us. "While I am tending to all of that, someone should purchase David's return plane ticket."

He turned his back again and started to whistle as he left the B&B. He was practically skipping as he went through the door.

21

That evening I plodded up the stairs to my room. I felt like leaving the B&B right then, didn't even care about packing or anything. But when Tate had called my airline, he was told that the first decent flight with available seats didn't leave for three more days. So I figured I'd be spending a lot of time hiding out in my room until then.

The first thing I saw when I opened my door was Snarffle. The day had been so long, and so mind-blowingly messed up, that I had forgotten about him. The poor little guy must have been banished to my room after Scratchull told Grandma what a danger his appetite was to her furniture.

It had certainly been a danger to my room. Apparently I wasn't the only one who had forgotten him in all the chaos, because it looked like no one had fed him all day.

He was hunched over in that classic *Bad dog!* way: head lowered near the floor but eyes raised up at me, tail twirling tentatively at half speed, body shivering slightly all over. He sat in the middle of the empty room.

And I mean *empty*. He had eaten the bed, the nightstand, the lamp, and the bookshelves. Along with all of the books.

I sighed. "Well, at least you didn't eat my clothes." They were piled up in the corner. "Thanks, my man. I know you were hungry, and that probably took some restraint." Then I noticed that he had decided to finish off the suitcase, however.

Snarffle took a couple of subdued steps in my direction. "It's okay, boy," I said. "You don't have to feel bad. I'll do enough of that for both us." His tail-twirling picked up at that and he scurried over to me. I sat on the bare hardwood floor and took him into my lap. He nuzzled into my chest, and I even let him lick my cheeks as much as he wanted. It felt so good to be with someone who wasn't totally disgusted with me.

"Don't worry about the bed. I doubt I'll be able to sleep, anyway." But I was wrong about that. Apparently ruining all of the relationships that ever mattered to you in a single day is pretty tiring work. I slumped against the wall and Snarffle curled up on my lap.

"I'll get you a snack in a minute. Just let me rest, okay?" Snarffle gave me a few more licks, which I took as an affirmative.

I tilted my head back. The only reason I could even think about relaxing—the only reason I could even *breathe* normally—was because I had seen Scratchull smash his little machine into mangled bits. We had all watched that. And then, not trusting him to leave the pieces alone, I hiked back down to the Nooksack and threw them into the river, which was flowing once again. The mechanical fragments had bobbed on the surface for a few moments before they smashed into river boulders and got all churned up in the white water. They were finally scattered and swept downriver toward the bay. There. Let's see him try to put all of *that* back together.

Maybe I had to leave this place, and maybe nobody really wanted me around here anymore, but I still wanted to be sure he wasn't going to cause any more trouble after I left.

I tried to think of other things I could do to mess with him, but exhaustion took over. Snarffle and I slept huddled up on the bare floorboards of my soon-to-be-ex-room.

The best thing I could say about the next couple of days was that it was easy to avoid having to talk to anyone. The mob of researchers and military personnel never materialized after the river got unfrozen. There's a chance that they might have been up at the glaciers, studying the source of the river, but they never zeroed in on Forest Grove. And the locals were in full gear-up mode for the Pioneer Day Festival, which would take place the day I left town.

(And, by the way, I didn't bother to kid myself. I knew I'd be leaving for good. I mean, how could I possibly come back next summer after it had all ended like this? Even if

Scratchull found a way off the planet before then without trashing the place first.)

Anyway, people were way busier than usual. Tate was consumed with prepping security measures for the big day. He had decided that with all of the excitement generated by the frozen-river incident, no off-world Tourists would be allowed to attend the festival. So he stalked around the house giving gruff instructions about staying inside the B&B and out of sight that day. He also spent a lot of time at the top of his watchtower, scoping out the town and making notes in his journal.

Grandma completely threw herself into baking for the contest. Scratchull used his homemade gadgets and a pile of old bricks to slap together a couple of long wood-fired ovens in the backyard. "Now you can make enough of your blue-ribbon goodies for every man, woman, and child in town," he had told her. "In fact, there will be enough for them all to have seconds!" Man, what a suck-up.

Amy offered some sort of activity for Tourists just about every hour of the day. She set up shuffleboard tournaments for the seniors, story time for the little kids, and led informational Earth nature walks for everyone in between. It was almost like she wanted her schedule to be so filled up every minute that there would be no chance she'd accidentally bump into me and have to actually, you know, talk about what had happened. Whatever.

I watched all of this from the sidelines. I spent most of my time taking Snarffle for hikes in the forest, where he found all sorts of berries and roots and bushes to chow down on.

That led to another minor confrontation with Scratchull before I left, however. Snarffle and I were sitting in the shade of a maple tree at the edge of the backyard, resting after a long hike, when the little purple alien's nose tendrils snaked out of his face and sniffed the air. Then he hopped up on all six legs and strained at his leash, whistle-growling deep in his throat. I let him pull me around to the side of the house.

And sure enough, there were Scratchull and his wobbly green assistant, sneaking around, each carrying a wooden crate. They were walking right up against the side of the house; Greenie was glancing furtively in every direction as they made their way to the backyard.

No more sneaking around or eavesdropping. Who cared if anything bad happened to me? In fact, it might make Grandma snap out of it and at least be a little suspicious of Scratchull. I ran right up and confronted them.

"What are you guys doing?" I said. Snarffle whistled angrily in agreement. I glared at Scratchull but jerked my thumb at Greenie. "What did he bring you this time?"

Scratchull's eyes went wide and his mouth fell open. "Oh, no! He has found us out!" Scratchull gaped at Greenie. "Behold Earth's greatest underage detective. He has foiled us yet again. Quick, hide these dangerous supplies!"

Greenie shuffled back and forth, his jelly body wiggling all over. He seemed very confused.

"What's going on back here?" Tate marched around the side of the house. He stopped and crossed his meaty arms over his chest.

"Good afternoon, Mr. Tate," Scratchull said. "This is the associate I was telling you about." He inclined his head toward Greenie.

"He don't exactly look capable of fitting into an earthling disguise."

Scratchull chuckled. "No, you are certainly correct about that. But I will keep him shielded from the natives. He has been good enough to bring me something that will help with the great baking experiment."

Scratchull set the crate on the ground and pried off the top. The wooden box was filled with what looked like tiny grapes, except they were bright yellow. "These exquisite fruits are the pride of the planet Mooglah. They make a jelly that will go perfectly with the Kerntaberries being used in the festival treats."

"Kerntaberries? Mixed with Mooglah fruit?" Greenie said. "Really? But won't those—"

Scratchull elbowed Greenie hard enough to dislodge a few wobbly chunks. Greenie had to set the crate down to pick them up off the grass and smooth them back into his head. Scratchull addressed Tate again. "We were just taking them to the ovens. David here was offering his assistance."

"Sure he was," Tate said. "Come on, I'll help y'all carry those. The girls are baking out back right now."

Tate bent over and lifted one of the crates with a grunt, then walked toward the backyard, all without so much as looking at me. Greenie and Scratchull followed.

I peered around the side of the house and watched as the little procession approached Grandma and Amy at the ovens.

I told myself I was doing it for security purposes—what if those were, you know, pieces of exploding death fruit?—but I guess it was really more so I could wallow in self-pity or something.

Grandma and Amy applauded when Scratchull swept the lid off the top of the crate to reveal the fruit. Everyone tried a few bites, even Tate, and they were all clearly enjoying themselves. Scratchull even put on a big, corny chef's hat and a KISS THE COOK apron and helped Grandma with the baking.

It was a disgusting train wreck of a spectacle and I couldn't look away. That is, until Scratchull looked over to where my head poked around the side of the house. He offered me a broad smile and a finger-waggling little wave.

I couldn't wait to get out of here.

22

When my last evening in Forest Grove rolled around, I knew I should probably stop hiding and take care of a few things, even though I didn't really want to. Everyone would be up early and in town for the festival, so I was going to be on my own in the morning. And there were a couple of things I had to say to Amy before I left.

It wasn't hard to find her. She was leading a music class for aliens of all shapes and sizes, and I just followed the noise.

She was sitting on a rug in the middle of the third floor lounge with a guitar on her lap. Surrounding her was a circle of Tourists, all blowing or banging or plucking at a variety of thrift-store instruments.

Amy was trying to strum her guitar and conduct the action at the same time. "One-two-three-and-*now* you come in." She nodded at a black alien holding a battered trumpet. "No, I meant you, Mrs. Farkwell. One-two-three-and-*now* you start to—no, no, hold off on striking the triangle until the second part, Xeeneehardeen. I know you're excited." The musical instruments all bonged and popped and tooted at seemingly random intervals.

Maybe "harmony" and "rhythm" were earthly concepts, impossible for visitors from beyond the stars to grasp. It's the only thing that would have explained something sounding that bad.

Amy saw me watching from the hallway. She set her guitar on the floor. "All right, take five, everybody."

"Five what?" said one alien.

"Take them where?" said another.

"Just rest for a few minutes," Amy said. "I'll be back soon." She stood and motioned for me to join her in the alcove at the end of the hall.

"That's quite a band," I said. "Sounds like they're ready for a national tour of all the big arenas."

"Aren't they funny?" Amy said. "They mostly come from planets where instruments are rigged to be played by mind control. You know, like thought rays or something? Anyway, they get the biggest kick out of actually holding the instrument in their hands."

"All part of the roughing-it experience Grandma provides here at the B-and-B, huh?"

"Exactly," she said.

For a minute there it felt natural again. Comfortable inter-action that came easily, just like old times.

But then there was a lull in the conversation. Amy chewed on her lip and watched the floor. And I was reminded just how awkward and messed up everything was now.

"I never thanked you the other day," she finally said to the rug. "You know, taking the blame for the illegal language translator in that monitor."

I shrugged. "Not much point in both of us getting in trouble, right?"

"I guess."

More silence.

"Besides," I finally said, "I never apologized to you for taking it without asking."

She sighed. "I guess we've both done things the last couple of weeks that we're not too proud of."

"Yeah."

I studied the little patch of freckles across her nose. She got more of them when it was sunny out, like it had been this week. I loved that.

But something about the sight made it hit me for real this time: I was never going to see those freckles again.

"I'm leaving tomorrow."

"I know." Although her tone of voice was neutral, I thought I heard a little catch in her throat, a sign she might be at least a little bit sad to see me go. But maybe I just imagined it.

I decided to just get through what I had to tell her. Stick to the basics and keep it businesslike; I definitely did not want her to see me start crying, especially if it was going to be her last memory of me. "I need to ask you for a couple of favors before I leave. First, can you feed Snarffle for me? Until his rightful owner comes to pick him up, I mean?"

"Of course."

I gave her the rundown on how many times a day he had to be fed, and how much he needed. Her eyes got a little bigger at that. I don't think she realized what a chore it was to keep that little guy satisfied. I don't think anyone around here did. Then I got to the most important point.

I took a deep breath. "And I need you to keep an eye on Scratchull," I said. "I know you don't exactly trust me right now, but you really are the last line of defense when it comes to that guy."

"It's not that I don't trust you, David. You know that." Hard to believe when she wouldn't even look me in the eye, but whatever. "It's just . . . a lot of weird stuff happens around here, you know? It's so easy to take something the wrong way. I've done it myself a thousand times."

Yeah, I know that, Amy. You can spare me the lecture. Man, did anyone even remember that I worked here all last summer?

"Look," I said. I tried to keep my voice even—nothing good was going to come out of getting into a big fight right before I left. "Let's assume the whole thing's just in my imagination, okay? It still wouldn't hurt anything for you to keep an eye out for that guy. Or for any other alien that might try to mess things up around here. Would it?"

"You're right. I can do that." Amy nodded. "I *will* do that."

"Great. Thanks."

We had an Awkward Silence Contest then, and we both won. Or maybe lost.

Finally Amy gestured back to the lounge and her music students. "I should probably..."

"Yeah, me too," I said. "Time to feed Snarffle. Maybe take him for one last walk."

"Okay." Amy let out a long and shaky breath. "I'm really going to miss you, David. I'm sorry we didn't get very much time together, and I'm sorry things got so messed up, and... Well, I'm just sorry."

"Me, too."

We both sort of reached for each other at the same time. But it was as awkward as the silence had been. Felt like hugging my mom. And then it was over.

Amy wiped at her eyes. "Good-bye, David." She turned and hurried down the hall to the lounge.

Girls. No matter how many females I meet from however many millions of planets all over the universe, I swear I'll never understand them.

23

Back in my furniture-free room I found a sleeping bag laid out across a series of couch cushions with a note on top:

Dearest David,

I wish I had known sooner about your bedroom. Please tell me that you haven't been sleeping on the bare floor—I would lose my grandmother license over that one for sure! I hope the makeshift bed I set up will suffice.

I've missed you at mealtimes around the communal table. (Truth be told, I've missed you at every other time, as well, my dear. I deeply regret having to tend to all of these preparations for the festival, especially when things have gone so wonky around here.) Have you been getting enough to eat? You'll find a special dinner wrapped up in tinfoil in the refrigerator. I hid it in the vegetable drawer so there would be no chance that Tate would stumble across it. :)

Love and Blessings,
Grandma

I managed half a smile as I tucked the note in my pocket. At least she was trying. I was going to miss that about her.

Snarffle licked at my hand. He seemed to sense that something was wrong. For one thing, his appetite was down—he only had four sandwiches, two bags of chips, and a single gallon of ice cream for dinner. He was also pretty clingy; he followed so closely while I was gathering up my stuff that it was a constant struggle not to trip over him, and whenever I sat down he wanted to jump up on my lap and stay there.

"I'm going to miss you too, buddy." I scratched at the patch of bright blue polka dots on his back while his little tail twirled like crazy. "I wish I didn't have to go. But I do." It was still hard to say it out loud.

When I was all packed up we sat on the cushions, looking out at the nighttime sky. The rest of the house was quiet; the guests had gone to bed hours ago. "You know, even though I'll be three thousand miles away this time tomorrow, we'll still be looking up at the same stars. At least that's what my parents used to tell me when they went away on business trips, so I wouldn't get too lonely." Snarffle looked up at me with sad eyes and gave me a halfhearted lick. "I know. It never really worked when they said it, either."

I let my gaze drift over the sweep of stars overhead. I wondered what Ursa Major would look like from Snarffle's home planet. If he were seeing those stars from a totally different angle, they probably wouldn't resemble the big bear at all. I suppose his planet had their own constellations with their own matching stories. I suppose all planets did.

A flash of movement and light caught my eye. I leaned out the window and looked up. There. That little TV satellite dish thingy on the roof. The contraption I had seen Scratchull affix to it was coming to life. The silver handle rose up until it was pointing straight at the sky, and then the tip of it extended—an antenna?—until the whole thing doubled in size. Then a pattern of bright green dots shot up the length of it, like lights on an airport runway. They kept doing that, over and over.

"Stay right here, guy. I'll be back in just a minute. I promise." Snarffle whistle-whined at me shrilly. "It's okay. I'll bring you back a treat or two. And yes, I'll be careful." I scratched at his sweet spot some more until he calmed down.

I eased my door open and tiptoed down the hall. When I got to Scratchull's room I inched as close as I could and laid my ear against his door. I could hear Scratchull in there, talking to someone, but he was using the screechy, knife-against-glass language from his home planet. Without a translator I had no idea what he was saying, of course.

Then someone answered him. It was also in an alien tongue, but this was lower and more guttural. It sounded like the words were deep in somebody's stomach and had to be dredged up and retched out to carry on the conversation.

Who could be in there with him? It certainly didn't sound like any Tourist I had met around here recently.

The conversation went on, with Scratchull's voice getting louder and more insistent. And I noticed something different about the other alien's voice. Even though it was harsh, it sounded tinnier than Scratchull's, and maybe there was a slight echo to it, almost as if the person were standing in a tunnel rather than a bedroom. Or kind of like they were talking long-distance with a bad connection to—

That's it! The satellite thingy with the flashing lights—Scratchull had built some sort of interstellar phone! But who could he be talking to? It certainly wasn't Greenie, with his soft, underwater vowels. Maybe I could—

I half fell into Scratchull's room as the door was jerked open wide. The tall white alien towered over me and sneered, all of the hate that he had been hiding so well finally painted all over his face.

But then he composed himself and smiled politely. He was holding some sort of jury-rigged microphone, which must have been the receiver for his phone. He opened his mouth, and the high-pitched screech that came out felt like a cold dagger jammed in my ear. I winced and backed away several steps.

Scratchull's eyes went wide in mock surprise. "Oh, dear me. I must have forgotten. You can't speak my language, can you? I suppose that renders your favorite hobby quite meaningless." I just glared at him. "However, it's your last night here, so you might as well enjoy it. I am not familiar with this particular earthling custom, but if it brings you pleasure to stand out here and caress my bedroom door with your ear, then be my guest." He said a few more parting words in his squealy native tongue and then slammed the door in my face.

My next move came to me in an angry flash of inspiration. He wasn't the only one around here who could communicate with people from distant planets. I marched down to the sitting room and grabbed the paper and pen from beside the telephone.

Dear Commander Rezzlurr of the Intergalactic Police Force,

   We met a year ago on Earth when you came here on an emergency distress call. I work at the secret transporter location, an inn that caters to off-world guests.

   I wanted to alert you to a possible dangerous situation down here. There is a new employee at the Intergalactic Bed & Breakfast. He is going by the name "Scratchull," but that might be an alias. I have reason to believe he is a rogue scientist, banished from the Collective and forced to spend time on this planet. He hates all earthlings and is determined to escape from here, even if it means causing great harm to the planet.

   Please come right away. He has already brought powerful illegal technology to Earth, and I am afraid he will do much worse soon. He has fooled the humans who work here, so they will probably not be much help to you. But he needs to be arrested and taken off-planet for detainment and interrogation immediately.

Thank you,
David Elliott
Milky Way Galaxy
Earth
Latitude: 48.8 degrees north
Longitude: 121.9 degrees west
(Near the snowcapped mountain)

I reread the letter half a dozen times, making sure it sounded official, believable, and urgent. And not like a kid wrote it. Was it going to mean trouble for Grandma? Would Rezzlurr shut down the transporters, like last summer? I decided that I didn't care.

Well, okay, I cared about Grandma and her business, obviously. But I had to at least try to do everything I could to protect her. Along with everyone else in the whole world, I suppose. If Rezzlurr had to make things uncomfortable for her to do that ... well, she should have been a little more careful during the whole interview-and-checking-references thing. That might sound harsh, but I didn't really have any other choice.

I found directions for getting in touch with IPF headquarters—kind of an interstellar 9-1-1 call—in Grandma's storage closet, then used the transporter on the first floor to send the note along. If last summer was any indication, it would probably take Rezzlurr a month or so to show up, but at least I could leave with a conscience that was a little more clear.

Now, time to grab my dinner and some Snarffle snacks from the fridge, and then I would try to get a little sleep. I made my way down the dim hallway to the kitchen and heard someone thumping around in there. For a second I feared it was Scratchull, but then the heaviness of the footsteps registered somewhere in my brain, and I figured it was Tate, scrounging around for a midnight snack.

I definitely did not feel like having to talk to him, but before I could hide anywhere, the door swung open and Tate lumbered out into the hallway. His eyes were glazed over and his mouth hung open. He looked right over my head, no recognition on his face. Was he sleepwalking? Then he shuffled into a patch of moonlight, which made him look ghoulish and also illuminated the little crumbs stuck to his cheeks. Ugh—was he sleep*eating*? What a nasty habit.

The big man trudged straight toward me. When he got close I expected him to stop, or at least angle sideways to get past, but he looked determined to plow right into me. I held up a hand to stop him, but his slippered feet pounded the floorboards, and he hit me belly-first, driving me backward.

"Whoa. Stop it."

Tate immediately halted, body and limbs frozen in place. His eyes were still glassy, but his head shifted, and they were at least aimed in the general direction of my face. "UNNNHHHH," he said. His mouth remained gaping even after he was done making noise.

"Wow, you're really out of it," I said. I waved a hand in front of his face, and he didn't flinch. I don't even think he blinked. "UNNNAGGHHGHNN," he added.

It gave me the shivers. He looked like a lost extra from a

zombie movie. I suddenly became a little worried about the potential tastiness of my brain.

I stepped aside and pressed myself against the wall, giving him plenty of room to maneuver by me. He didn't take the cue—just stood there. "Why don't you go back to bed?" I said.

Tate immediately lurched into action and staggered past me and up the stairs. But he had something to share with me in parting: "AAARRRGHGHNNGH."

"Thank you, I'll remember that," I said to the darkness. I desperately tried to see the humor in the situation—a sleep-walking zombie-Tate should have been pretty funny, after all —but I just ended up feeling severely creeped out. I grabbed an armload of food and rushed back up to my room.

Snarffle was staring longingly at my pile of laundry, a trickle of slobber trailing from the corner of his mouth, when I stepped through the door. "Sorry it took me so long, fella. Thanks for sticking to your no-clothes diet."

Snarffle vacuumed up all of the food and then sniffed at my hands for more. "All out, guy. But don't worry, Amy will bring you more food tomorrow." I patted his head and he nuzzled up next to me. "She'll be a sucker for that hungry puppy look of yours. Just give her that big-eyed gaze and twirl your tail a little bit, and she'll give you anything you want."

He whistled in agreement and nestled in closer. Soon he was asleep, and there was no one left to confide in. I closed my eyes and tried to join him, but for a long time all I could hear was the unnerving sound of Tate's tortured air-gargling as it echoed through my mind.

When I woke up the next morning, Snarffle was still whistle-snoring heavily, a warm bundle on my lap. I eased myself out from underneath and laid his beach ball body on the ground as gently as possible. He stirred restlessly until I gave him a final scratch and he settled back into sleep. Good. I hate sad good-byes.

I checked the time. Under an hour until my taxi was supposed to pick me up. I showered, threw my clothes into a battered suitcase from Grandma's basement, and went downstairs.

The house was empty. The contrast between this silence and the frenzied getting-ready activities of the last few days was eerie. My footsteps sounded too loud as I walked along the deserted hallways.

I thought maybe I was going to slip away completely undetected when I saw Grandma on the couch in the sitting room by the front door. She looked so tiny, sitting all alone in that big empty room with her hands folded neatly in her lap.

"Busy morning," I said.

"I think the Tourists must have just gone home early so they wouldn't have to listen to Tate hounding them to stay out of sight." She tried to give me a smile, but it was a small, sad one. "He doesn't know quite what to do with himself. This is the first Pioneer Day Festival when he hasn't been the sheriff, you know. Used to be one of his busiest days of the year, directing traffic all day and helping kidlets who had been separated from their parents." She sighed and looked out the window. "I think he misses it sometimes."

"Where is he now?"

A batch of worry lines bunched up around Grandma's eyes. "Well, he slept in past six a.m. today, which is very unlike him. Didn't get up until almost eight. And he was pretty groggy for a spell."

I thought of him lurching around in the dark, sleepwalking up and down the stairs in the middle of the night. No wonder he was so tired this morning.

"I was a bit worried, but two cups of my special coffee perked him right up and then he went into town. Probably to direct traffic and help the lost kidlets." She smiled again and it looked a little more genuine this time. "I do hope you can forgive him his gruffness over the last few days. He's been pretty fidgety with all of the activity around here."

I nodded. "Amy?"

"I haven't seen her at all this morning. She probably went into town to make sure everything with our little booth is just so. You know how she is, that little overachiever. A real sweetie, but very determined." The look on my face must have shown what I was feeling, because Grandma added, "Don't be too hard on her, David. Having you leave like this is tearing her up inside. She probably didn't want to get all upset right before she had to face the hungry masses of Forest Grove."

"It's no problem," I lied. "We said good-bye last night. Sort of."

Grandma patted the couch cushion next to her and then opened up her arms. I dropped the suitcase and went to her. I let her hug me for sort of a long time.

When I finally trusted myself to talk without, you know, getting all emotional or whatever, I said, "Shouldn't you be down there with them? The festival starts pretty soon, doesn't it?"

"In a few minutes, yes. But I had to stay and say good-bye properly." She squeezed me around the shoulders again. "I feel just awful about all of this, David. I haven't slept in three nights for mulling it over, and I still don't know if we're doing the right thing."

"It's okay," I said. It was another lie, of course, but I knew she was only doing what she thought was best. It's not like she was trying to be mean or anything. I don't think she was even capable of having a negative thought . . . but then again, that was probably the root of the problem when it came to seeing Scratchull for what he really was. "You've been running this business and keeping it a secret for a long time. I get that you're trying to protect all of that. I really do."

"Oh, David. Why must you be so understanding and good-natured? It only makes it harder to say good-bye." She took off her big pink glasses and dabbed at her eyes. "I remember your father getting on an airplane to go off to college in Florida. Seemed like he wasn't much older than you are right now." She sighed shakily. "I didn't see him again for ten years. I don't want that to happen to us, David."

"It won't." I genuinely hoped I wasn't lying this time. I had to cling to the belief that Commander Rezzlurr would get here before Scratchull had time to cause any more trouble. If the white alien was taken out of the picture, and if Grandma could ever forgive me for tipping off the police, then maybe I could come back. Now that I was about to walk out the door, I realized how desperate I was to return someday.

Grandma hugged me again. And I hugged her back. Finally I pulled away and said, "You should probably get into town for your first customers, huh? You might not be eligible for that big blue ribbon if you're not actually at your booth." My taxi was going to be here soon, anyway. Besides, it was just going to be torture for both of us to drag out this good-bye any longer.

"I suppose so." Grandma used a hankie to blow her nose, then readjusted her eyeglasses and smoothed down her hair. "But first, here's a little something for the road." From the coffee table she picked up a paper plate piled high with baked treats, and handed it to me.

"Thanks," I said. "How'd they turn out?"

"Honestly? I don't even know. Scratchull helped me with the baking on one condition: he said that nobody could sample the goods until the day of the festival. Promised it would be the baking masterpiece of my lifetime, and he wanted everybody—including me—to be surprised. I know he's not your favorite alien, but you must admit he has a flair for the dramatic."

There were so many things I could say to that, but I swallowed them all. "Well, it's the day of the festival. You can try one now."

Her small, sad smile came back. "I'm afraid I don't have much of an appetite at the moment." I could relate. "But you could probably ask Tate about how they taste." Grandma rolled her eyes. "If I know him, I'm sure he has snuck a few here and there."

An image of the sleepwalking security man with crumbs all over his cheeks came to me. At first I almost laughed out loud, but then that sense of unsettling creepiness came flooding back, and I just wanted to get out of there.

"Thanks," I said again, trying to figure out how I was going to carry the plate and my luggage at the same time.

"You're most welcome, David. And I do hope I see you soon." We walked out the front door together. "All of this will blow over sooner rather than later, you'll see," Grandma said as we descended the porch steps. "In fact, maybe you could come back during your Christmas vacation. And your parents could come with you. Oh, that would be wonderful."

"Sure, Grandma." But I knew she was just playing the eternal optimist. I doubted I would be able to come back so soon, and I doubted even more that my parents would come with me. Especially Mom. Someone who scheduled her life in five-minute increments in a daily planner and watched C-SPAN for entertainment was probably not ready to believe in aliens, much less kick off her shoes and hang out with a group of them on vacation.

Grandma took one long, last look at me, then kissed my forehead before she hurried down the road toward town.

I just stood there, all alone. Was there actually a time when I had daydreamed about moving out here after I graduated high school and making this my career instead of just a summer job?

I turned away from the Intergalactic Bed & Breakfast and stared down the empty road. Time for a new life plan. Now that I was outside and about to leave, I could feel it: I was never going to see this place again.

Half an hour later, I watched Grandma's place fade into the distance through the back window of the taxi. I tried to recall the shock of seeing it for the first time last summer, but it was impossible. The memories of the good times I had spent within those walls, and the great friends I had made there, smoothed out the wackiness of the exterior. It just looked like a normal house to me now. Like a home.

But that thought hurt too much. I pushed it out of my mind and turned back around to face the windshield.

"Nice day for the festival they got going on in town," the

taxi driver said. He was built like a fire hydrant, short and squat, with a bushy black beard.

"Yeah, it is," I mumbled. I hadn't really noticed the blue sky and warm temperature until he mentioned it.

"Guess you're missing out, though, huh?"

"Time to get out of town."

"Got that right. You and me both, kid."

The taxi was rolling through the residential streets that led into Forest Grove's downtown section when I saw something strange. "Hey, pull over for a second, okay?"

The driver shrugged. "It's your dime."

We pulled up to the curb and I rolled down my window. Greg, Eddie, and Brian—these three high school guys I had met last summer—were down on all fours in the middle of a vacant lot. They crawled all over the grass like they were playing some bizarre teenage version of I'm a Little Horsey.

I watched them for a minute. All three were so focused on their task that they didn't even notice the taxi. "Got another one!" Eddie shouted. He stood, raced over to a plastic container, and dropped something into it. Then he got back down on all fours and crawled around again.

"What are you guys doing?" I called. All three heads snapped up. Eddie and Brian looked confused at first, then sort of glared at me, and finally went back to their lawn-scrounging, but Greg stood and walked over.

"Hey. Scrub, right?"

"Yeah. Or David, actually. Whatever. And you're Greg?"

"Right. I didn't even know you were back in town. We haven't seen you at the park or anywhere."

"Yeah. Been pretty busy at Grandma's place. But I'm on my way to the airport right now. Just a short trip this time."

"Look us up next time you're around, okay? We still need to have a hoops rematch." Greg jerked his thumb at the lawn. "I think Eddie's had enough time to cool down after the last one."

"Sounds good." I thought of what Mr. Harnox, one of Grandma's guests, had done to the guys in that ball game, and half smiled at the memory. I had been so worried about it then, but after the events of the last week, it seemed pretty tame.

"Well, I should probably get back to work," Greg said.

"What's going on?"

"Oh, I thought maybe you knew. It kind of has to do with your grandma's place."

"Really?"

"Yeah. You know that new guy who works there? The albino-looking dude?"

I nodded. I hoped my face still looked calm, because inside I was suddenly all twisted up and jittery again.

"He said he'd give us ten dollars for every slug we found. Isn't that crazy?"

"That *is* crazy." *Especially if you knew what he was planning on doing with them.*

"I know. We just have to bring them in alive, and make sure to deliver them by ten o'clock. He wants us in town in time for the judging of the baking contest. We're supposed to vote for your grandma." Greg checked his watch. "Anyway, that only gives us fifteen more minutes." He turned back to the lawn.

"Wait a minute. How long have you guys been doing this for him?"

"Just today. He said it was a onetime thing. But ten bucks! For *each* slug! I mean, can you believe that?"

I exhaled and the anxiety drained away. It wasn't world domination this time, only Scratchull's warped taste buds.

"A ten-spot each, huh? You could probably make some serious money around here."

"Totally. We started early and we're up to four hundred bucks. Apiece. Now maybe my mom will stop nagging me about finding a job this summer."

"Look at this one!" Brian called. "Biggest catch of the day." He held up a fat green slug, its slimy body glistening in the sunlight.

"Nice. Might be a twenty-dollar special," Eddie said.

"You think?"

I waved at Greg. "All right. Well, good luck."

He gave me a thumbs-up and returned to crouching over the grass. The taxi pulled away. When I remembered Scratchull biting into those slimy things, my stomach clenched up and I had to fight the gag reflex. It looked like he was going to have a big new batch, probably for a celebratory meal, now that he had gotten rid of me.

The taxi slowed as it approached downtown. The main road was blocked off for the festival, and the driver had to take a detour down narrow side streets that were choked with parked cars and a steady stream of pedestrians. I got glimpses of downtown through the cracks between the buildings, though.

There was a big banner stretched across Main Street

proclaiming this to be the Super-Centennial version of Pioneer Day. The people working the carnival-style game booths and the food stands were dressed in Northwest pioneer outfits; the men in flannel-and-denim lumberjack garb or rugged "mountain man" pelt coats with coonskin caps, the women in plain cotton dresses and bonnets.

The taxi stopped when the town's only stoplight glowed red, and suddenly I had a clear view of Grandma's booth. Banquet-style tables had been set up in front and were piled high with baked treats. They were the same as those on the paper plate beside me: sugar-dusted scones dotted with purple Kerntaberries, with a yellow jelly center made out of the alien fruit that Greenie had brought in those crates. Mooglah fruit, I think he called them.

Grandma's head just barely poked up above the mountain of baked goodies. Scratchull stood out front like a circus barker, waving people over and shouting. A big crowd had formed around the booth, with more folks funneling over as I watched.

I scanned the mob for Amy but couldn't find her. Then the light turned green and we rolled out of town.

The ride down the mountain and back to civilization is usually great for looking out the window. Every break in the trees offered panoramic views of the snowcapped mountain peaks of the Cascade Range, while the sunlight made the white water of the river sparkle. Sometimes the side of the road abruptly gave way to a plunging cliff, and it felt like being in a flying car.

But I didn't notice any of that this time. I don't really know how to describe it, but I just didn't feel right. I mean, I knew I wouldn't exactly be feeling *good* today. I expected the anger at Scratchull, of course, and obviously sadness about having to leave the B&B. But underneath that was something else. I figured I would feel at least a little relieved to be moving on from a situation that had gotten pretty bad, but there was none of that.

I closed my eyes and tried to let the twists and turns of the mountain road lull me to sleep. It wasn't working. I had an itch somewhere in my brain that I just couldn't scratch, kind of like when you have something right on the tip of your tongue but can't quite remember it. Only I had no idea what I was trying to remember in the first place.

What was it? Maybe I was unsettled because that skull-faced jerk was my last image of Forest Grove. Seeing Scratchull under any circumstance was disturbing, of course. The way he felt about humans, there was no reason for him to be in town at all, and it was especially out of character for him to be hamming it up at Grandma's baking booth. But he was probably just doing it to suck up to her, as usual.

I pressed the heels of my palms into my eyes, took a deep breath, and let it out in a long, slow exhale. I just wanted to forget all about this stuff. That was the only way I'd be able to get out of this funk when I got back to Florida and maybe salvage the rest of the summer. And the rest of my life, I suppose. But some annoying little part of my brain wouldn't let me.

So why is he sucking up to her this time? it asked. *Why would he even want to help out with the festival, anyway? You've learned the hard way that he has a reason—a plan—for everything. He's selfish and cruel, and he only does things to help himself. So how, exactly, is he helping himself at the festival today?*

I don't know! I almost yelled it at myself. Thankfully I kept it inside, though, because that would have freaked the driver out. He definitely needed all of his concentration to keep us alive on this road with all of its snaky switchbacks.

Wait . . . maybe Scratchull pureed his sickening little snacks in a blender and snuck some slug shake into Grandma's recipe. Nasty. I looked down at the treats beside me in disgust and almost threw them out the window . . . but with my luck this summer, I'd probably get arrested for littering.

Anyway, that must have been what was gnawing at the corner of my brain: tainted treats. Scratchull would have a big laugh at the expense of all those hungry humans on their special day of celebration. And he had used up all the slugs in his aquarium for the scones, and now he needed a fresh supply for his personal enjoyment. So now he was at the festival booth for the chance to see the looks on all of those human faces when they took a big bite of slug surprise. Case closed.

I leaned back against the headrest and closed my eyes again. But that nagging sense of something being not quite right wouldn't leave me alone. As much as he didn't like humans, Scratchull would consider a practical joke like that as beneath him, wouldn't he? And besides, he seemed to genuinely love the taste of slugs—he told Greenie that earthlings were "wasting their greatest delicacy" or something like that —so feeding them to the humans wouldn't seem gross at all to him. In fact, he would probably see it as a gift wasted on the unworthy.

Revulsion sucked me into the land of sense memory, and suddenly I was back in the closet, crouching painfully and peeking through the slit in the door as Scratchull shared his slimy snacks with Greenie. He had slurped a stray slug off of his chin like the last spaghetti noodle, and then looked at Greenie and said, *When I finally leave this planet, these delicious creatures will be the only things worth taking with me.*

My eyes flew open. That really must be it! Scratchull was leaving. He had a backup plan. Of course he had a backup plan. And if he was having the teens gather up the slugs this morning—*a onetime thing,* Greg had said—then whatever he was going to do, he was going to do it soon.

That lingering sense of unease disappeared but was instantly replaced with an overwhelming sense of dread. He had to be stopped.

But what could I do? I considered telling the taxi driver to turn around and drive back to Forest Grove, but only for a second or two. What would I be able to accomplish back there? I didn't exactly have the best track record when it came to stopping Scratchull. I just made things worse. Grandma, Tate, and Amy were tired of hearing about my suspicions. And Scratchull would just find a way to make me look like a fool again.

The farther down the mountain we raced, the more my dread turned into panic. Panic quickly morphed into desperation. And desperation forced the unthinkable to pop into my head.

What if I called the police? The human police, that is. Told them the whole story. The alien guests, the transporters, Scratchull's plan for destroying the world. Everything.

Pro: They might actually do something to stop him. If I could get somebody to believe me, they could send in a S.W.A.T. team, the National Guard, a secret army of ninjas, whatever and whoever. Scratchull might be brilliant and powerful, but I doubted he was invincible. And he would have lost the element of surprise. Team Humanity would at least have a chance.

Con: Grandma loses her business. Tate makes hunting David down his life's mission. Amy hates David forever. David spends a lifetime of friendlessness and regret.

I took my cell phone out of my pocket and stared at it. Sure, my life might be lonely if I made the call . . . but at least I would have a life. And so would everyone else on this planet. I'd rather have those three hate me and be alive than love me and . . . you know, not be alive.

I pressed the power button. The status bars flickered and faded. No phone service.

Crud. I clutched the cell phone in both hands, my knee bobbing up and down with fidgety energy. I didn't want to lose my nerve. I forced myself to look out the window as long as I could stand, and then I checked the cell phone again. One bar lit up. Not enough.

"Beautiful country up here, huh, kid?" My body jerked in surprise. I had been so deep in my own world that I had forgotten all about the driver.

"Oh. Yeah."

"We don't get many calls up this way. It's nice for a change, you know?"

I checked the phone again. All the service bars were lit up now. My heart instantly went crazy. There's no way I could make that call. What was I thinking?

On the other hand, if I didn't ...

And back and forth I went. The next several minutes of driving in and out of the shadow of Mount Baker were brutal. Every time I made up my mind to call, the taxi would drive out of cell phone range. And every time the bars lit up, I lost my nerve.

Finally I decided to take my brain out of the decision entirely. With the bars dead I dialed 9-1-1 and then put my thumb on top of the send button. As soon as the bars lit up again I would simply push down.

Waiting ... waiting ... one bar lit up ... then two more ... pretty soon four of the five would be in range ... that would be enough. ...

"Hey, kid. This is kind of a long drive, isn't it?"

"Huh? Oh, yeah." Down to two bars again.

"Well, I was just wondering ... are you, um, planning on eating all of those goodies you got back there?"

The third bar lit up. Almost there.

"Because I can't help but notice they smell pretty good," he said. "Must be fresh."

Two bars disappeared. Down to one. *Crap!*

"So, like I said, I was wondering ..." The lone bar flickered. "If you're not going to eat all of those, maybe I could try a bite? You know, one for the road?"

"Huh? Oh, sure." I kept my eyes fixed on the phone but handed the plate of treats over the backseat. "Have as many as you want." I wondered fleetingly if I was right about Scratchull saving all those slugs for himself, but mostly I was focused on the phone.

"Thanks, kid. Forgot my lunch today, you know how it is."

"Uh-huh."

We rounded a corner, the trees parted, and sunlight streamed in through the windshield. Suddenly all five status bars lit up. I automatically mashed my thumb down on the button.

It rang once. I had just enough time to realize I had no idea whether I wanted to go through with this—I had spent so much time trying to keep Grandma's secret that my whole brain cramped up in protest at actually giving it up—before someone answered.

"Nine-one-one. What's your emergency?"

"Um..." Good question. They probably didn't have a police shorthand code for Unspecified Alien Attack.

Slight pause. "Yes? How may I help you?"

Oh, man. Was I really going to do this? I put my thumb on the End button. But I didn't push it.

"Sir?"

"Yeah, I'm here."

I couldn't let Scratchull do anything disastrous. I just couldn't. One deep breath, and then forge ahead. "I need to talk to somebody about...a secret." Now that I was actually doing this, how could I put it into words?

"Yes? Go ahead, sir."

"It's a secret that could turn into an emergency pretty quick if we don't—"

"UNNNNGGHHARGHH."

The driver turned to look at me, but I'm not sure if his glassed-over eyes even recognized what he was seeing. There was no spark of intelligence behind them at all. His mouth hung open, and crumbs from Grandma's treats were stuck all over his beard. I dropped the phone.

The taxi was hurtling down the mountain at over sixty miles an hour. Driven by a zombie.

And he wasn't even looking at the road.

26

"Turn around!" I shouted.

Zombie driver obediently faced the windshield, but that didn't do much to improve his driving. The road was curvy, and with his arms locked onto the steering wheel in an unwavering death grip, the taxi moved in a straight line, the yellow center stripe weaving from one side of the car to the other.

When we drifted into the left lane we scraped up against the guardrail, its thin band of metal the only thing between us and a sheer cliff that plunged a thousand feet straight down. When we swerved back into the right lane we were in danger of smashing into the craggy wall of the mountain. Back and forth we went. It was lucky we were the only car in sight—usually there were huge semis on this road, hauling tree trunks down the mountain.

We came up on a bend in the road. "Turn right!"

The driver swung his head and shoulders to the right so that he was staring out the passenger side window. "UHHGNGHHNNN!"

"No, the steering wheel! Turn the steering wheel to the right!"

His arms jerked stiffly at the wheel. The taxi lurched into the right lane and kept going, over the white line and onto the narrow shoulder between road and mountain. The edge of the bumper clipped a bit of jutting rock, and the impact rattled my teeth painfully. The taxi scraped by and continued tearing down the mountain.

But coming up was a series of sharp S-curves. There was no chance of our making it if I kept steering this thing by remote control. Mr. Night-of-the-NASCAR-Undead was not exactly a finely tuned instrument.

I leaned my torso over the seat and grabbed the steering wheel over the driver's shoulders, but it was locked in place.

"Let go!" I shouted. His arms shot straight up in the air. I could steer now, but I couldn't actually see much.

I caught a glimpse of the guardrail rushing up to meet us, and yanked the wheel to the right. The paper plate slid off the seat and the zombie treats scattered all over the floor. The driver turned his head to tell me something very important— "HAGGNNGHGH!"—and I could feel his hot breath on my face. I lunged forward to get a better view of the road and nearly smashed us into the rocky side of the mountain.

Finally, the right thing to say came to me in a blinding flash of the obvious.

"Stop the car!"

"UNH?"

"The brake. Stomp your foot on the brake!"

The engine revved and the car shot forward, the speedometer needle shooting up to 90 mph. Trees and rocks rushed by in a muddled blur. The whole car started to shake.

"No, the other pedal! Step on the other pedal!"

Eeeeeerrrrrchh! The taxi skidded to a halt, its side resting squarely against the guardrail. The wooden posts creaked, and the metal siding groaned under the weight of the car.

I chanced a look out the driver's side window. A hundred feet below us was a bird. Another several hundred feet below the bird was a jumble of rocks. They looked...hard. I sort of forgot how to breathe for a few moments.

The car's engine hummed steadily, still very much alive. I had to be extremely careful about what I said next—if the driver took his foot off the brake he would send the car crashing right through the guardrail.

"Don't. Move."

The zombie driver's body and limbs obediently remained stiff. A drop of sweat dribbled down my forehead and stung my eye.

How was I going to talk him through this? He wasn't exactly the best student, and I wouldn't be taking Driver's Ed for another few years.

But then another idea—one that should have been obvious —kicked me in the head. I pushed with my legs and extended farther into the front seat. I jerked the emergency brake all the way up. Then I lunged forward, grabbed the keys hanging from the ignition, and turned off the car.

The engine noise died, along with the possibility of death by flying taxi.

But the dread remained. I had to get back to Forest Grove, fast. If everyone in town tried one of those treats, then what was Scratchull planning to . . . ?

No time to finish that thought now. The first thing to worry about was getting back to town. Walking would take forever. And I couldn't just leave the driver and this taxi sitting here on a curve in the road. Somebody whipping around the corner would smash right into it.

Right. I'd have to drive back by myself. Which meant I had to get in the driver's seat.

The driver couldn't get out of his door—it was pinned against the guardrail. So I had to get creative.

I climbed over into the passenger's seat. "Okay, you're going to have to sit still for a minute."

And then—*eeewwww*—I had to push myself up and across until I was more or less sitting on his lap. My legs had to go under the steering wheel, which pinned me against the driver.

"HHHNNNUGH!"

"I know, I know. Trust me, I don't like this any more than you do."

I lifted myself off him as much as possible, my head jammed up against the roof of the car.

"Slide over. Quick."

"UNNHH." The zombie driver wedged himself up against his door. A distant part of his foggy brain got frustrated when he couldn't go any further, and he started banging away at it. I swear I could feel the center of gravity shift and the taxi tilt in that direction, grinding against the metal guardrail.

"No! Stop! Other direction! Slide to your right! This way!"

I reached around and grabbed his jacket and tugged him toward the passenger's seat. He finally figured it out and lurched over. I plopped down behind the steering wheel, the edge of the cliff just a foot away. My whole body shook. I remembered about the importance of breathing, just before I would've passed out. I sucked air in ragged gasps.

After all of that, getting the car up the mountain again was actually pretty easy. It was just like video games—fire up the ignition, press on the right pedal, and use the steering wheel. I didn't like being too close to the edge of that cliff, though, so I straddled the center line the whole time and prayed another car wouldn't come barreling down at me. I was thankful that the road was so quiet...until I realized what that must have meant: people in Forest Grove were in no shape to drive.

27

I had just enough brain cells still working to realize I probably shouldn't go racing down Main Street in a bright yellow taxi. If Scratchull was indeed unleashing his new plan at the festival, then my approach needed to be a little stealthier.

I hit the brakes too hard and brought the car to a skidding stop behind the sign that read WELCOME TO FOREST GROVE: YOUR OASIS IN THE WILDERNESS at the outskirts of town.

The driver directed his vacant gaze in my general direction. "AAAAGHGHNN."

"Thanks for asking, but I actually have no idea what I'm going to do. Any suggestions?"

"UNNNGHGHNN."

"Sounds good."

I stepped out of the taxi and shut the door. Then I turned and looked back through the window.

Hmmm. What to do with this guy?

"Stay."

The driver remained planted in his seat but continued to stare at me. What if he saw something that caught his interest and wandered out of the taxi?

I remembered Tate staggering to bed after his little zombie episode. Grandma said he had slept in and been groggy but normal in the morning. Well, normal for Tate, anyway.

"Lie down."

The zombie driver tipped over and spread out on the seat as if he'd been waiting for the invitation all along.

"Now, go to sleep." Within a minute his breathing became deep and rhythmic. "Good zombie."

I set off for downtown, approaching the festival area carefully. I jogged in a half crouch behind parked cars and tried to keep buildings between me and the town common. The element of surprise was the only weapon in my pathetic arsenal at the moment.

I heard it before I actually saw anything: hundreds of Forest Grove's finest doing the ol' zombie air-gargle in unison. It sounded like the whole town had an urgent complaint about a very important matter but had forgotten how to use actual words. Extremely creepy.

I dashed over to the brick city hall building and peeked around the corner.

It looked like a scene from a horror movie, with hundreds

of mindless zombies roaming around the open common area with their mouths gaping open.

But this was way worse, because horror movies don't really try to look real. You never see the little-girl zombie holding a helium balloon on a string. Or the old-woman zombie in a pioneer costume, dragging a purse. Or the guy-in-a-wheelchair zombie spilling ice cream all over himself. But all of these—and more, so many more—were on display before me.

And in movies, you never sense the real person trapped behind the listless zombie mask. In this case, innocent folks who had only been trying to enjoy a sunny day at a small-town festival.

And okay, so maybe I've made better friends with the aliens at Grandma's place than with the humans in town, but it still killed something inside me to see all these people like this. Time to move.

I had no plan—it's kind of hard to make a plan when you have no idea what's happening—but I at least had a first step. I had to get over to Grandma's booth to see whether she was a zombie, too, or if she was being held hostage or something. And after that, of course, I would have to face Scratchull.

Yikes. Best just to think about step one right now.

I was working my way through the crowd when a sound cut through the static of incoherent zombie babble.

"David!"

I wheeled around and saw nothing but the shuffling masses.

"Over here!"

I whipped my head around and stumbled in the direction of the voice. There! Under the wooden steps of the bandstand. A glimpse of a face and a waving hand.

I sprinted over and crouched down to get a look.

"Quick, get under here. You have to get out of sight!"

I scrambled underneath the stairs, where it was dim and cool. All of a sudden I was being grabbed and pulled by several hands. Fierce whispers in my ear: "David, thank the Creator you're all right!" and "You came back! I knew you'd come back!"

I untangled myself and pulled back for a better look. Grandma and Amy were gazing back at me, as hunched over as I was. Their eyes were wide, and deep worry lines creased their faces.

"Oh, David," Grandma said. "I'm so sorry I didn't listen to you."

Amy nodded vigorously. "We both are."

I followed their lead and whispered, "What's happening?"

"The festival is not going well this year."

"Yeah, I guessed that much. But what happened?"

"Scratchull got the whole crowd gathered around my booth to kick off the judging for the silly baking contest," Grandma said. "Passed out a scone to every man, woman, and child. Told them to hold off on eating until he could deliver a proper opening address to start the day's festivities." Grandma shook her head and sighed. "Of course, everyone listened even though we've never had an opening address. Not once in a hundred years. Anyway, he let loose with a lot of fancified speech—you know how he is—and then lifted a scone high in the air and proclaimed the Centennial Pioneer Day to be officially in session. Two minutes later we had this." She gestured to the crowd of zombies stumbling past the bandstand.

"But you didn't eat any?"

"Saying good-bye to you left me without much of an appetite, and thank goodness for that. As soon as I saw what was happening, I realized you had been right about him all along, of course. I ran away and hid here. I've been trying to think of what to do ever since." Grandma took off her glasses and wiped at her eyes. "I still can't believe anyone from off-world could do something like this."

"So you don't know what he's planning?"

Grandma shook her head.

I turned to Amy. "You didn't eat one, either?"

"No, I wasn't even down here yet. After we said good-bye last night I just couldn't sleep at all. I was in bed, staring at the ceiling, when I remembered something that teenage alien guest had told me about the translator. You know, the one who helped me rig up the baby monitor?"

"Yeah?"

"Remember how I didn't want us to say anything incriminating around that thing? That was because he said that it not only translates, but it records as well. Stores up the audio file for playback."

"Really? Then that means you could—"

"Go back and listen to the conversation you overheard. Exactly. I stayed up until three in the morning but couldn't figure out how to make it work. I slept in way later than normal, and even though I knew I'd be late to the festival, I tried again this morning. And I finally got it to play."

"So you heard?"

"Everything." Amy reached into her pocket and pulled out the baby monitor.

"Where did you find that, anyway? Didn't Scratchull have it?"

"He just left it lying around in the sitting room after our meeting in there. He doesn't need a translator, of course, so I think he just sort of forgot about it."

I shook my head. "He doesn't forget anything. He just thinks so little of humans that he didn't even consider the possibility that anyone would be able to figure out how to use it. He didn't see you as any kind of a threat to him at all."

Amy's eyes went dark. "Last time he makes that mistake."

She fiddled with a few knobs and then pressed a button. Suddenly the voices of Scratchull and his nervous green assistant filled up the crawl space underneath the bandstand steps.

"*It is very simple. I want to escape from this planet first, and* then *annihilate it, you graxx-for-brains.*"

"*Yes, yes, of course . . . but . . . I thought you said . . .*"

"*Pay attention!*" I heard a *splat!* and pictured blobs from Greenie's head splattering around the guest room. "*My first priority remains getting off this forgotten space island.*"

Grandma's eyes went wide, and she put her hand over her open mouth. Amy turned off the monitor. "I ran down here to warn Dad and your grandma, but I was too late, obviously. Oh, David, you were right, and I can't believe I didn't trust you more. I am so, so sorry."

"No time for apologies. Speaking of your dad, where is he?"

Grandma scoffed. "Are you kidding? He had a scone in each hand. Could hardly wait for Scratchull to finish making his speech so he could be the first one to dig in."

"So he's out there somewhere?" I gestured toward the shuffling crowd.

"I'm afraid so."

Amy smacked her fist into her palm. "If I had just twenty-four hours and some decent lab equipment, I bet I could come up with an antidote for those stupid zombie scones." Her eyes narrowed to slits as she stared out at the shuffling mob. "Or at least a poison deadly enough to take care of that traitorous jerk."

"I don't think we're going to get twenty-four hours." I rubbed at my temples. "Just give me a minute to think."

Okay, keep it simple and start with what I know. One: Scratchull wants to get off the planet. Badly. Two: I ruined his first plan. Three: He must have made another plan . . . but what did that have to do with temporarily turning everyone in Forest Grove into a zombie? Sure, the town was isolated, but he must know that sooner or later the outside world would find out that—

"PEOPLE OF EARTH." Scratchull's voice boomed out over the crowd noise. It had that electronic echo that comes from using a bullhorn. "STOP WHERE YOU ARE."

The zombies lurched to a halt.

"VERY GOOD. NOW STOP MAKING THAT INFERNAL RACKET." No change in the volume of the group air-gargling. "I MEANT *SHUT UP!*"

The hideous chorus stopped as if a switch had been thrown. The sudden silence was intensely eerie. To make it worse, somehow, a few birds started chirping, as if this were an ordinary summer day.

"YES. THAT'S MUCH BETTER," Scratchull said through the bullhorn.

"I'm going to see what he's doing," I whispered.

"We're coming with you."

"No, it's too dangerous," I said.

I crept out from under the stairs. Amy and Grandma ignored my warning and followed right behind me. We crawled up the steps onto the elevated platform of the bandstand. Crouching below the level of the banister, we watched the town common through the narrow slits between wooden slats.

"There he is," said Amy.

I followed her pointing finger. Scratchull was standing on the ledge of a fountain on the outskirts of the open common area.

He spoke deliberately, enunciating each word with care. "WHEN I SAY 'GO' YOU WILL MOVE IN A SLOW AND ORDERLY FASHION TOWARD THE SOUND OF MY VOICE." The heads of hundreds of zombies turned in unison and faced more or less in Scratchull's direction. "GOOD. I DARESAY YOU FEEBLEMINDED CREATURES MIGHT ACTUALLY BE ABLE TO PULL THIS OFF. ARE YOU ALL READY?"

A multitude of gargling groans were directed his way in unison.

"EXCELLENT. *GO!*"

The crowd lurched as one toward the fountain.

"Come on!" I said. "It's our only chance of getting close to him undetected."

"What are we going to do then?" Amy said.

"One thing at a time," I said. "We'll figure it out when we get there."

Amy hesitated. Grandma looked at her. "I'm through with not trusting David."

"Good point," Amy said.

We ran down the bandstand steps and waded into the crowd. "Walk like they do in case he looks over here." We let our mouths hang open as we lurched and shuffled along with the mob, but at a faster clip, getting nearer and nearer to the white alien.

The first zombie to reach the fountain was a big man in blue overalls and a John Deere cap. Scratchull reached down and palmed the man's head like it was a basketball. The zombie stopped in his tracks.

"LINE UP BEHIND THIS PERSON HERE, AND THEN STOP MOVING." The zombies bunched up near the fountain. "SINGLE FILE, EARTHLINGS. THERE IS NO NEED TO CROWD TOGETHER. I ASSURE YOU, THERE WILL BE PLENTY OF ROOM FOR EVERYONE WHERE YOU ARE HEADED."

There was still some stiff-bodied jostling here and there, but the mindless drones eventually aligned themselves into a loose single-file formation. The Forest Grove undead were nothing if not obedient. Soon the line stretched out of the common and all the way down a side street. Every person in town must have been in that line.

"This way," I whispered. We staggered zombie-style toward the line, then broke off and scurried to a hiding spot behind a cluster of picnic tables near the fountain. I saw a suitcase and an aquarium full of slugs propped up on the ledge of the fountain near the white alien.

Scratchull pulled something out of his pocket and raised it to his dark lips.

"What's he doing now?" Amy whispered.

The white alien spoke into the thing he was holding, then paused and cocked his ear toward it as if he were listening.

"It's the receiver!" I said.

"What?"

"He made some sort of an interstellar phone from a satellite dish on top of the roof. I saw him talking on it last night."

Grandma shook her head and looked at the sky. "What has been going on at my place of business? And right under my nose?"

Scratchull spoke in his screechy native tongue.

"The translator, quick," I said.

Amy fished the baby monitor out of her pocket again and switched it on.

"—and all clear for landing," Scratchull was saying. Amy fiddled with the volume and we heard the next part loud and clear. "Everything is prepared and ready for a quick loading and then immediate takeoff again. You will not encounter trouble from any humans whatsoever."

An enormous shadow fell across the city hall building. I

looked at Amy and Grandma. Their faces grew darker. Soon the whole town was immersed in the dull gray of twilight.

I looked up. An enormous spaceship was dropping straight down on the common from out of the sky. It was so big it blotted out the sun.

The next sound to come out of the baby monitor was knife-against-glass laughter. It needed no translation.

The bulk of the spaceship was an enormous black globe. No lights, no portals, no distinguishing features at all: just a dull, unmarked surface all the way around. It looked dead, like a black hole had solidified and fallen from the darkest depths of space.

The spherical ship was encased in a red triangle. Surrounding the globe at equator level were massive red wings, three long, straight extensions that met at their tips.

"I don't suppose there's any chance they're from the Collective?" I whispered to Amy.

She just shook her head and stared up at the ship.

"Are you sure? Because Scratchull said they'd come back with ships if there was a natural disaster or something." I was desperately clinging to any scrap of hope I could think of. "Maybe they found out about the frozen river and figured out that Scratchull got hold of his invention?"

"No chance. There's no Collective insignia, see?" Amy pointed at the ship. "No markings of any kind to alert anyone as to what kind of ship it is, what its mission might be."

"What's that mean?"

Grandma, mouth hanging open as she gaped at the sky, found her voice. "It means that it's a rogue ship."

"Rogue?" I said.

Amy nodded. "Lawless. They don't answer to any governing body." Her face went even darker in the encroaching shadow of the spaceship. "It means anything goes."

The craft continued to descend. I cringed, certain that the buildings all around us were going to get smashed. But as the ship lowered, it squeezed into the town common, just barely missing the structures around the perimeter. It made the three-story city hall building look like a dollhouse.

When the bottom of the black ball touched down, the bricks of the common walkway were ground into dust. The ship threatened to roll out of the common like a giant's bowling ball and level the buildings of downtown Forest Grove, but the tips of the triangle wings folded down and formed a stabilizing tripod. The massive vessel nestled into the depression it had made.

Then a hatch opened, and a ramp fell down from the belly of the ball and crashed onto the ground.

A dozen of the fiercest-looking aliens I'd ever seen marched out.

Their faces were mostly teeth. Fangs as long as daggers, too big for their slobbery mouths, jutted out at odd angles. A row of intense black eyes across the top of the forehead was the only sign that maybe these weren't completely mindless eating machines.

They leaned forward when they walked, as if their thickly muscled torsos were too heavy for their tree-trunk legs. Or as if they were eager for a fight.

And they all carried ten-foot staffs, each of which ended in a knotted club covered in swirling dots of red light.

"Look at that armor," I breathed.

"Actually, I think that just might be their bodies," Amy whispered back.

I looked closer. I had thought the mottled green, gray, and dirty tan that covered them was a synthetic camouflage suit, but maybe it was just the coloring of their skin. And Amy was right—on closer inspection, the thick plates that covered their shoulders, forearms, stomachs, and shins looked like natural growths for protection, like dinosaurs.

"Evolution can get pretty weird on other planets," Amy whispered.

"But what kind of a world could lead to beings like that?" I gestured at the hideous creatures.

"Someplace where they fight." Amy swallowed. "A lot."

I put my arms around Grandma and Amy and tried to scrunch us all down even further out of sight behind the picnic tables.

The new arrivals pounded the bricks with cinder-block feet

until they drew near and formed a semicircle around Scratchull and the fountain. Thick gobs of drool spilled over the sides of their overcrowded mouths and splattered on the ground.

"Good afternoon, gentlemen." Scratchull spread his long arms out to indicate the surroundings. "Welcome to Earth, such as it is."

The biggest, ugliest alien stepped forward. "You one who called?" This was the voice I had heard last night, with words that sounded like they were deep in his stomach.

"Indeed I am." Scratchull stretched his dark lips into what he probably thought was a welcoming smile. "And you must be the captain of this fine vessel. An Arslaggian slave ship, is it not?"

The camouflage alien grunted in the affirmative.

"Excellent. May I ask what you would like—"

"Your offer. Better be real." The Arslaggian captain shook his staff menacingly. "Better be good."

"Of course, my dear sir." He swept a white hand toward the line of Forest Grove zombies stretched out behind him. "One thousand human workers, precisely as advertised. Delivered at the exact time and place that I promised. And they'll all be joining you without a bit of a struggle, as you can clearly see. I assume that the acquisition of indentured servants has never been so effortless for you, yes?"

The Arslaggian captain sneered at Scratchull—one long, jutting tusk nearly lacerating his own bulging eyeball in the process—and stalked over to the head of the line of zombies.

The big alien jabbed the lead zombie in the middle of his blue overalls with a thick, gnarled finger.

"UHNNGHNGHN."

The captain turned his head to glare at Scratchull.

"What wrong? They look worthless."

Scratchull jumped down off the fountain to approach the pair. The dozen armed aliens growled and closed in as a unit. Scratchull hurriedly put up his hands in a calming gesture of peace. The captain waved his henchmen away with a flash of his staff.

"Oh, no, they are perfectly capable, I assure you," Scratchull said. "They are only temporarily incapacitated. You see, they recently ate a mixture of Kerntaberries and Mooglah fruit."

"Huh? Why for? Everyone know that make you stupid."

"Well, now, please remember I never said they were the smartest creatures in the universe. But they will snap out of their stupor in less than twenty-four hours, and I do guarantee they will be able to take simple commands. Also, they have good, strong backs. I am confident you shall find them well suited to a lifetime of menial labor on your planet."

The Arslaggian captain strode up and down the line of zombies. He stopped near an old woman, leaned in close, and sniffed her all over.

"Ah, yes, I see where you're going there. Indeed, they would also make great snacks," Scratchull continued. "I've never tried one myself, but many of the beings on this planet are quite soft. I am certain they would be most succulent."

"This one. Too old."

"Come now. Certainly someone with your refined palate knows that a well-aged cut of meat is always the finest, yes?"

"Hmmph." The captain looked over the population of

Forest Grove, then sneered at Scratchull. "And you. In return. You just want hitchhike ride?"

"That is correct. My home planet is conveniently located on your path as you return to Arslag. You only have to drop me off there and our account will be settled." Scratchull stuck his hand out for the Arslaggian captain to shake. "Do we have a binding agreement? I daresay this will be your easiest pickup ever."

The captain ignored Scratchull's hand and took one more look up and down the length of the line. He grunted and nodded once. "Load them on ship." He turned to one of his henchmen. "Open dungeon."

"Excellent. You will not be disappointed." Scratchull got out his bullhorn. "WALK SLOWLY FORWARD AND GO UP THE RAMP. SOMEONE ON BOARD THE SHIP WILL SHOW YOU TO YOUR QUARTERS." As the line lurched into action, Scratchull added, "AND THANK YOU FOR FLYING ARSLAGGIAN AIRLINES."

I felt all hope drain out of me as the residents of Forest Grove staggered toward the gigantic dark orb. Amy gripped my hand, hard, her fingernails digging into my skin. Grandma started to sob and shake.

There was no one to call for help. As soon as the humans were on board, the ship would lift off and be gone, and no one from Forest Grove would ever be seen again.

I watched the zombie in front, the guy with the overalls and John Deere cap. Only it wasn't just a zombie, of course. He was a real person. I even thought I recognized him from around town. When his leather work boot hit the spaceship's ramp with a metallic clang, something broke inside me. I jumped up and ran toward Scratchull and the Arslaggian captain.

"Stop!" I screamed at the zombies. "All of you! Stop!"

29

The lead zombie halted abruptly, and the rest of the line accordion-squeezed together. The Arslaggian captain pointed his staff at me. The swirling red lights merged together to form a glowing ball on the end of the club. My chest got hot. I looked down and saw a laser sight centered on the front of my T-shirt, big as a cannonball.

The big alien glared at Scratchull. "What this? You said no trouble."

A look of surprise flashed across Scratchull's face, but he quickly masked it. "Oh, this one won't be any trouble at all." He hurried over, arms outstretched and long white fingers gnarled up, ready to grab me. "In fact, he will be quite useful. If any human gives you trouble on the ride home, you can torture this one to send a message."

I ducked away from Scratchull and ran right over to the Arslaggian captain. I had to crane my neck to look up into his face. I only had one card up my sleeve and it sure wasn't an ace—more like a deuce or maybe even the joker—but I had to play it.

"You better leave these people alone, get back in that ship, and fly away in a hurry," I said. "I have made an emergency call to the Intergalactic Police Force. Directly to Commander Rezzlurr himself. Ever heard of him?"

I could tell by the way all of his black eyes got a little wider that he had.

"He'll be here any minute. And even if you load up and get out of here before he arrives, he'll be able to track you down. It's a straight shot from here to Arslag, and his police ship can go a lot faster than this thing. What do you think he'll do when he boards and finds all of your illegal cargo?" There were a lot of details in there I wasn't too sure about, obviously, but if you're going to bluff, then you better bluff big.

The Arslag captain looked at Scratchull standing behind me. "No good. Trouble with police not part of deal."

Oh, man. Was this actually going to work?

"You better just get back on that ship and get out of here right now," I added. "It's the only way you're getting out of this."

Scratchull stepped in front of me and pulled a slip of paper out of the pocket of his coveralls while the captain watched. "Pardon the intrusion, but is this the urgent message to which you were referring?" He unfolded it and held it up for both of us to see. It was the note to Rezzlurr, in my own handwriting. I was suddenly so deflated that I could hardly stand anymore.

"The first thing I did was rig the transporters up so that any emergency messages sent to the police would be rerouted directly to my room." Scratchull waved the sheet of paper in my face. "Did you honestly believe that I wouldn't figure out how to do something like that? I practically *invented* the transporter system!"

"So . . . Rezzlurr not coming?" the Arslaggian captain said.

I was close enough to hear Scratchull mutter under his breath, "Nice detective work, chief. You're about as quick as the humans."

But then he flashed that winning grimace at the captain and said, much louder this time, "That is correct. I suggest we begin boarding immediately." His hands clamped around my biceps like iron bars, pinning my arms to my sides. "I would be more than happy to deliver this young human to your dungeon facilities myself."

Scratchull hoisted me into the air and marched toward the spaceship. The open hatch loomed bigger and bigger, the gaping mouth of a space beast ready for the kill.

"Let him go!" Oh no. It was Amy, running up to us, with Grandma right behind her.

"Run away!" I shouted. "Save yourselves!"

"I'm not letting them take you!" yelled Amy. "And they're not getting my dad, either!"

Amy reached down and scooped up half of a broken brick, then cocked her arm back and fired it right at the Arslaggian captain. It plinked harmlessly off the plate covering his stomach.

The big alien looked down at the brick and then growled at Scratchull. "More human trouble?"

Scratchull sniffed. "A girl throwing rocks and a feeble old woman? I hardly think so." He inclined his skull head to indicate the circle of henchmen. "Have your colleagues escort them to the dungeon. I personally guarantee that this will be the last nuisance requiring your attention."

Amy and Grandma tried to run, but they had no chance. With just a few loping steps, a pair of Arslaggian guards was on top of them. They were thrown over broad shoulders like sacks of potatoes and marched toward the spaceship.

"I am so glad you returned," Scratchull whispered in my ear. His breath was freezing. "If you survive the ride with the Arslaggians—which I highly doubt, by the way—I believe I'll take you with me when I depart at my home planet. There are so many pain-tolerance experiments I have been meaning to perform. Just how much physical misery can one being endure before death takes over? I'm delighted the field of science will have a thoroughly well-tested answer."

I struggled and swore and bit and kicked and threatened and spit. Scratchull laughed.

The open hatch got closer.

30

Scratchull dragged me right up to the spaceship. The realization that I would never see Earth again hit me so suddenly, and with such finality, that it knocked the wind out of me.

The Arslaggian guards carrying Grandma and Amy were ahead of us, just a few steps away from the ramp. Our new lives were about to begin.

"Aahhhhh!"

Three Arslag warriors screamed and ran past us toward the ship, elbowing zombies out of the way in their rush to race up the ramp. Two of them dropped their staffs and didn't even bother to stop and pick them up; they just dashed into the ship and out of sight.

When the two guards holding Grandma and Amy turned to look at something behind us, their arms went limp, sending their prisoners tumbling to the ground. The Arslaggians' black eyes tripled in diameter while those fang-filled mouths dropped open. One of them let out a terrified squeak that I might have found funny under less dire circumstances.

Amy helped Grandma to her feet and they backed away from the ramp. The guard that had dropped Amy pointed at something but remained rooted to the spot. His partner grabbed his arm and tugged at him in the direction of the ship, but he remained paralyzed.

Finally the partner backhanded the frozen one across the face, hard, until black blood poured down his forehead. The trance was broken and both guards dashed up the ramp.

"What is it now?" Scratchull growled. He turned us both around.

Oh, no. Snarffle was tearing along a side street, headed straight for the common. How had he gotten out?

"Go home, boy!" I called. "Turn around. Get out of here!" No use in his getting captured, too.

But he kept racing right toward us. The Arslaggian captain staggered backward several steps and leveled his staff right at Scratchull. "You trick us. This is trap!"

"What are you talking about?" Scratchull had dropped the fake politeness, and his words came out in an angry screech.

"Lure us here. Unleash monster. Bad trap." The club at the end of his staff lit up, and Scratchull's gleaming white face glowed an eerie red.

Scratchull let go of me and held up his hands, trying to calm the captain. "That thing? A monster? Not at all, my good fellow. That is only a snarffle. A common house pet. Surely no cause for alarm."

The captain continued to back up toward the ship. He kept the laser sight on the white alien but pointed to Snarffle with his free hand. "House pet? Do you not see markings on back? Can you not count legs? That is the Monstrous Mouth of Morglarz! Everyone know that!"

Snarffle ran right up to me. I dropped down and scooped him up in my arms. He whistled happily and licked me all over.

The Arslaggian captain stopped in his tracks. His mouth dropped open so wide I thought maybe he had unhinged his jaw. "A child?" It came out in a choked whisper. "A child commands the Monstrous Mouth of Morglarz?"

"What in the galaxy are you talking about?" Scratchull shouted. "He doesn't *command* anything. He walks that stupid thing around on a leash and gives it treats."

Snarffle hopped down off my lap and whistle-growled at Scratchull.

"Do not anger it!" the captain cried. The half-dozen guards who hadn't run back onto the spaceship moved to huddle behind their leader, staffs poised at the ready in two-handed grips.

"What are you afraid it might do?" Scratchull said. "Lick you to death?"

"You crazy?" said the captain. "Is most destructive beast in cosmos! Used in many wars. Could eat entire spaceship!"

The first spiderweb lines, faint and gray, spread across Scratchull's throat and jaw. He was losing it. I winked at Grandma and Amy, huddled together near the hatch.

"Well, well, well," I said, walking casually over to the white alien, followed by Snarffle. "Have we found something that the wise and all-knowing Scratchull has never heard of before?"

The spiderweb lines crept past his jaw to cover his cheeks. "Nonsense." He whispered so only I could hear. "That is a simple house pet, and you know it. These Arslags have just spent too much time drinking fermented zandeen juice while they listen to space legends. As soon as I—"

"Maybe I'll give them a little demonstration," I said. The spiderweb lines stretched to his forehead and burned black. I turned to Snarffle. "Hey, boy! You hungry?" The purple alien wriggled in joyous anticipation. I pointed to a line of cars parked near the common. "Snack time, buddy. Go nuts." Snarffle's little tale twirled and he raced over to the cars.

A pickup truck, an SUV, and a convertible vanished beneath a purple blur in just a few moments. The huddled group of Arslaggians took several shuffling steps backward. One of them was shaking so hard that his staff rattled against the bricks.

"Snarffle! That's enough!" I called. The blur stopped instantly, and Snarffle sat calmly on the sidewalk, half of a tire sticking out of his mouth. "All right, you can finish that up, but then come back over here, please." Snarffle gulped down the rest of the tire, then trotted over to me. I picked him up and he panted heavily.

An Arslag guard grabbed the captain's shoulder and pointed at us. "He give orders! To Monstrous Mouth of Morglarz!"

"And Monstrous Mouth of Morglarz obey!" said another.

Snarffle burped happily and licked me on the cheek. I carried him in the crook of one arm and approached the group of Arslaggians. They started to shrink away. "Stay where you are. I will not let him harm you." I tried to make my voice a little deeper and sound all official and stuff. I think I did a pretty good job, too, because they all froze up and stared at me.

I marched until I was standing directly in front of the Arslaggian captain in the shadow of his spaceship. "Should we talk about you getting back in that ship and flying far away from here?" I said.

I didn't get a chance to say anything more, though, because Scratchull wormed his way in between us. "Do not listen to anything he says," the white alien screeched. "He's a mere child, just a stupid, prattling human boy who—"

"Stop talking." The captain stuck the glowing end of his staff against Scratchull's chest and pushed him out of the way. Then he pointed at me. "I negotiate with him now."

I smiled at Scratchull, then cleared my throat and addressed the Arslaggian captain. "As I was saying, I think it's time for you to leave now."

"What we get? In return?"

I shifted my stance so that Snarffle was closer to the Arslaggians. The guards backed away, but the captain held his ground. "Well, you get to keep your ship. How about that?"

The captain shook his head. "If he eat ship, we stuck here. Then we make war. Is Arslag way."

Then he extended his club so that it was pointed at the line of cars that Snarffle had started devouring. A laser shot out the end of the club, and three nearby vehicles were encompassed in a circle of red light.

The captain jerked his arm upward, pointing the staff in the air. The cars shot a hundred feet above the road, tethered to the staff by a ray of red light. The captain flicked his wrist this way and that and the cars zigzagged all over the sky. Finally, he brought his arm down, fast, and the cars plummeted back to Earth and shattered. A millions bits of twisted metal exploded into the air and then rained down all over the street, and you couldn't even tell they had once been cars at all.

The captain looked back at me. "Ten thousand Arslag soldiers on ship. All have weapon. Mouth of Morglarz mighty, but not get all. You want war?"

"Ummm... no." It looked like we had hit a stalemate.

The captain sneered. "So what we get? In return?"

Good question. What did we have that these guys could possibly want?

The Arslag guards, bolstered by their captain's confidence, closed in on us in a rough semicircle. Snarffle whistle-growled and I patted him to calm him down. The air was electrified by pre-fight tension.

"Perhaps I could make a suggestion?" Grandma said. She and Amy walked over to join our little group. She looked perfectly comfortable, just like she was serving brunch to a family of alien Tourists back at her inn.

The Arslag captain looked at me. You know, because I was in charge. I nodded. "Go ahead, Grandma."

"How about you take this fellow right here?" She smiled sweetly and pointed at Scratchull. "He wanted to go along with you anyway. This way you just keep him."

Scratchull's spiderweb lines smoldered darkly. He stepped toward Grandma. "How dare you—"

"Shut mouth," the captain said. He slammed the club into Scratchull's chest this time, knocking the white alien backward until he fell, sprawling, across the bricks. "Keep it shut."

The captain looked back at me. "We come far. For thousand slaves." He made a dismissive gesture at Scratchull. "He just one. Not fair. No deal."

"Actually, that's not quite true, sir." Amy stepped forward and pulled the baby monitor out of her pocket. "If you don't believe us, just listen to what Scratchull himself has to say about his own trade value."

She fiddled with the buttons on the monitor until Scratchull's voice came booming out of the speaker. His words had made me so angry the first time I heard them, crouching in his closet, but they sounded pretty sweet right now: "*Having the humans die so that I may continue my valuable work is a small price to pay. If you spent any time here at all it would be plain enough for even you to see: A single one of me is worth billions of these earthlings. Indeed, an entire planet of them.*"

Amy flicked off the monitor with a satisfied smile. How did I get lucky enough to meet the coolest girl in the universe?

"I would take his word for it if I were you," I told the captain. "He's extremely intelligent. Just ask him."

"Yeah," Amy said. "There's so much he can do for you. Tell me, do you ever have any trouble with the technology on your ship?"

The captain shrugged. "Sure. Sometimes. Everybody does."

"Well he can fix it for you, no problem," Amy said.

"Right. You heard him a few minutes ago: *I practically invented the transporter system!*" I did a pretty fair Scratchull imitation, if I do say so myself.

"And he's a wonderful cook," Grandma chimed in. "I'm sure it's a long flight home. Scratchull could bake your entire crew all sorts of wonderful treats. He has a real knack for serving large crowds."

The captain tilted his head and looked a question at his guards. The guards glared at us. The decision hung in the balance.

"Oh, and he doesn't have to sleep, so he can work around the clock for you without ever taking a break. He's very efficient that way."

"Hmmmm." The captain mulled everything over, scratching at his hideous face with a thick talon of a fingernail. He looked at Scratchull, then at the line of zombies, then back at the rest of us. "Hmmmm."

I whispered into Snarffle's ear. "Give him something to think about, buddy. Scare 'em a little."

Snarffle whistle-growled deep in his throat and wriggled as if trying to work his way out of my grip. Then he looked up at the ship and licked his lips greedily.

"Deal," the Arslag captain said abruptly. He turned and walked up the ramp. The biggest guard grabbed Scratchull by the back of his coveralls and pulled him toward the ship. The white alien was dragged heavily across the bricks of the common.

I expected screaming and swearing and threatening. But Scratchull had finally lost his words. The spiderweb lines drained from his face, leaving it not just white but blank. His eyes were dull and his jaw was slack. I realized that he looked just like one of the zombies.

And then he was hauled up the ramp and out of sight. The hatch closed, the tripod unfolded itself to become wings again, and the dark globe shot straight up in the air, so fast it was out of sight in just a few seconds.

"That was the coolest Pioneer Day Festival ever," Amy said.

31

I set Snarffle down and scratched at his sweet spot. He wriggled all over and twirled his tail. "Nice job, buddy. Yes, that's a good boy, Snarffle."

Amy knelt down to pet him, too. "I guess we have to stop calling him that, huh? What is it, the Big Mouth of Something?"

"I think he likes Snarffle better," I said. "Don't you, boy?" He panted happily in answer.

"But what are we going to do with him?" Amy said.

"He should live with us. What about it, buddy? You don't want to go back to wherever they were using you and be in any stupid wars, do you? You like it right here. You want to stay with us. Yes, you do." I patted and scratched him some more. His answer came in the form of enthusiastic licks across my face. "That is, if Grandma doesn't mind."

Grandma laughed as I tried to dry myself off. "I think he's earned his room and board and then some." She put both hands in the small of her back and stretched. "Well, I guess we've got some cleanup to do," she said. We all looked at the line of a thousand zombies.

"What are we going to do with *them*?" Amy asked.

"They're nice and obedient," I said. "I think we should just sort of herd them home and tell them to go to bed. If they're anything like Tate, they'll just wake up a little groggy in the morning with no memory of what happened."

"Sounds like a plan to me," Amy said.

It took us the rest of the afternoon to herd everyone back home. Grandma thought we should make sure they were safe, so we split up and escorted everyone to their individual houses. I walked back to the taxi and parked it at the little campground just outside of town. That was going to be one very confused driver in the morning.

I met Amy back at the empty town common before Grandma got there. "I guess Earth might have to wait a little longer to join the Collective, huh?"

"Yeah, I suppose so." Amy shrugged. "At least we have great jobs, right?"

"And we get to do them together."

"Good point." Amy stepped closer. "Thanks for saving my hometown, David. Oh, and the rest of the planet, too."

She gave me one of her lopsided grins. "That's probably in my all-time top ten for nicest things that a guy has ever done for me."

"Top ten, huh?" I smirked back at her. "Let's not forget who saved your life at the dam."

Amy drew closer. "Maybe even top five."

"I'll try to be a little faster about it next time."

Amy got about as close as she could and put her arms around my neck. "And David? Thanks for not saying I told you so."

I wanted to say it then, for a joke, but my lips were kind of busy for the next few minutes.

Grandma came walking into the town common after a while with Snarffle bounding along beside her. Tate followed, dragging his feet with his mouth wide open. "They're all safe at home," Grandma said.

Amy looked at the crushed brick in the middle of the common. "I'm not sure how we're going to explain that," Amy said.

"Or the disappearance of a few cars," I added.

Grandma studied the scene before us and then threw her hands in the air. "I don't see why we have to explain anything. We'll wake up tomorrow as groggy as everyone else, right?" Amy and I smiled and nodded. "Besides, every small town deserves to have a few mysteries. Now let's get home, I'm famished."

We were walking out of the common when I heard something from behind a patch of bushes near the road. A soft whimpering. I walked behind the thicket to investigate.

"Please don't hurt me!" Greenie wailed. He was crouched as low as he could make himself, his entire jelly body shivering. "He forced me to do it! I promise! I'm so glad he's gone! You must believe me! You must!"

"What do we have here?" Grandma said as she, Amy, and Snarffle joined us.

"Scratchull's assistant," I said. "Looks like he got left behind." Snarffle whistle-growled deep in his throat.

I watched Greenie. He couldn't stop quivering and his eyes bulged out of their sockets as they searched my face.

"Please, good humans, please. I am not even liking the Master. Everything I do is in fear only, never with love, you must believe me. I will never seek him out or help him ever again." Greenie's eyes scanned the sky nervously. "Especially where he is going. Oh, please. You must believe." He implored us all for mercy with his bulging eyes.

Grandma turned to me. "I think we should let David decide what's to be done with him."

I appreciated Grandma's trust in me, but I also felt so tired. Responsibility is exhausting.

I shrugged. "Well... it's going to take us a while to walk back to the bed-and-breakfast," I said. "If someone were to race back there and jump in a transporter before we returned ... I don't think there's much we could do about it."

"Oh thankyouthankyouthankyou!" Greenie slithered forward, grabbed my hand, and planted slimy kisses all over it.

"Ugh. On second thought, maybe we should—" But Greenie dashed away and was out of sight before I could finish.

We all strolled back to Grandma's place together, Tate

shuffling along to bring up the rear. Everything was so peaceful with the entire town of Forest Grove at home, in bed.

"You know, David," said Grandma. "I lost an employee recently. Do you think you might consider canceling your flight home and interviewing for a summer job around here?"

I scratched at my chin, pretending to mull it over. "I don't know, Grandma... The minimum wage is pretty good back in Florida. What's in it for me if I stay?"

"All the Kerntaberry-and-Mooglah fruit scones you can eat, for starters. I still have hundreds left over for some reason."

"And don't forget the joys of scrubbing alien germs off the floor for my dad," Amy said.

"Hmmm... that's a pretty tempting offer, ladies."

Grandma laughed. "Actually, I'm sure we'll be able to find more important jobs for the person responsible for saving the planet." She put her arm around me and squeezed. "And we'll need to start attracting a clientele base again. We're in the middle of our busiest season, and Tate chased all the customers off before the festival."

"Yeah," said Amy. "I miss the senior activities and movie nights with the kids."

I grinned. "I'll see what I can do."

The setting sun was still warm, the rest of my summer stay at the B&B was spread out before me, and none of us was on a spaceship heading for a lifetime of slavery on planet Arslag. All in all, it was a perfect evening.

When we walked up to the inn, the first thing we all saw was the gaping hole in the wall up on the second floor where Snarffle must have chewed his way out of my room.

"Yikes. Sorry about that, Grandma."

"Oh, no matter. It will give Tate something to do when he wakes up and snaps out of it."

"ANNGHGHN?"

"Yes. That's a good boy," Grandma said, patting him on the back. "I know you'll like to have a manly job, won't you?"

"UHNNGHGHN!"

"Are you totally sure he'll snap out of it?" I said.

"Oh, yes, I'm quite confident." Grandma saw the look on my face. "What's the matter?"

"Oh, nothing." I glanced at Amy out of the corner of my eye. "It's just that I think I might like him better this way."

Grandma and I burst out laughing. Amy swatted me on the arm, but she was smiling, too. Snarffle whistled happily.

Yep, it was a perfect evening at the Intergalactic Bed & Breakfast.

ACKNOWLEDGMENTS

A galaxy-sized thank you to the following people:

All of the great teachers of writing I've had over the years: Pam Morehouse, Peggy Stephens, John Lehni, Carole Anne Wiseman, Tom Lockhart, Lalani Pitts, James Bertolino, Richard Emmerson, Victor Yoshida, Jen Peel, Uma Krishnaswami, Tim Wynne-Jones, Julie Larios, Cynthia Leitich-Smith, Alan Cumyn, Margaret Bechard, Leda Schubert, Ellen Howard, Shelley Tanaka, Sharon Darrow, Kathi Appelt, Marion Dane Bauer, and Rita Williams-Garcia.

Marcy Waite and Jeff Clark. Teaching journalism to middle/high school students and advising the school newspaper is one of the most selfless, noble (and probably crazy) things that a teacher can do. I realize now that all of our arguments over what might or might not be considered "appropriate content" for a student publication were signs that you were taking my work seriously. (Sorry about the occasional insolence coupled with the frequent sarcasm. I'm a little bit better now, I promise. With the insolence, anyway.)

Martine Leavitt, who gave me the gifts of confidence

and wonderful editorial advice during the process of putting together a first draft.

Bob Peeples, who helped me out of a tight writing spot with a timely suggestion.

Mark Wright. Thanks for all the conversations about keeping the dream alive, my baroque friend.

Illustrator Christian Slade. Thanks to his fine work, I have no problem with people judging my book by its cover.

My agent, George Nicholson, along with Erica Silverman, Caitlin McDonald, Kelly Farber, and everyone at Sterling Lord Literistic.

The amazing team at Disney-Hyperion Books and Disney Publishing Worldwide, especially Hallie Patterson and Tyler Nevins.

My editor, Stephanie Owens Lurie. When two grown-ups have this much fun discussing the names, eating habits, and general motivations of goofy space aliens, you know they have found the right jobs.

Myra, Logan, and Cameo. I'm sure that I smiled before I met you people, but I can't remember exactly why.

The members of the Whatcom County Council, circa 1992, who passed a resolution officially declaring the county as a "Sasquatch Protection and Refuge Area." I've never been more proud to live here.